FORBIDDEN EARTH ANGEL

Published by Spines
ISBN: 979-8-89383-199-3

FORBIDDEN EARTH ANGEL

EARTH ANGLE TRILOGY BOOK SERIES

NATOYA WAYNE

CONTENTS

GLOSSARY OF SUPERNATURAL BEINGS AND ANGELS

Different types of Angels

- **Seraphim** - Highest rank of angels that are the most powerful and beautiful. Lucifer was a Seraphim that fell from grace.
- **Cherubim** - Celestial record keepers.
- **Thrones** - Angels that maintain the cosmic balance of universal laws and celestial magic.
- **Dominions** - Angels of justice, judgement, and order. They oversee the management of lower rank angels.
- **Virtues** - Angels that maintain order of the natural world, inspire science, and different types of arts.
- **Powers** - Warrior angels, also known as the celestial police force in the Supernatural community and the unseen protectors of humanity. They apprehend rogue angels and demonic forces.
- **Archangels** - Govern all affairs for humanity and Earth. The Council of Archangels consists of seven Archangels: Michael the warrior, who is the head of the Council; Raphael the healer; Gabriel the messenger; Uriel the master of knowledge and wisdom; Azrael the angel of death; Chamuel the angel of love, matters of the heart, relationships, and mate bonds; and Ariel the angel of nature.
- **Gregori Watchers** - Sentinel angels that were sent to observe and teach humanity. They were the first angels to create Nephilim offsprings with humans.
- **Principalities** - Angels that govern spirituality, religions, and politics.
- **Cherubs** - Not to be confused with Cherubims. Cherubs are third-class angels that usually serve as attendants for higher rank angels. Some serve as matchmakers in the supernatural

community and are skilled in the art of beauty, love, and passion. They are not plump, childlike beings with a bow and arrow.

- **Angels** - Regular angels that are guardians of humanity. Guardian angels are part of this category.
- **Earth Angel** - A human that was transformed into an immortal angel created on Earth due to the blood seal of the seven most powerful Archangels altering their DNA. The Warrior King Zanael of the Desert tribes was the first Earth angel.
- **Nephilim** - The hybrid offspring of an angel and a human. They are not immortal but have the longevity of slow aging. They have some angelic abilities and white wings. The Council of the Archangels had wiped out all Nephilims and strictly forbid their creation. The Earth angel Zanael's daughter Seraphina and Lord Gideon's manservant Cael are the only known Nephilims in existence.
- **Fallen Angels** - Angels that have been corrupted by the energies of hell. Their wings were burned off as punishment for aligning with Lucifer.
- **Unaligned Angels** - Angels whose allegiance is to their own self-interest. They have no allegiance to Heaven or hell and have not lost their wings.

Supernatural Community

- **Fae** - Human-sized beings (often taller than most humans, slim, and beautiful). They dwell in a dimension parallel to Earth, but many often try to blend with humans on Earth. There are many species of Fae. They are mostly immortal with powerful types of magic, usually of the elemental variety, psychic abilities, or healing. They like to wager and bargain, and some are often tricksters, cruel, or mischievous. Queen Mab is an ancient Fae Deity.
- **Sidhe** - Some of the most powerful types of fae. They rule the Seelie and Unseelie Courts.
- **Brownies** - A type of Fae whose abilities are superb domestic duty skills.
- **Dwarves** - Usually short in stature magical beings that are the treasure miners and carpenters of the supernatural community. Nobility rank Dwarves have the ability to detect the magical properties of magical objects.
- **High Witch/High Mage** - Humans born with rare advanced magical abilities that became immortal after giving up something they most valued. They are very knowledgeable with spellcasting, enchantments, healing, potions, and hexes. They can hex weapons that can harm celestial beings. Some have psychic and seer abilities.
- **Regular Witch/Mage** - Humans born with magical abilities that have longevity of slow aging but not advanced abilities to become immortal. They are very knowledgeable with spellcasting, enchantments, healing, potions, and hexes but cannot hex weapons that can harm celestial beings.
- **Demonic entities** - These come in different categories and species: 1. Captured Angels who were tortured and experimented on with dark and twisted magic in the hell dimension. 2. Corrupted human souls that have been combined with various magical and non-magical animalistic creatures in gruesome experiments using dark and twisted magic. 3. Captured supernatural beings that have been

corrupted and experimented on using dark and twisted magic.

Note 1: Fallen angels are not demons. They are still angels unless they have been experimented on with dark and twisted hell dimension magic.

Note 2: Enochian Wards and Runes: Powerful protection wards powered by celestial runes in the angelic Enochian language. Enochian runes can be tattooed as a last-resort protection on an angelâ€™s body. Still, they must be tattooed with celestial ink from the divine angelic scribe, Metatron. The spell to activate Â Enochian rune tattoos has a high probability of inconsistencies, hence why many angels avoid getting Enochian rune tattoos.

PROLOGUE

Eons ago, before the pyramids were built, there was civil unrest on Earth after the powerful Seraphim Lucifer and his rebel angels fell from Grace. Lucifer was the most beautiful and powerful of the Seraphim class, but he betrayed his brothers in his lust for power and dominion over the creator's favorite creation—humans. Michael, the warrior Archangel with whom he shared a close relationship, begged him not to betray the forces of heaven. Still, with his unyielding pride, Lucifer would not listen to reason. Being the charismatic one out of all his brothers, he gained a following of angels who shared similar beliefs that they should have dominion over Earth and humankind.

Many of the fallen angels that were once beautiful were severely scarred in the fall from the heavens and, furthermore, in the rebellion civil war. The forces of heaven led by Archangel Michael were able to force the rebel angels to retreat.

Lucifer decided to set up his stronghold in a dimension that religious texts referred to as hell and appointed a hierarchy of rulership similar to heaven forces. Lucifer still retained his ethereal beauty because, being a mighty Seraphim, the fall did not scar him. But some of the other rebel angels' visages became grotesquely twisted versions of their heavenly beauty and, over time, became more corrupted. Some regretted following Lucifer with his rebellion but could not return to heaven once cast out. So, they chose not to dwell with Lucifer and the other rebel angels but formed their own factions on Earth, refusing to further ally with Lucifer or with the other angels who refused to allow them back into heaven.

Lucifer appointed seven princes to rule beside him, and these seven princes were his personal henchmen and assassins. These seven princes, Azazel, Ramiel, Dagon, Leviathan, Astaroth, Belial, and Abaddon, were mistaken for gods on Earth by several tribes of humankind in the early Earth years and were worshipped and revered. With the power of sacrifice and worship, these seven princes became very powerful and unleashed unspeakable chaos and horrors upon humankind.

Lucifer knew the seven most powerful Archangels, Michael, Gabriel, Raphael, Uriel, Azrael, Chamuel, and Ariel, would not interfere with the free will of humankind to prevent them from worshipping these princes, hence why he allowed his princes to do as they will with humans.

Archangel Michael led the Powers, a class of warrior angels, in battle to capture and subdue the seven princes of hell. Michael, the ever-strategic general and leader of the Archangels, had an abyss built in another dimension to serve as a prison for the seven princes to hamper Lucifer's power. According to the laws of celestial magic, each of the seven most powerful Archangels had to give some of their divine blood to create a seal to bind the prison of the seven princes. Half of the seal was bound to the prison abyss, while the other half of the seal had to be kept in a human vessel and merged into the life force of that chosen human to maintain the balance of celestial magic used to create the seal.

The warrior King Zanael of a desert tribe, which is now modern-day Saudi Arabia, was the only human to survive the process of the blood seal of the seven Archangels among the chosen ones that had the potential to carry the power of the seal. This process altered his genetics to transform him into the first created Earth angel.

The Earth angel Zanael, along with some of the Powers, Dominions, Principalities, Virtues, and Gregori Watcher angels were assigned to various posts on Earth where portals to travel to other dimensions can occur to ensure the prison abyss for the princes of hell stays undisturbed. These angels that were assigned on Earth formed different factions to maintain order among the supernatural community. They are also the unseen protectors of humanity.

Lord Gideon, the most powerful and beautiful of the Powers, a warrior class of angels, was handpicked by Archangel Michael and some of the Powers to be assigned to Earth. His fellow Powers saw him as a protege of Michael and rendered him with the same respect they gave the warrior Archangel. Gideon was assigned to serve as a Guardian for the Earth angel and train him to use his angelic powers. Gideon is a fierce warrior who is a force to be reckoned with when it comes to battling demons and other rogue angels, but he cannot stop specific forces, especially that of his charge, the Earth angel, from falling in love.

The Earth angel Zanael was permitted to live as he pleased, whether in a supernatural society or with humans, as long as he stuck to the rules and stayed protected. As ancient times switched to modern times with more technological advancements, Zanael wanted to do more with his life, so he decided to attend college, where he obtained his Ph.D. in Anthropology and Archaeology. Zanael was then offered a job position as a professor of Anthropology and Archaeology at Emerlyn University in Connecticut. He went by the alias Dr. Zane Abner.

In the early 2000s, during his tenure as a professor renowned for his successful expeditions, he fell in love with a beautiful human woman named Dr. Athania Kebede, who was also a professor of anthropology and archaeology. They met on one of his archaeological expeditions to Ethiopia.

Zanael remembered how he fell in love with her stunning beauty at first that rivaled that of a supermodel, but he loved her brilliant mind and engaging personality the most. Athania stood at five feet eight inches with long kinky dark hair, a flawless dark brown complexion that seemed to glow in the sun, and a defined face with high cheekbones, but when she smiled with perfect white teeth, it felt like the sun was shining. Her smile seemed to light up any room. Her build was athletic due to years of professional ballet, and she walked with an effortless grace and dignified posture. He knew that he was forbidden to have any love relationships per the Council of Archangel's orders for his own protection, but being with Athania felt just right.

He was alive for thousands of years and saw the rise and fall of different civilizations were known by many names and had liaisons with numerous women, but Athania was the one woman he fell in love with. He always had a wealth of knowledge to share, having lived many lives, and she was fascinated by it all with her thirst for knowledge. Zanael and Athania's chemistry was compared to fireworks on New Year's and Independence Day celebrations with endless stimulating conversations between two brilliant scholars. Zanael knew he had to marry her, although the marriage was forbidden to him. Athania always told him there was something "angelic" and "regal" about him but never tried to investigate his true identity because she accepted what he was willing to divulge about himself.

As a mortal King, he was known to be very handsome, with dark curly hair, brown eyes, a chiseled face, and an olive complexion, and he stood at six feet four inches with a muscular physique from being a warrior. He was the tallest man among his tribespeople. Becoming an Earth angel only gave his already handsome visage an ethereal look.

After a year of dating, he was forced to reveal his true identity when she saw his brown irises turn a glowing silvery color after rescuing a young man from a demon attacking him in an empty park area. He quickly dispatched the demon with his scimitar celestial weapon, which materialized in his hand like it did for most angels. After an evening lecture, his angelic senses urged him to follow the demon to a nearby empty park, and he had to intervene to save the young man from being drained of his essence by the demon. He did not count on Athania following him to the park to give him his cell phone and house keys, which he had forgotten in her office. He quickly assessed the young man he saved for any injuries that needed healing, and since there were none, he compelled him to forget everything he saw and send him on his way home. Healing abilities and compulsion are perks of being an Earth angel.

He hoped she did not see anything since it was nighttime in the empty park, and dispatching the bottom-feeder low-level demon happened so fast. He asked her to return with him to his house so he could explain everything away from prying eyes. She mutely complied, somewhat in shock, but not the type that he repulsed her. He also did not sense any fear from her given that she briefly saw him kill a demon that turned to ash and his irises glowing an unearthly silver color.

He will never forget how she gazed upon him awestruck as he revealed his shimmering silvery white angelic wings and glowing aura as he told her his story. She took in everything he told her with a calm demeanor that he had not seen in most humans. She was ever more fascinated by his appearance and kept asking curious questions about his story. He had seen many humans lose their senses over the existence of angels, demons, and other supernatural things.

Still, Athania's reaction to his true identity was that of wonder, astonishment, and curiosity. She was not scared of the demon she briefly saw after he dispatched it and made it clear that her love for him had not changed. She said she knew something different about him but could not tell what it was. She also had an open mind that the supernatural world existed and felt that most people would not react well if they knew supernatural beings were real. Athania knew that the knowledge of the existence of supernatural beings was not meant for many human minds to process. Some might try to pretend that they do not exist and go about their mundane lives; some might lose their minds and end up in psychiatric wards, while some might panic, and some might want to conduct gruesome experiments on these beings for the origin of their abilities. So, she understood why he had to keep his true angelic identity a secret from her and everyone else. They spent the entire night talking, and he answered her numerous questions as best he could. He admired how she processed everything he discussed, which only made him fall deeper in love with her.

Zanael was able to ward himself off so that Gideon and

the other angels of Gideon's faction could not detect him. He had the help of a witch who was familiar with angelic runes. He eloped with Athania, and they married in a small, intimate ceremony in her friend's backyard. Athania became pregnant shortly after. She gave birth to an infant girl after a long and challenging labor. Zanael knew the Council of Archangels forbade a Nephilim child, so he stayed hidden with his family.

It was due to this divine phenomenon of the birth of a Nephilim that alerted some demonic acolytes of Lucifer and the worshippers of the seven princes. Gideon got the aid of a powerful High Witch named Celeste, who goes by the alias Dr. Celeste Chevalier, a holistic clinical psychologist with her practice, to detect the energetic aura of the angelic protection runes. After a year or more of trying, Gideon got Zanael's location and went with his elite group of Powers to retrieve the Earth angel and his family. But it was too late. Some of Lucifer's demonic acolytes had already killed Athania. They tried to drain Zanael of the Archangel blood seal, but he transferred the Archangel blood seal and his angelic powers to his infant daughter. Judging by the various piles of ashes from demons that littered the floor, it looked like Zanael did put up quite a brave fight even though he was severely outnumbered. Gideon saw him clutching Athania's lifeless body while surrounded by the remaining demons. He had also used the last of his life force to create a protection barrier to protect his infant daughter as Gideon and the Powers quickly dispatched the remaining demons. Zanael, with his dying breath, told Gideon that he had passed on the blood seal of the seven Archangels and his Earth angel powers to his infant daughter and that he must protect her at all costs. She was his responsibility now. He named her Seraphina and released the protective barrier before dying so that Gideon and the Powers could take her to safety.

Gideon took the crying and hungry babe to be raised by the High Witch Celeste, who helped him detect Zanael's off-grid ward. Celeste had always wanted a child and was happy to adopt her. He even gave a large sum of money for any expenses for the baby since this surprised Celeste. She placed a protective ward powered by angelic runes to glamour her Nephilim and Earth angel aura so she could blend with humans. She also bound her celestial powers. The Archangel council felt it was safer for Seraphina to be raised as a human hidden in plain sight.

Gideon stayed in the shadows, watching over Seraphina like a Guardian angel bodyguard as she grew from an infant to a statuesque young woman enrolled at Emerlyn University, where her father was once a successful professor. She had Zanael's brown eyes but looked more like her beautiful human mother. She had her mother's height, athletic build, and a defined face with high cheekbones and long curly hair. Her flawless golden brown complexion glows with an ethereal, healthy glow. She had a brilliant smile that lit up a room. She was a bit reserved in high school and now even more in college. She seems to have inherited her parents' scholarly brilliance and excelled in her studies. He watched from afar as many human males tried to date her in high school and college. She would go on dates with a few but rebuffed any further advances. He watched as she attended a few parties and school activities like any typical teenager. He admired how she pursued her studies and extra-curricular activities in ballet and gymnastics with ardor and diligence. He even attended some of her gymnastics meets and ballet performances. She was such a beautiful dancer and was captivating to watch on stage.

Gideon has always been honorable and respected her privacy by never intruding on her private moments. Besides, Celeste, with her motherly instincts, had already threatened to hex any male angel if she found out they were intruding on Seraphina's privacy. A powerful High Witch like Celeste or any witch's magic cannot kill a celestial angel, but some hexes can cause severe damage if the witch knows what she is doing.

Gideon would visit Celeste for regular updates so he could report back to the Council of Archangels but never revealed his presence to Seraphina. He would often leave Celeste with gifts for her. He knows that the days are numbered when the demonic forces and rogue angels will try to find her and come for her as she holds the key to the prison abyss of the princes of hell. The blood seal of the seven Archangels holds immense power, and many angels from unaligned factions will want to get their hands on it for their purposes. But for now, he will do his assigned duty and watch over her from the shadows and will intercept any forces that will try to attack her. As always fate and destiny usually conspire to mess with the best-laid plans…

CHAPTER I

SERAPHINA

The same recurring dream happened again as I dozed off in my mythology, folklore, and occult studies class, which was a fun elective class I chose to take out of interest in those subjects. In my dream, I saw myself standing in a scorched grassy area. It was nighttime, and the full moon had an otherworldly blood-red hue. Angelic beings were battling each other with such ferocity and intensity that some were moving so fast in a blur that my eyes could not keep up. Around me, the ground was littered with angelic beings. Some looked like they were dead, and some were severely injured. Cries of agony, along with the clashes of weapons, filled the air. In my dream, this battle scene always looked like something from a video game. Just as one of the angelic beings was approaching me in my dream, I felt a tug on my hair.

I woke up startled. Victoria Sharma, also known as Vicky by everyone, was looking at me with a cocked eyebrow and an amused smirk. "You know you were muttering in your sleep, right?" She whispers to me." And you have a bit of drool going on, too."She gestures at the corner of her mouth. I was aghast and quickly wiped my mouth with my hand. I know, very unladylike. Professor Katsipolous was teaching a death by PowerPoint lecture about Greek Mythology and the Greek's early civilizations.

One might assume that he would approach Greek mythology and their civilizations more enthusiastically and not in such a monotone voice because he was of Greek ethnicity and was raised in Greek culture, but that was not the case. I was glad that we were at the back of the vast classroom. Professor Katsipolous had dimmed the lights for the PowerPoint lecture. Some students looked bored, while some seemed genuinely interested. "What were you dreaming about that caused such a drool fest?" Victoria asks with a wicked smile. I shush Vicky to keep her voice down." Was it about Nathan?" She wags her eyebrows. I smack her arm lightly. "Stop with the gutter thoughts, Vicky. I did not get much sleep last night. I was up late working on my final term paper due before spring break." I shush her. I was tossing and turning all night, having that recurring dream about those angelic beings. That dream happens occasionally, and I don't know what to make of it. "Really Seraphina? Oh, come on. We both know you do not even have to try hard on all your papers, and you will get straight As. You sure you were not up with Nathan?" Vicky teases. I shake my head at her, clearly a bit annoyed. "Nathan and I are not an item. We barely went on two dates, and he tried to kiss me. I did not return the kiss and promptly exited his car. After that, we have not seen each other much except in hallways and between classes." "But he is really into you though. He will be at Laurel's birthday bash tonight. Are you still coming?" She whispers excitedly.

Laurel is the president of the Delta Phi Gamma sorority, and her yearly birthday parties, I heard, have always been the talk of the campus. This was the first time I got invited to Laurel's birthday party. Vicky's bubbly personality is exceptionally infectious. She makes people forget they are annoyed and mad at her, even if they want to stay angry. We have been friends since starting our first year in high school when she moved from New York. Her dad is an East Indian immigrant who owns quite a few banks and investment firms, while her mother, who is a very talented surgeon, is of Irish ancestry from New Jersey. Vicky has three other siblings and grew up wealthy and privileged. She considered herself not as spoiled as her other siblings and a better fashionista than them. Her much slimmer and taller siblings often teased her about her height and weight. She was only five feet, curvy and plump, with a pretty round face. She usually wears her long black hair in a messy bun. She often radiates positivity and is very outgoing. She has a reputation for being very blunt and always talks fast. Sometimes, I wonder if she ever pauses to catch her breath. She always knew where the best parties were being held and would often get invites to these parties.

I watch as Professor Katsipolous wraps up the lecture

and dismisses the class. "Yes, I will be there," I tell her as I pack my tote bag. "I have to stop by Celeste's place first to pick up a few things, then I will make my way there." "This will be the biggest party before spring break, and most of all, Nathan will be there. Maybe the two of you can finally talk and get the awkwardness out of the way." She suggests as she follows me out of the classroom and shoves books and stationery in her Prada backpack. Vicky loves luxury designer goods, and her parents often indulge her whims. I knew she was only taking Mythology, Folklore, and Occult studies because I was in them. She was not interested in it, but it was an easy elective that gave us more time to spend together. She has many acquaintances, but I am her only close friend. Most of the time, she babbles about every topic in the class. "Maybe I will talk to him and clear the air," I mutter. I asked her for a ride to Celeste's house since my car was getting some repairs. My old Toyota Camry transmission car gave out on me. Vicky drives a Tesla that her parents gifted her when she started college. She was gifted a luxury condo to live in off-campus while I was in a two-bedroom house. I zoned out as Vicky babbled excitedly about the upcoming party.

The house I currently live in belonged to my father, the late Dr. Zane Abner, Professor of Archaeology and Anthropology. According to Celeste, both of my parents tragically died in a freak accident on an archaeology expedition when I was still an infant. When that happened to them, I asked her where I was, and she said angels had saved me. I remembered the strange looks kids used to give me in elementary school when I told them I was saved by angels when my parents died. My teacher thought it was touching that some compassionate people saved me and brought me to Celeste. I inherited my dad's house and some inheritance money for education expenses. Not enough to be rich, but just enough to cover necessities and bills. I use the cash sparingly and rarely splurge on anything substantial.

Celeste was the only mother I knew; she made sure I knew who my parents were and their legacy. She was left as my legal Guardian and raised me on her own. She was of Italian and French ancestry, average height, and built with bushy, curly, dark brown hair. She had kind, startling green eyes and the most soothing voice. Her personality radiates wisdom and tranquility. Although in her forties, she did not look a day over thirty-five. She usually dresses in knitted clothing during the cold months and bohemian-style flowing dresses and skirts during the warmer months. Her family lives in Massachusetts, and Celeste moved to Connecticut to open her Holistic Clinical Psychotherapy clinic. Her relatives refer to her as the "hippie" of the family and often refer to her alternative treatments as a trip down to *Woodstock* and the *burning man.*

Celeste was also a Wiccan and part of the Circle of the Full Moon coven. They would often have meet-up group events, which I have attended a few times. She also does Tarot cards and palm readings. She has a room in her house dedicated to those services. I was forbidden to go into her psychic reading room. She would often have clients over for readings. One day, I took a peek inside the room and saw a chart full of strange-looking runes that seemed to glow. I wondered if it was a trick of the light or if it was glow-in-the-dark ink she used to write them. When she found me staring, it was the first time I saw her visibly upset at me. I was around fourteen years old. She grounded me for a week. Vicky called her the kooky hippie therapist when she found out I was grounded just for that.

Celeste has no children of her own and is unmarried, but she has a long-term boyfriend named Jebediah Silver Feathers, who is of Cherokee ancestry and a homicide detective. I remember him sleeping over occasionally and having some of his belongings at her place, but they still did not live together. He always treated me like a daughter and often gave me my favorite R.L. Stine books for birthdays and Christmas. Everyone calls him Jeb, and Celeste would only call him Jebediah during arguments. But for the most part, they seem to have a loving relationship. Jeb was around the same age as Celeste and did not look a day over thirty-five either. He was well over six feet tall, built like a well-muscled, burly linebacker with dark eyes and military-styled dark hair. His face's sharp, angular features make him seem like he is always scowling. Vicky will sometimes jokingly ask what their anti-aging secrets are or who their plastic surgeon was. I grew up calling him Uncle Jeb.

Vicky pulls me out of my thoughts by warning me not to miss the party. As I exited her car, I quickly told her I would see her later. I pull my coat tight around my body as I walk toward Celeste's house. The evening air was still chilly, although spring was approaching. Celeste's house was a beautiful two-story house with an old colonial brick veneer revival. I saw her Subaru SUV in the driveway, which means she was home, and a brand-new silver Mercedes SUV was also parked. Whose expensive ride? And who is the visitor? If it was one of her clients for psychic readings, I bet they were probably wealthy. I still had a key to her place and opened her front door. Celeste and some strange markings on her door that she called "protection runes," along with a few amulets.

As I step into her house, the smell of sage incense bombards my nose. There were various crystal decorations in different areas of her home. As a child, I loved playing with her crystals and stones; she would tell me what energy each possessed. Celeste was laughing in the kitchen in her high tinkling laugh at something a man's deep baritone bass voice was saying. That certainly does not sound like Jeb- or a client. Those two seem like old friends! I did not know Celeste had any male friends. And even if she did, they would have had to be pen pals or online because many would be too scared of Jeb's linebacker size and his usual broody dark scowl to even step a foot into her driveway. Her tuxedo cat, Nyx, ran upstairs as I approached her kitchen. That little ungrateful kitty did not greet me with any meows and purrs for ear scratches.

As I walk into the kitchen, a pair of hazel gold-flecked eyes and green eyes both look at me. "Seraphina, I forgot you were coming over," Celeste beams with her brilliant smile. Her eyes lit up as she quickly came over and hugged me, smelling of sage incense and lavender essential oils. She has always been a hugger; her expressive eyes often speak volumes. I am lucky that such a sweet maternal woman was my adopted mother. I turn my attention to the man sitting on one of her kitchen bar stools gazing at me with quizzical hazel eyes with flecks of gold, and my breath caught in my throat.

CHAPTER 2
SERAPHINA

I was unprepared for the god of a man sitting in front of me, assessing me from head to toe with this look like he was surprised to see me. He quickly stands up and extends a large, bronze complexion, muscular hand to me. I felt my eyes widening and my cheeks flush with heat. He was so tall. He was at least six feet-six inches, and well-built like one of those Greek heroes and Greek god statues in the photos of my Greek culture lecture earlier.

His clothing was impeccable. A black button-down shirt with sleeves rolled up halfway way, exposing bulging biceps and a few top buttons undone, showing a glimpse of a smooth, muscular-looking chest with an intriguing-looking tattoo that looks tribal. The tucked-in dress shirt looks tailored to his body, framing a well-proportioned torso. I did not have to guess if abs were rippling under his shirt because I am sure they were. His matching black pants also was tailored to his slim hips. It was hard not to stare at his athletic build. He had broad shoulders, bulging biceps, a slender waist, and hips. He was wearing matching, expensive-looking black leather dress shoes. They look like the type of expensive shoes Vicky's dad usually wears.

I was trying not to make it evident that I was staring at him with my breath still caught in my throat. I was like a moth to a flame. His jet-black hair was flowing in waves, slightly brushing his shoulders. His hair seems like it should belong in a shampoo commercial. His well-chiseled face with an angular jawline, straight nose, and sensual-looking mouth was the most gorgeous face I have ever seen. The five-o'clock shadow gives his face a somewhat harsh and aloof rugged look. I mean, Nathan Beckett was the most handsome man I have seen around campus, but this man's face would make him look like a plain medieval kitchen serf.

He had a very regal confident aura, and his mesmerizing hazel eyes framed by dark eyebrows were still gazing at me. They were the most beautiful-looking hazel eyes I had ever seen. They had unusual flecks of gold, which was a startling contrast to his jet-black hair. He looked roughly around his late twenties, perhaps about thirty, but an air of wisdom about him belonged to someone much older. He oozes sex appeal but, at the same time, has a very classy and edgy vibe, especially with that strange tribal-looking chest tattoo peeking out of his shirt. Is it even possible to have all those traits all in one man?

It feels so wrong for a man to be this good-looking and sexy. Vicky would be proud if she only knew my current thoughts. She was the only supportive friend who did not judge me, while most just regarded me as a bit of a prude that needed a good lay to loosen up some tightly wound screws. I do not consider myself a prude.

"You must be Seraphina," He says, taking my hand in his with a smile showing a hint of brilliant white teeth that look too white to be authentic. If those are not veneers, I would like to know his dentist. His fingers closed over mine, and they felt wam. I briefly felt a jolt of electricity and brushed it off as static electricity. His handshake felt warm with a bit of firmness as his fingers were caressing my own. The handshake lingers a bit longer than it should have been. I quickly release his hand, not wanting him or Celeste to notice how much I like his fingers touching my own. "Celeste told me so much about you. I am Gideon," He says to me, his eyes never leaving me. A voice like his should do phone sex gigs as a side hustle or film industry voice-over work. If his devastating good looks could not make any woman throw their underwear at him, his deep baritone bass voice certainly would. I didn't detect a Northeast accent, so it's probably not from around here. But there was a hint of a British accent.

Hmmmm intriguing. My ability to speak slowly returns. "Nice to meet you, Gideon." I managed to respond neutrally. "Gideon is a consultant working with Jeb's detective unit," Celeste says quickly. "He has been a friend of Jeb and mine for a while but was away on business and just returned to town." she continues as she grabs her wine glass. "Well, it was nice to meet you, Gideon. Welcome back to town." I give him a quick smile and turn to focus on Celeste instead. I did not want him to notice how his devastating good looks affected me. "So... how are your studies coming along? Celeste told me you were studying anthropology and genetics." Gideon asks, his gaze still on me. "Classes are going well. We are about to be on spring break soon," I briefly respond. I was hoping that the nervousness in my voice would go unnoticed.

I am usually a bit confident about men, but something about Gideon made me feel like a giddy high school girl with a crush. "She is quite brilliant and talented like her parents were." Celeste smiles at me and then at Gideon between sips of her red wine. "I hoped to borrow your car for a birthday party tonight. May I borrow it?" I asked Celeste as I rested my heavy tote bag on her kitchen counter." I need my car to meet with my Wicca group later tonight, but Gideon can drop you off. I trust him to get you there safely." She responds with an off-hand gesture at Gideon but seems to emphasize the word 'safely.' I glanced at Gideon to see his reaction after Celeste had volunteered him to be my Uber, but he did not object. "That is OK with me." He nods in agreement. I tried not to allow my breath to be caught in my throat again. "Great. Thanks, Gideon. I will be ready in about thirty minutes." "She means in an hour," Celeste teases with a laugh. I scoffed at her and gave him a quick smile as I left the kitchen to get ready upstairs in my old room.

The room I grew up in looked precisely how I left it. Celeste maintains it by ensuring everything is kept clean and not covered in a layer of dust and cobwebs. I left my mahogany dresser, nightstand, and queen-sized bed because my current house already had that furniture. It was just a sparsely decorated, normal-sized room. There's not much to it since I took most of my belongings when I moved. What can I say? I like simplicity. I still had some clothing and toiletries that I left just in case I needed to stay over. I have not slept over since I moved out when I started college. A full bathroom was inside my room, which was a nice perk compared to the other upstairs bedrooms.

I was supposed to stop by briefly for some books that Celeste got for me, and now I will be driven to Laurel's party by the most gorgeous man I have ever seen. I should not be having such thoughts about Gideon. Maybe he is married and has a wife and kids! No-wait, there was no wedding band on his ring finger. Or does he have a girlfriend or something because there is no way such a good-looking man like him is still on the dating market? He looks wealthy, too, with the way he dresses and the expensive Mercedes-Benz SUV. Why am I speculating on all these scenarios about Gideon anyway? There is no way he will want to date a twenty-one-year-old college student. I am sure he prefers women in his age range.

My thoughts kept rambling about different scenarios about Celeste and Jeb's mysterious friend Gideon and his relationship status while taking a nice warm shower. I selected a lovely form-fitting sparkly navy color merino wool sweater dress with a side slit and some ankle boots. The dress was a Christmas gift from Celeste. It was the most expensive and luxurious piece of clothing I owned. I smile, thinking about how Vicky and the other ladies at the party will react when they see Gideon dropping me off. I will have a lot of explaining to do with Vicky later on. She will ramble off, asking all sorts of nosy questions about Gideon. I apply light makeup and tame my long, curly hair into a fishtail braid. I fastened the gold collar necklace with the amethyst stone Celeste gifted me for my birthday. I thought about what questions I should ask Gideon so that the car ride to Laurel's sorority house would not feel awkward. I was feeling butterflies doing somersaults in my stomach, thinking about being alone with him in his car. "OK, Seraphina, just be your charming, friendly self. There is nothing to worry about. Gideon is just a handsome guy who is probably not single. Treat him normal like how you treat members of Celeste's coven."I mutter to myself in my dresser mirror. I stare at my reflection, a defined face with sharp, high cheekbones and almond-shaped brown eyes framed by long lashes staring back at me. I get many compliments about my face, especially Vicky, who says it will give a supermodel a run for her money. I have received many jealous compliments about my slender, athletic, well-proportioned figure from other girls I trained with in gymnastics and ballet. After high school, I stopped competing in gymnastics and only danced ballet as a recreational workout. I was built very slender, but there was no way I would have made it professionally as a ballet dancer unless I could have gone on a diet to lose the boobs.

Although I was pretty, I have never had a serious

boyfriend or relationship. My thoughts refocus on Gideon. Maybe since he is that good-looking, he probably has a terrible personality. But perhaps I am wrong about that since Celeste or Jeb would probably not be acquainted with him if he was a total douchebag. I wonder why Celeste seems to trust him to be around me so quickly, even though tonight was the first time I met him. Celeste has usually been extremely overprotective of me when it comes to boys since I was a teenager. She barely met Nathan once and immediately disliked him. She said he had "bad vibes" and "chaotic energies." But with Gideon, who is way better-looking than Nathan, she casually asked him to give me a ride to Laurel's party like he was a family member she knew all her life. She mentioned that he is a consultant who works with Jeb's homicide unit but failed to mention his existence before tonight. Maybe later, I will grill her about Gideon, but for now, I will let my butterflies stick to their landing, calm my nerves, and go downstairs.

"Your carriage awaits," Celeste teases as I descend the stairs. "Well, aren't you a sight for sore eyes? I am so glad you finally decided to wear that dress." She clasps her hand, smiling at me. "I am glad I found a special occasion to wear it to. "I smile at her while I put on my wool jacket and cross-body clutch. "Shall we?" Gideon says to me as he walks to the foot of the stairs. He already had his coat on—a nice, luxurious-looking, long black leather jacket. Vicky would love to know who his stylist is because Gideon seems to have great style. He glances at me, and I swear he was checking me out with a nod of approval at my outfit, but his face quickly returned to a neutral expression. "Have fun, be safe, and I will see you tomorrow for your books," Celeste says as she ushers us toward the door. "Keep her safe, Gideon," she says in a firm whisper to him with a warning look.

I could have sworn there was something an unspoken code language spoken between them as Gideon nodded his head in response. Huh? How close of a friendship do these two have? Maybe I will have to ask Gideon. He quickly opens the door for me as Celeste gives us a wave and shuts it behind us. "So, where is this party?" He asks as we walk toward his SUV. The night air was even colder, and I shivered under my coat. I should have worn my warm puffer coat, but Vicky said that coat belonged in the wardrobe of the abominable snowman and I should burn it. I give him the address to Laurel's sorority house. "Allow me." He graciously opened the passenger side door for me, and I was more than eager to step into the warm car he had already started as soon as we walked out the door. Opening doors- what a gentleman. Chivalry still exists. His car was immaculate and luxurious inside. I settle myself in his leather car seat and hug my arms. It was a very comfy seat. He noticed I was cold and turned up the car heater. "Celeste asked me to drop you off, although we never met. I hope that did not make you feel awkward." He turns to face me with those mesmerizing eyes. "I was more than happy to oblige," he says as he settles in his car seat. "It was either you or an Uber. So, where do you live around here, and how long have you known Celeste and Jeb?" I blurt out frankly. I just wanted to get the truth from the horse's mouth." I live close by," He answers curtly. "And I have known Celeste and Jeb for a while." "Then why have we never met before? They have failed to mention you." I glance at him furtively. "I am usually on special projects," He casually replies, his eyes straight ahead, focusing on driving.

I knew I was not going to get much out of him. He was being very cagey and not a chatty person who would talk to fill the silence. A bit of awkward silence fell between us. But I decided to break it. So finally, I ask, "What do you know about the culture of ancient Athens, Gideon?" I was thinking about my Greek lectures earlier. Gideon glances at me with a solemn look, and then his lips curl into a hint of an amused smile. I instantly felt more at ease, and he seemed to find my question somewhat amusing. "Do you mean the philosophers, scholars, and cowards? I prefer the Spartans to them." He scoffs. I was surprised how his demeanor changed from a serious look to amusing sarcasm. "I bet you like the Spartans because of the movie 300." I shake my head at him. That bro-code movie 300 is the only reason most men I know like the Spartans. "Never seen it. "He frowns, looking a bit confused. "But King Leonidas was quite a formidable king. It was not 300 Spartans like in the movie you mentioned. Not much I can say about Pythagoras in Athens." He says, his tone of voice dripping with sarcasm. "You mean the triangle guy who made high school math a nightmare for me?" I gasp with a short, sarcastic laugh. I was a bit terrible at trigonometry but somehow passed it. Another grin of amusement spread across his gorgeous face at my reaction. "I did spend some time in Greece," he says as he drives down a well-lit dark street. The streetlights illuminated the hazel-gold flecks in his eyes. Such mesmerizing eyes. We continued our banter about the Greeks and the Spartans. I laughed when he referred to the Greek deities as a "bunch of petty pagans." I found his sarcasm quite funny, and his wit was charming. I felt more at ease conversing with him, but whenever I tried to ask him questions about himself, he would deflect and change the subject. The mystery of his persona just made him even more intriguing.

Vicky, Laurel, and a few of the Delta Phi Gamma sorority girls were on the porch of the Greek revival structure sorority mansion when Gideon drove up behind a few parked cars. Laurel's wealthy parents donated the brand-new sorority mansion to Delta Phi Gamma and had it renovated to resemble a two-story Greek revival-style house. It was not a huge party but an exclusive by invitation only. The sorority house even had a few maids, a gardener, and a housekeeper. That is how affluent and exclusive it was. I even saw a few waitstaff going around with drinks and finger foods on platters on the enormous front porch.

Both Vicky and Laurel stared as Gideon got out of his SUV, opened my side of the car door and offered his hand to help me out of the car. The other sorority girls saw where Vicky and Laurel were diverting their attention, and they all openly stared. Some looked like they were swooning, and I even saw Laurel lick her lips. Vicky's eyes widen, looking like two saucers. Gideon seems oblivious to his effect on these ladies because he barely turns briefly in their direction. He gave me his cell number so I could contact him if I needed a ride home or if any issues arose. I asked him to help me with my Greek culture assignment since he sounded like a history brochure. I also asked if we could meet at the cafe near campus where I usually study. I tried hard to contain my excitement when he agreed with a smile. I thanked him for the ride with a hug and walked toward the front porch as he drove off.

As soon as I made it to the steps, Vicky pounces upon me and loops her arm with mine with lots of barely audible word vomit pouring out. All I could decipher was, "Who was the hottie?" Why didn't you invite him in? Where did you meet him? What does he do? He looks loaded." She did not pause in between questions. Laurel and the other sorority girls circled me like pretty predators closing in on prey, all asking nosy questions about Gideon. Some of them could not even contain their jealousy of why an older-looking god of a gorgeous man would want anything to do with a prude like me. I felt a bit possessive when Laurel commented about all the "bad things" she would love to do to his body. She shut up when I told her with a smug smile that he barely even glanced in her direction and would meet me at the cafe near campus to help me with my assignment. "That is not even a date." She sneers, rolling her eyes. "If I see him again, I will make him notice me. "She huffs and folds her arms.

If Barbie were a human, she would look like Laurel. She was tall and beautiful with long, wavy golden blonde hair and sparkling blue-green eyes. Her short, long-sleeved, sparkly pink dress fitted her slender form like a glove. She has a reputation for being spoiled, arrogant, and pampered. Laurel usually stops at nothing to get her way; most of the time, she does. Vicky was familiar with her more socially than me. Most of the time, she barely acknowledged my existence, and tonight was the most word she had ever spoken to me. She was a legacy because her mother and aunt used to be Delta Phi Gamma. Her parents are also generous donors to the sorority, hence the fancy sorority mansion in which all the sorority pledges live. She was beautiful but had the intellect of a doorpost. "So, what's all the commotion out here?" A male voice drawls. I turned around, and there Nathan was, leaning casually in the doorway, looking at me with a half-smirk. He was tall with lean muscles and short blond hair. His face was gorgeous. Cold. His icy light blue eyes were fixated on me as he strolled toward me.

CHAPTER 3
GIDEON

I was in my translucent phased form as I observed Nathaniel walking toward Seraphina. I had one of the Cherub angel servants take my car back to the compound so I could conduct my surveillance. I have lived for millennia, watched civilizations rise and fall, and had many liaisons, but nothing could have prepared me for the effect that Zanael's daughter had on me. When I first touched her hand, I felt electricity surge through my body. I remembered how easy it was to converse with her during our car ride. She had quite a sense of humor. Her voice and tinkling laugh were infectious. Not only was she a sight to behold with a toned, graceful dancer's body, but she was also intelligent, charming, and witty. I found her slender and willowy dancer's body quite attractive. She had curves in all the right places, beautiful slender-toned legs, and perky full breasts. Oh no, I should not be having these inappropriate thoughts about her attractive body, not about her gorgeous and toned legs or her breasts.

I have had many beautiful human women, fae women, witches, and other angels assigned to Earth as lovers. Some even more beautiful than her that ignited feelings of lust- but none ever had this effect on me where I felt both a stir of lust and an intriguing cosmic pull like what I feel for her.

Celeste should have warned me that she was coming over. I have watched her grow from an infant to a young woman from afar, like a silent Guardian angel, but being in her presence and talking to her was a whole different story. The attraction I feel for her caught me off guard. It was definitely unexpected given that I had known her all her life so far. I observed that she had grown into a beautiful young woman, but no inappropriate thoughts crossed my mind until I was in her presence tonight.

She was not supposed to see Celeste and me together. Although a gifted High Witch, Celeste can be pretty forgetful sometimes. She does have a disdain for many angels, especially the Powers class of warriors, and thinks we are a bunch of beautiful, arrogant pricks, but she has even worse disdain for demons and fallen angels. She calls us Powers Heaven's anti-demon task force, which technically we are the celestial police force. The Powers, warrior angels, are the strongest of the supernatural community. We maintain order on Earth and in the supernatural community. The celestial jail cells are full of rogue angels because of us. She has proven to be a valuable ally and has our respect and gratitude. Being a powerful

High Witch and seer, she is immortal, but the ritual comes at a price where she cannot produce a life of her own. The law of magic used by High Witches to gain immortality is that they have to give up something of value to balance the scales. Having at least one child of her own held the most value for Celeste, but she wanted immortality, so she gave up her ability to have children.

She and my most trusted second-in-command, the warrior angel Jebediah Silver Feathers started a relationship right after I sought her help to locate Zanael. The Council and I allowed their liaison since Celeste cannot give birth to children. She was reluctant at first to help me, stating she wanted no part in the business of angels, but Jebediah convinced her. Even though she is dating one of the Powers, she still thinks most of us are a bunch of celestial assholes.

Celeste has been an excellent foster parent for Seraphina and raised her well to be the beautiful and intelligent young woman she is. Zanael would have been proud. Jeb is also like a pseudo-uncle to her and helps out Celeste. I feel much at ease for her safety with a powerful High witch and my most adept warrior, Jeb, looking out for her. I was only supposed to watch her from afar. As the Lord of all the Powers, I was not supposed to do tasks a lower-ranking angel was supposed to do. But I made a promise to Zanael as he lay dying in my arms to look after his daughter. I remember her as a beautiful and vulnerable infant. Her cries of hunger and distress were heart-wrenching as I held her in my arms and teleported with her to Celeste's place.

My mentor, the most powerful Archangel Michael,

assigned me to Earth after the rebellion as the Guardian of the Earth angel Zanael. He was like a brother to me, and I still grieve for him. Zanael was quite eccentric and always found humor in everything. He always made me laugh. He always loved teasing me that I was a broody soldier and needed to lighten up. So Zanael's way of getting me to lighten up was to take me to the midsummer festivities that the fae folks usually celebrate, exclusive festivities held by the nobility classes in the Roman empire and the bacchanals the ancient Greeks usually had hosted by no other than the pagan God of Debauchery himself, Dionysus. For many centuries, we had some fun times.

Being assigned to Earth, I could indulge in certain human pleasures. However, the Council of Archangels strictly forbade me from having marriages or long-term relationships and from fathering any Nephilims with humans. The only unions they would permit are mate bonding ceremonies if it is with another angel. It also has to be with someone they approve of, but those rarely occur and are even rarer for Powers since we are Heaven's warrior class and police task force. We can indulge in pleasures but usually don't fall in love or have long-term liaisons like Jeb and Celeste's arrangement. Jeb has been one of those rare exceptions where one of the Powers has a long-term liaison with someone from the supernatural community who is not an angel. The Council of Archangels approved his union with the High Witch Celeste because she is a valuable asset, and an alliance with her was beneficial. We are warriors, first and foremost.

Being incarnated on Earth automatically made us celestial angels feel some human emotions, and we disguise our true celestial visage, especially our eyes, to blend in with humans. Zanael taught me and many other angels assigned to Earth to manage the influx of earthly emotions that bombarded us. Zanael... how could you have been so stupid to fall in love? And with a human, too. You were immortal, while she would eventually succumb to the ravages of age and time. Then you fathered a Nephilim, who is now the new Earth angel after you got yourself killed. I assumed the Human Scientist was just another of his many conquests and a fleeting phase, but I was wrong. When I saw that he was falling in love with her, I told him to end it before the Council found out, which upset him. Zanael eloped with her because he feared I would tell the Council. He should have trusted that I would have done everything possible to help him.

Zanael was also sterile, being the first of his kind, so everyone, including the Council of Archangels, was baffled when he was able to impregnate a human. Seraphina was not supposed to exist, but she does, and she is my responsibility. Zanael married the human right under my nose and hid his love for her. But now his lovely daughter is being raised as a human and is unaware of her celestial heritage, thanks to Celeste binding her angelic powers at the request of the Council of Archangels to make her blend in among humans. If it were up to Archangel Michael, Seraphina would probably be locked away in a tower.

Archangel Raphael and Chamuel suggested she should be glamoured as a human hidden in plain sight.

I watched as she squirmed uncomfortably under Nathaniel's gaze. Ah, Nathaniel. If you much less as touch her without her consent, I will run you through with my sword. Nathan Beckett, as he calls himself among humans, is a rogue, unaligned Gregori Watcher. He was one of the first Watchers who had fathered forbidden Nephilim. The Council of Archangels had his Nephilim offspring massacred along with all the others. Nathaniel took no sides in the rebellion, although Lucifer's forces tried to recruit him. He prefers to be unaligned to neither Lucifer's forces nor Heaven's. He is one of the leaders of the unaligned Gregori Watchers faction on Earth. A powerful one up the highest echelons. He and his other faction members prefer to live a hedonistic lifestyle, taking their lewd pleasures with human women, fae, and witches as much as possible. Now, his latest conquest seems to be Seraphina. No, not her. I had already failed her father. I cannot fail her and allow this rogue Watcher to get his hands on her.

Nathaniel's faction knows Seraphina is different because her aura still shows that she has an angelic heritage, but they don't know how special she is. Celeste could only have done so much to disguise her Nephilim aura. But for the most part, Seraphina can pass for a human. Nathaniel's faction wants their hands on her to figure out what she is. Celeste knew he would be at this party for his nefarious purposes, so she asked me to drop Seraphina off so I could watch her and him closely.

I watched her lithe form move effortlessly, backing away from Nathaniel's predatory gaze. My protective instincts for her kicked into high gear. That Watcher was such a lout. Although many angels assigned to Earth, especially those under my leadership, were afforded many earthly luxuries and pleasures, I ensure my warriors live disciplined lives. Some angels like Jeb prefer to hold earthly jobs and blend in with humans to keep watch over things better.

Even Michael and the other Archangels, whenever they visit Earth, are usually dressed in the most luxurious designer suits and will stay at my mansion with servants at their disposal. Our clothing had to adjust to modern times. We only wear heavenly ceremonial robes for special rituals and occasions and gleaming celestial battle armor for battles. Being the Lord of the Powers, the warrior class of angels assigned to Earth has perks because I had millions of Earthly funds to ensure the angels in my faction needs were well taken care of on Earth. My mansion is the most opulent one among the factions, and it is the only place the Archangels like to stay whenever they visit Earth because it is also heavily protected with lots of wards. They have every lavish whim at their disposal in my mansion. Prepping for the Archangels' visit usually feels like prepping for the arrival of royalty.

The Powers that live with me are my faction's handpicked best warriors and the elite squad. Even though the angels on Earth have glamoured themselves to pass for humans, many humans cannot help but be mesmerized by us. Some humans can even sense something otherworldly about us. I know the effects I can have on human women, so I kept my distance from Seraphina. I can feel that she immediately had an attraction to me when she first saw me. I saw the desire in her eyes, but she had not tried to act upon her desires when we were alone like many other human women I encountered would have done and had done. I didn't expect I would feel attracted to her, too.

I remembered how much I wanted to caress her full-looking lips with my own and showed her the pleasures she had never experienced before when she hugged me to thank me for the car ride. Her body against mine felt so warm and inviting, although it was a simple platonic hug. It took some willpower to keep my arousal in check and to refrain from tipping her face to mine and kissing her. Supernatural libido can have its downsides. Our sexual desires can be in overdrive because we experience emotions and pleasures way more intensely than humans. No, I cannot think of these inappropriate thoughts about Zanael's daughter. She is innocent of the supernatural world around her, and I do not want to hurt her. Intimacy is something I don't partake in with any female I take to my bed. Just carnal pleasures. I am her Guardian, so it would be deemed very inappropriate.

I did not know what came over me to accept her offer to meet her at the cafe to assist her with her Greek culture assignment, but I had to cancel it because I didn't want her to get the wrong ideas. I don't want to mislead her in any form. Besides, Celeste and Jeb have parental love for

Seraphina, and Celeste will find a way to make me pay if I hurt her in any form.

Over the centuries, it has been difficult for human lovers because I cannot give them the intimacy that many of them crave, but only temporary carnal pleasures. I am an immortal celestial angel, and they will eventually succumb to the ravages of age and other things that come with mortality. So, I stopped taking human women to my bed to avoid the complications that come with such liaisons. To take care of my sensual pleasures, I only take other supernatural women to my bed. There is a thorough vetting process for who gets selected.

I watched as Nathaniel tried to converse with Seraphina. I tuned into my supernatural hearing so I could hear their conversation. Of course, I should have known that fae women were hosting this college party. The fae loves to lead a very hedonistic and lavish lifestyle. They are great entertainers that always throw the best parties and orgies but are a tricky lot to deal with—always trying to make pesky deals and bargains. Every supernatural knows that thanking a fae makes you indebted to them, and if you do something for a fae, they will always try to return the favor. I knew that this gaudy Greek revival sorority mansion had fae written all over it and recognized those sorority girls as fae glamoured as humans. As an angel, I can see through the glamour of every supernatural species that tries to blend in with humans. It comes in handy for demons that disguise themselves as humans.

Some fae love to glamour as humans so they can attend

colleges and institutions and infiltrate human jobs to make their bargains. I immediately recognized the favorite of the fae King Aodhan's daughter, crowned Princess Laureliana. She calls herself Laurel Sanders, a college student and Delta Phi Gamma sorority president. Her royal parents cater to her every whim, hence the gaudy sorority mansion as her earthly dwelling.

The fae dwells in a supernatural dimension parallel to Earth, which I have visited many times, but they love making Earth their playground. They mostly stay out of the business of angels unless they are trying to seduce us. The fae usually find us angels very fascinating and try to act like our groupies. They especially find the Powers more challenging to seduce, given that we are the warrior class and usually don't indulge in emotions and pleasures much.

Princess Laureliana immediately recognized me as soon as I exited my car. She has been trying to cement her status as my lover for centuries. I have only given in to her seduction once under the influence of too much fae ambrosia during one of their Queen Mab midsummer festivities in the early tenth century. Angels are impervious to human afflictions, many enchantments, and spells except for High Witch hexed weapons, but fae ambrosia drink does give us a heady buzz if we drink too much of it.

Although Laurel's seductive beauty can stir the arousal of many supernatural males and human males, I do find her quite fickle, spoiled, and vapid. Ever since that one night, I took her to my bed centuries ago, she has been trying to seduce me again, looking to cement her status as a regular lover. I remembered how Zanael had ridiculed me for making the "social climbing hussy" fae princess obsessed with me after a one-night stand. That was a stupid mistake on my part. I have been very selective with the vetting process of lovers for my bed, but she was the result of a one-time lapse of judgment on my part. Zanael. I miss you so much, especially the great times we had.

Laurel and her fae entourage seemed insulted that I did not even acknowledge their presence. I ensured I was a decent distance from the mansion to survey Nathaniel so she and the other fae would not sense that I was still nearby. They have very keen senses, like angels.

I heard Nathaniel asking Seraphina to walk with him outside for a bit. I watched him take her arm and lead her down the pathway to some trees behind the mansion. I decided to follow in my phased form. I saw Nathaniel pulling her toward him and kissing her. I felt a pang of jealousy as she allowed the kiss and wrapped her arms around his neck. But when Nathaniel glides a hand on her slender thigh under her dress, she quickly ends the kiss and pushes him away, telling him to stop. Nathaniel glares at her in confusion and frustration at her reaction. He calls her a cocktease prude and grabs her arms. Whatever jealousy I had toward their make-out session quickly switched to protectiveness as I advanced toward them to intervene, my hands curled into fists. I stopped when she yelled at him to get his hands off her and kicked him in the crotch area.

She is definitely Zanael's daughter—a force to be reckoned with. I smiled to myself, approving the way she was handling the situation. She is no damsel in distress and can take care of herself. Caught off guard, Nathaniel quickly releases her as he drops to one knee on the ground. Fuming, she hastily walks toward the mansion. I watch as Seraphina quickly takes out her cell phone and calls her friend Vicky to come outside to take her home immediately. She told her about the situation with Nathaniel. She was so furious that she was visibly shaking. I saw Vicky running out to meet her, grabbed her into a consoling hug, and led her to her car. She could have contacted me, but that is fine. I need to deal with the rogue Watcher.

I materialize my celestial broadsword, unphased my body, and walk toward Nathaniel. He quickly stands up, straightening himself casually as if expecting me. "Ah, come on, Gideon. I can smell your self-righteous stench from miles away." He rolls his eyes with a crooked, sarcastic smile. "You have always been such a party pooper. Had to spoil my fun." He scoffs as his celestial weapon materializes in his hand, and his eyes start glowing with an icy blue angel-fire. His celestial weapon was a Viking's sword.

Watcher's angelic eyes' natural form is usually icy blue angel- fire while my eyes' natural form is gold angel-fire as the Lord of the powers. Unlike the fallen angels, unaligned angels have not lost their celestial wings. "I think the human girl that just gave you a swift kick to your nether regions has a different idea of fun." I give him a smug smile. "Trying to force yourself on human college girls is a new low, Nathaniel. What happened? The fae women are playing fickle with you again?" I goad him mockingly.

Nathaniel shrugs off my comments as he glares at me. "Quit the bullshit, Gideon. We both know that the girl is not fully human, the High Witch is not her birth mother, and you are her Guardian. I've got my sources to confirm this." He waves a dismissive hand as he watches me stop abruptly. As much as I would gladly like to run my sword through him for trying to force his advances on Seraphina, I have to keep my cool. He seems to know something. Too much about Seraphina already. I need to know what he knows. "Besides, there is no way she could have kicked me without breaking her leg if she was fully human." He continues. He got a point there. Our bodies are technically invulnerable. Humans hitting us have zero effect on our bodies. "Relax. I am not here to fight." He raises his palms as if surrendering as his celestial sword de-materialized and his glowing blue angel-fire irises returned to their glamour of human icy blue. "Despite your battle prowess, we both know you would not be able to take me in a fight Nathaniel." "Ah, you Powers are a pompous lot. Especially you-Michael's goody shoes, Tin soldier," He retorts, his voice dripping with sarcasm. Before Nathaniel went unaligned, he always teased me about being Michael's protege. One thing that has not changed about him is that he loves to hear himself talk.

"I know that you have been watching Seraphina for a while now. The question remains: What is so special about her that the Lord of the Powers, the mighty Lord Gideon, is doing the task of a lackey to watch over her?" He probes, stroking his chin. I know I must be careful with my response because Nathaniel is slick. "What I do is of no business to your unaligned faction," I respond curtly as my celestial sword de-materializes. I knew Nathaniel would be foolish to attack me right now, so retracting my weapon was safe. "This is your last warning. Stay away from Seraphina," I warn him through clenched teeth. "And if I don't, my Lord?" He curtsies mockingly. "You always have a penchant for the dramatics, Nathaniel." I shook my head at him. "Then I will run you through with my sword if you lay a hand on her again without her consent," I say to him, glaring at him. "Possessive, aren't you? We both know that prudish college girls are not to your taste. She is pretty sassy, and I will have her with or without your consent." He seethes, eyes blazing with fury. "I will find out what she is." He teleported in a blast of blue angel- fire before I could slug him for his offensive comments about Seraphina.

CHAPTER 4

GIDEON

"You were supposed to watch over her!" Celeste yells shrilly at me over my cell phone after a series of swear words and profanity. She is the only one who can get away with talking to me like that. I gave her a pass because Celeste only reacted like any mother would, especially after hearing about what Nathaniel tried to do to her daughter. She is usually mild-mannered, but when it comes to anyone who tries to harm Seraphina, she seems to transform into the Goddess Kali, ready to chop someone down. Nathaniel was already on her shit list when Celeste first heard that Seraphina had gone on a few dates with him. She threatened to pluck his wings like a rooster if she ever saw him again. And she probably could, given her knowledge of magical hexes that can cause severe harm to celestial beings.

I heard Jeb trying to calm her down in the background, chastising her for yelling at me and telling her it was not my fault what happened. She calmed down, and her voice switched to a graver tone when I told her I think Nathaniel knows more than he leads about Seraphina. And that he threatened to find out what she was. She said that she would need to strengthen the Enochian protection wards around Seraphina's house and that, more than ever, I need to be vigilant in watching her or assign a detail of angel guards to do it. Jeb also agreed. As soon as I got off the phone with Celeste, I saw a text message from Seraphina. She held me to that tutoring meet-up promise and asked if I could meet her in a few days. I responded that I had heard what had happened to her and asked if she was OK. She said she should have called me to take her home but didn't know if I was available. I told her I would never be too busy to help her and would be there if trouble found her again.

It was around midnight when I decided to teleport to my mansion's compound. I will have to brief everyone to keep a close watch on Nathaniel, but most were either out at their various patrol posts or in their private quarters. The mansion felt eerily quiet tonight. Most other angels do not know about Seraphina's true heritage except for Jeb and my elite squad, who were there that fateful night when Zanael died and transferred his Earth angel essence and the blood seal of the seven Archangels into her. The Council of Archangels wanted it to remain that way, so they had the Council of the High Witches make all the others there that night swear a blood oath to secrecy about Seraphina's true identity. Celeste was the one who led the ritual and administered the blood oath.

Cael, my manservant, was startled when I materialized

in front of him in a burst of gold angel-fire. "Cael?" I arch an eyebrow at him, amused by his jumpy reaction. Cael was one of the first and only Nephilim that I know of who survived the great massacre of his kind. Nephilims are a liability in the supernatural world. They were unpredictable and volatile, with many often seduced by demonic forces. These sinister forces frequently used Nephilims who chose to ally with them to oppress humanity.

When I first met Cael and saved his life, he was a mere boy who looked around ten years old. I saw goodness in his aura and the potential for greatness. He refused to partake in the macabre rituals and the horrors his family committed and ran away from home. I found him dirty, starving, and scavenging for food. I could not bear to allow the other angels to kill him. Michael punished me with a few hundred years of hard labor for saving one of the Nephilim abominations. Michael pleaded on my behalf to the Council of Archangels, and they allowed the child to live under the conditions that I kept a close watch on him and that I stay assigned to Earth. I miss my brothers and sisters in Heaven, but I feel more of a sense of purpose being assigned to Earth to protect humanity.

I offered Cael his freedom, but he decided that he wanted to be my manservant. Nephilims are not immortal but have longevity, slow aging, and some angelic abilities. Cael was ever grateful to me for saving his life and swore loyalty and allegiance to me and my faction. He has proven to be highly skilled and has mastered many earthly trades that are valuable assets to my faction. He looks like a human male roughly in his early fifties, although he is a few millennia years old. He stands about five-ten, average, with grey eyes and grey, streaked sandy hair.

"My Lord," He bows his head reverently as he reaches to take my coat. "Her Royal Highness, the fae princess Laureliana is here to see you," He says in a low, nervous voice. I whirled around in irritation. "You know she is not allowed to come here? How did she get past the Wards?" I ask him sternly. Cael flinched a bit but quickly composed himself. "She has her ways. Kemuel let her in. There was nothing I could have done to stop him." He lowers his head sheepishly with a sigh. Kemuel is one of my lieutenants in my elite squad. "I will deal with Kemuel later. Where is she?" I inquire as I walk up the stairs leading to my private quarters. "She is in your private quarters." He responds by trying to catch up with me. I was infuriated. Not only did the presumptuous fae princess come over unannounced, but she was in my private quarters! I strode toward my bedroom door and unlocked the door.

Laurel was sitting on my four-poster Cal King bed wearing a pink silk dress held by thin straps that didn't leave much to the imagination. Her pink nipples were hard under the silky material. She smiled seductively at me, batting her eyelashes as she crossed her long, slender legs. She looked so desirable in that silk dress. Many male angels found her desirable, and they couldn't understand why I wouldn't have her. The fae King, her father, King Aodhan, would love for a union between her and myself to build an alliance, even if it is not a formal marriage. Her body was glowing with ethereal light. The fae tend to have elemental powers, but she is a light fae, hence the glowy light display she was doing with her body. Some of the upper echelons of fae also have a keen sixth sense, which humans call psychic abilities. Laurel has some clairsentient abilities, which are as good as many angels, so I must be cautious. I usually have an energetic block, so no fae or other angels can read my feelings.

Although I was in the mood for some sensual pleasures, she was not the one I wanted in my bed tonight. The one whose long, slender legs I would prefer to be wrapped around me as I bury myself deep inside her, giving her pleasures that she has never experienced before was forbidden to me because she is my charge. Nope. I should not have such inappropriate thoughts about her. I would rather sleep alone tonight. "Get out, Laureliana," I command her, giving her a look of displeasure. She merely arches a well-defined eyebrow at me. "I feel slighted that you ignored me for that human prude on my birthday. I didn't know frigid college girls were your type, Lord Gideon," She pouts. "Laureliana," I scold, clearly annoyed about her comments about Seraphina. "Leave now before I have the guards escort you off the premises. You have permission to teleport out right now. I would not tolerate your disrespect to Seraphina." I scowl at her.

The protection wards only allow residents in the compound to teleport in and out, anyone else has to get my permission. She frowns at me. "You know, it always ends in disaster for you and human women. Seraphina is a prude and, according to Nathaniel, very frigid. So, not your style." She rolls her eyes. I could sense she was trying to read my feelings, but my psychic shields were up. "We had one night of fun centuries ago, and that was it. You are beautiful, your Highness, but that one night was it. Now leave." I gesture for her to leave. Although polite, saying "please" is not a word to say to a fae. "OK. I'll leave." She sighs with a petulant whine. "I don't know what is so special about that human girl. Nathaniel is obsessed with her; you are, too, because you have been watching her. I can sense you are hiding something about her, and I will find out what you have been hiding about her," she fumes, standing up from my bed, then teleports in a brilliant display of pink light.

I let out a breath of relief, now feeling less irritated that she was gone.

When she left, Cael entered my bedroom with bath towels and a decanter of my favorite wine. I dismissed him so I could be alone with my thoughts as I got ready for bed. I do sleep but don't need it as much as humans do. Sleep is more of a relaxing ritual for me than a rest and recovery one. There was so much going on in my thoughts. I sat on my bed, sipping some of the wine Cael brought for me. My bedroom was the most opulent one in the mansion. The servants decorated my Cal King four-poster bed with Renaissance revival-era drapes. My entire bedroom decor was a true Renaissance revival with some touches of modern amenities like a jacuzzi and a huge shower. The Renaissance era was my favorite time era with Zanael.

My thoughts wandered to Nathaniel and his lewd

obsession with defiling chaste human women and discarding them whenever he got bored. That vile lout. I will pluck his wings if he even tries to touch Seraphina again. The thought of him touching her against her wishes made my blood boil. It angered me what he tried to do to her, but I also found myself smiling when I remembered how she defended herself from his unwanted advances. She, indeed, was quite spirited. The moments of that kick she gave him should go down in history because no woman has ever kicked Nathaniel like that or rejected him. I contemplated whether I should cancel the meeting with her for that tutoring session I promised her. I have to keep a close watch on her. But not from a distance anymore. I felt myself drifting off to sleep as I saw a pair of brown eyes and full lips smiling at me.

CHAPTER 5
SERAPHINA

Gideon insists on picking me up to go to the cafe. I had just stepped out of the shower after a ballet workout dance session when I heard a knock on my door. I didn't expect him to show up this early. I quickly threw on a bathrobe and ran to answer the door. He was standing there in all his gorgeousness, gazing at me with those ethereal hazel gold fleck eyes. He wore casual jeans, a white tucked-in button-down shirt, and a black leather coat. His dark hair looks impeccable, as usual. Once again, Vicky would love to know who his stylist is. I felt self-conscious under his gaze and vulnerable in my nakedness in the bathrobe with my wet hair wrapped in a towel. I quickly usher him inside, telling him he can wait in the living room while I get ready.

We have been conversing with each other over the past couple of days over the phone. I found out that we shared quite a few common interests. There was lots of banter and friendly debates about literature works, art, music, history, and some novels. He was not really into movies and TV shows, which is why some pop culture references sometimes leave him quite puzzled in our conversations. Celeste even invited him over to dinner with Jeb when I visited her. I discovered he lived in that vast mansion on the hill that I had assumed belonged to a celebrity or something. Gideon was still quite cagey about the details of his job or family. So, I assumed that he must probably be in some top-secret service job that helps out Jeb and inheritance money to live in a grand compound. Vicky joked that he must be in some mafia organization.

I remembered how Vicky couldn't contain her excitement when I told her about the tutoring date with him for my assignment. She started cooking up all sorts of scenarios of what it would be like to make out with Gideon. I felt myself blushing at her lewd comments when I scolded her that it was just a tutoring session at a cafe. Although we had had many conversations, none were flirtatious or indicated that he was attracted to me in that way. She begged to differ and had me covering my ears when she started singing "Rolling in the Deep."

I was surprised that even Celeste approved the tutoring session with him, no questions asked, and did not seem to care that he was much older than me. She said that I am an adult and that she trusts Gideon more than that perverted Nathan. I shuddered as I thought about what Nathan had tried to do to me. He is a sleaze, and his good looks cannot compensate for his perverse personality. If I hadn't kicked Nathan and got away, goodness knows what else he would have tried to do to me. Nathan doesn't like hearing the word no. I hastily dressed in jeans and a fitted sweater and tried to tame my hair.

I certainly didn't want to keep Gideon waiting too long. When I entered my living room, I saw Gideon staring at some of my gymnastics and ballet photos on the wall. He was also gazing intensely at a framed picture of my parents that they had taken on one of their archaeological expeditions. I remembered that the photo was a gift from Celeste. My parents looked so happy and besotted with each other in the photo. My heart aches whenever I think about them, and I wish I could have met them. "I remembered this photo from their Tomb of Nefertiti's expedition," Gideon says as he tears his eyes away from the framed photo of my parents and turns to face me. "Celeste did mention some of their expeditions to me." I put my coat on, and then I saw his eyes surveying me from head to toe. "You look lovely." He says, nodding in approval at my outfit. I was blushing under his gaze, feeling shy about his compliment. "Thanks," I give him a small smile.

We left for the cafe, and Gideon mentioned that he would like to invite me over to dinner at his place. The cafe was not as crowded since Spring break just started, and many college students have left town for warmer temperatures, perhaps for it. It was my favorite place to study and get my sugar high on mochas with Vicky. Gideon was looking around the cafe with unusual interest. I wonder why? It's just a simple college cafe. Several girls were checking him out with flirty eyes, even if some were with a guy. A few even threw me some furtive scowling looks at me that said, "Why is she with such a hot guy?"

Gideon knows how to make quite an impression, even in casual clothing. Besides his gorgeous looks, I think it is his presence. He had such a regal presence that commands attention. A presence that screams that he is used to giving orders and commanding servants of gold.

The barista, a senior in college that I had seen around campus, looked star-struck, like she was seeing her favorite celebrity, and lost all form of speech when he spoke to her in that deep baritone bass voice of his about our coffee order. She looks like she is about to faint when he smiles at her, nodding his thanks as he takes our cups of coffee from her and pays for them. I saw her and the other female baristas watching his retreating form as he walked over to where I was sitting and handed me my coffee. They seemed a bit disappointed that he was with me.

I saw one of Laurel's acolytes at her party that night, giving us curious glances. I know she already called Laurel and gave her a full report about us. Instead of sitting across from me in a chair, Gideon sat on the couch next to me. His scent was so intoxicating. It was like a masculine mix of exotic musk, sandalwood, cedar wood, and another scent I didn't recognize. Whatever scent it was, it definitely smelled expensive. I remember my brief stint working in the fragrance department at Saks Fifth Avenue until gymnastics and ballet training got in the way. I remember smelling something similar in one of the expensive men's fragrance collections. Whatever it was, I was definitely enjoying his scent.

He stretches an arm on the top of the couch, holding his coffee with the other. It was the first time I ever sat so close to Gideon, except when I was in his car. I started asking questions for my assignment as I took notes to distract myself from how his nearness messed with my focus. He seems like a human history textbook. We kept going off-topic and discussing historical topics irrelevant to my assignment. He asked me about my plans after graduation, and I told him I would probably enroll in a PhD program. He seems pretty impressed. He also inquired about my spring break plans, and we discussed the archaeological and geneticist internship I wanted to do. Again, he deflected when I tried asking him questions about himself.

It was not until late evening when he dropped me off at my house. I unlock my door, then turn and hug him. "I still don't know anything about you," I murmur, gazing up into his face, my arms still around his torso. "Like, what is your favorite color? Even favorite foods or any family members around?" I question, arching an eyebrow. He gives a low chuckle at my questions. "I like red, Italian cuisine, and have some family around." He murmurs, gazing at me with those golden-flecked hazel eyes of his. As soon as I release his torso, he quickly encircles his arms around my waist, pulling me to him. His body felt like a warm bronze statue of muscles. "Does that answer your questions about me? I wouldn't lie to you, but I can't tell you everything about me." His eyes glisten with hypnotic intensity as he tips my chin. The mystery of him was such a turn-on. He lowers his face, and his mouth descends upon mine, his lips caressing in an intense kiss, making my legs feel weak. The kiss caught me off guard because he had made no flirtatious inclinations that he was attracted to me.

I was not prepared for the bombardment of pleasurable sensations his kiss was awakening within me. I felt that slight jolt of electricity again that I had felt when I first touched his hand. I have been kissed before, but never like this. Even Nathan was a good kisser, but not this good, and his touch was repulsive.

Gideon's fingers felt warm and pleasurable, tracing a line along my jawline as he kissed me. His lips felt so warm, soft, and sensual as they continued their caress on my own. I entwine my arms around his neck to pull his head closer when he abruptly pulls away, breaking the kiss. "Apologies. I shouldn't have," He mutters, his breath ragged as he lets his arms fall away from me. I was still reeling from the kiss. "I am not," I whisper, gazing at him, searching for answers, clearly perplexed about why he stopped kissing me. I was still trying to catch my breath, seeing desire burning in those ethereal hazel gold-flecked eyes. He looked like he was debating whether to walk away, and I was expecting him to walk away, regretting our kiss, but with a low growl in his throat, his hands cupped my face and kissed me again. This time, the kiss was hungrier, harder, his lips crushing mine as his tongue parted my lips to dance with mine. His intoxicating smell and taste made me giddy with desire. I felt a low moan escaping my throat as his hand lifted one of my legs to wrap it around his hips while the other pushed open my door without breaking the kiss apart. Gideon half-carried me inside, his arms around my waist. He pins me to the wall, still kissing me. I tighten my legs around his hips to stay balanced. His warm hands felt searing on my skin as he glided them up my sweater. The hardness of his erection was lengthening against my stomach and straining against his jeans.

His breath was hot and ragged, groans escaping his throat as his warm mouth kisses my neck and then returns to my mouth. He sucks gently on my bottom lip as his hands cup my breasts, and the searing sensation of his touch makes my skin hum. I glide my hands under his shirt. The sculpted muscles of his chest and abdomen felt smooth to the touch. I was right. He does have rippling abs under there. A low groan escapes his throat at my touch. He briefly breaks the kiss to slide my sweater over my head when his cell phone starts ringing. He was trying to ignore it so he could finish taking my sweater off, but his phone just kept ringing. It sounds urgent. He mutters a curse under his breath as he reluctantly releases me. "I have to take this call." He whispers, his forehead pressing against mine. Goodness, his voice was so sexy. "OK," I nod in between breaths. He quickly kissed me before he pulled away to answer his phone. I compose myself and fix my sweater, still bracing against the wall, waiting for my legs to start working again.

Gideon was pacing as he spoke in a hushed tone over the phone. His face was solemn when he hung up the phone call to return his attention to me. "There is something I need to go take care of," He says in a serious tone as he walks over to where I was standing. "Is everything OK?" I ask him as I give him a look of concern. His eyes say that everything is not OK. "It will be." He wraps his arms around my waist, pulling me to him. I liked the feeling of his warm, hard body against my own. "I want to see you again." He murmurs as he kisses my forehead. "I will contact you later with the details about dinner." His lips playfully tease mine before he kisses me. This time, the kiss was soft and sweet. "Good night, Seraphina," He whispers huskily against my lips. He quickly walks out the door before I can say anything else to him. I stood there, watching his retreating form. I was breathing in shallow gulps as I touched my lips, which were still tingling from his kiss, and the parts of my skin where his fingers had touched me still tingled with warmth. I was still reeling from what had just happened between us. Oh, I know what more would have happened if his phone ringing hadn't stopped us. And the thing is, I would have allowed him to take things further if he wanted to. I berated myself for being too weak with my attraction to him. I felt embarrassed that I should have had more willpower to stop moving so fast with Gideon. I acted like a wanton. What just happened between us will change everything.

CHAPTER 6

GIDEON

"Where are the others from your post, Kafziel?" I questioned the warrior angel in full copper-colored celestial battle armor that stood beside me. I was also in my full celestial battle armor. Mine was a dazzling golden color that denotes my status as Lord of the Powers. Kafziel was one of my best lieutenants and part of my elite squad who is quite proficient in espionage and intelligence. It was Kafziel who called me to report that there was a demonic disturbance at one of the portals that led to the fae dimension. It was rare for demonic activity to occur at a fae portal. King Aodhan usually has two powerful faes guarding all his portals, so I had to check this out.

"They are with Jebediah, currently subduing a few demons attacking humans, my Lord," He answers. "You could have contacted me in angelical. Why call me on the cellphone?" I ask, looking at Kafziel. I watch him pacing, looking pensive. He was always serene and not as rowdy as the other Powers. Although he seems like a tall college kid with curly red hair, he is quite a deadly fighter. His celestial weapon is a Halberd. "I had to improvise. You were with your human charge. We both know that angelic communication can affect humans negatively." He reminds me shrewdly, glancing at me. I nod at his answer. Angels communicating telepathically in angelical language gives off a high frequency that causes nose bleeds, hearing issues, and worse, even a brain aneurysm in humans if exposed to it for too long. I am glad he was considerate when he contacted me about this issue because I would have been upset with him if the angel radio frequency had harmed Seraphina.

"How many of them do you think are down there?" I ask him

in a low voice, gesturing at the groove of silver birch trees at the edge of an empty lot, one of the portals to access the fae dimension. We were on the rooftop of a building in phased form, scoping out the demonic situation below before we attacked. "Looks like about four of them, my Lord." He responds grimly as his celestial Halberd materializes in his hand. I peered into the silver birch trees grove to get a better view and saw a greenish light glowing around the portal area. The energy of the light felt like fae magic.

I counted four soul-sucker demons. Two male and female fae were lying on the grassy ground next to the silver birch trees—the Guardians of that portal, I assumed. I tuned into my supernatural hearing to check their heartbeats to see if they were still alive. I heard two faint heartbeats. They were alive but barely. A greenish light emanated from their bodies, which formed a dome of protection around them. They probably cast an energy protection ward around themselves before passing out. I watched in disgust as the four soul suckers' demons were trying to siphon the energies from the ward to get to the unconscious fae. The soul suckers were foul ghastly nightmarish demonic creatures. They stood about seven feet tall with their bodies, a humanoid mass of writhing tentacles. Their heads are an even bigger mass of tentacles, but worse was their gaping mouths, shaped like circles displaying rows of razor-sharp teeth. If their tentacles latch onto a body, they will siphon energies from supernatural folks in the most painful manner, and for humans, it's an even grimmer fate. They will siphon everything from a human, leaving them with a dry husk of skin and bones, then siphon their soul energies. These hideous creatures look like they are from a Lovecraftian nightmare. I wondered why they were in a fae dimension portal. "We must dispatch them before they can kill those fae Guardians." I materialize my celestial broad sword and leap from the building, landing softly on the ground. I walk toward the fae portal with Kafziel following me. We decide not to manifest angel fire on our weapons because the soul suckers will feed off those energies. The soul suckers were so occupied with trying to siphon the energies from the fae protection wards that they barely had enough time to react when Kafziel and I descended upon them, moving in a blur of gold and copper. There were unearthly shrieks as tentacles and black goo were flying everywhere as we slashed relentlessly with our celestial weapons. One of the soul suckers' tentacles tries to latch onto my leg, but I maneuver in the air with a twist and swipe at the thick tentacle with my sword. With a spray of black goo, the tentacle drops to the ground, writhing. I levitate in the air and flew toward the soul sucker like a missile with my sword and swipe its head off with a clean stroke. The soul sucker shrieks, and then its tentacled body collapses on the ground in a mass of black goo. One down. Three to go.

I was feeling pumped full of adrenaline as I dodged another tentacle from another soul sucker that Kafziel was slashing relentlessly at with his Halberd. I do enjoy the tasks of apprehending fallen angels and banishing demons. I always feel a thrill of euphoria whenever I am in battle. Within minutes, Kafziel and I took out the rest of the soul-sucker demons. Kafziel made a noise of disgust as he swatted a writhing tentacle off his shoulder. I survey the damage of the hacked pieces of tentacles, watching them disintegrate, leaving behind traces of black goo on the ground. I dematerialize my celestial battle armor back into the ether. I sent the two unconscious fae a telepathic message that the threat was over and that they should release their protection ward. They whisper their names, Floriana and Lachlan, weakly in my head, and then I watch as the barrier of greenish light dissipates from around their bodies. They remained unconscious. I promise them I will get them both to safety. "What do you want to do about them, my Lord?" Kafziel asks as he stoops down and examines the unconscious fae for injuries. "Take them back to the compound and see that they are comfortable, and send word to their retrieval faction. Their King, Aodhan, will need to know about this attack. Make sure he knows. I will request an audience with him later," I respond. Kafziel nods as he hoists both fae one on each shoulder and teleports in a flash of copper angel fire.

As soon as he left, I felt a prickly sense of dread. Something does not feel right. I scrutinized the area where both fae were lying unconscious when my danger senses suddenly started blaring. Before I could summon my celestial sword and celestial battle armor, I felt excruciating pain as something sharp pierced the flesh on my upper back. Stunned, I staggered, lost my balance, and fell to my knees. "You are getting complacent, Gideon." A voice chortles with disdain as Nathaniel emerges from the darkness with six other Watchers and the fallen Throne Angel Razziel. "The mighty warrior Lord Gideon is on his knees." He ridicules smirking. "Nathaniel, you coward. We both know the only way you can strike me is off guard." I grit my teeth at the pain from the attack. One of the Watchers had struck me with a spear, probably hexed by a High Witch. It was a spear that could pierce celestial flesh. Nathaniel's faction has a High Witch working for them. That cannot be good. He is usually unaligned. Why is the fallen Throne angel Razziel with them?

I could feel that the hexed spear had immobilized my ability to summon my celestial sword and armor. I felt my energies draining. I could hardly move my body. Nathaniel knows what I am trying to do and wags a finger. "Oh, no. Don't even attempt to tune into angel radio to call for backup. Sprout those wings to fly away or teleport. All accesses to your celestial powers is blocked. you're not the only one with a High Witch working for you." He mocks me smugly. I survey the other angels with him, quickly contemplating how to take them out without access to my weapon. The vile lout had ambushed me.

"We know the human girl is special because you have been watching her. What is she?" Razziel demands in a grating voice. I turn my attention to the tall, ash-blond, lanky Throne, who has a long scar from his forehead to his jaw on his thin face. I was the one who had given him that scar during the rebellion when he decided to side with Lucifer and burned his wings off with my angel fire.

"Ask Nathaniel how special she is for nearly neutering him for forcing his advances." I goad, almost laughing at that memory of Seraphina kicking Nathaniel. Despite my predicament, I smile with satisfaction as I watch Nathaniel's face contort in rage. One of the Watchers stabs me in the stomach with the hexed spear. I clench my jaw at the pain, refusing to show weakness by screaming.

"I will get my hands on the little lass and make her pay for her presumptuousness. Then, when I tire of her, I will let the others have their fun." His eyes blazed with blue angel-fire fury as he took the spear from the Watcher and stabbed me in the stomach again. I doubled over, bleeding from the excruciating pain. "Oh, it Hurts, doesn't it? All that bravado, even in the face of your demise," Nathaniel scoffs. "Kill me now so I can be spared from your insufferable chatter," I grunt, clutching the wound on my stomach with my palm. My shirt was blood-soaked. "No, we wouldn't kill you, Gideon." Nathaniel crouches down to look directly at my face. "Razziel here will take you to hell where your pretty visage especially will be tortured beyond recognition, and we will see how Seraphina will accept you like that. I can smell her scent all over you. Did you sleep with her? Does she know your true identity?" He stabs me deeply again with the spear, this time on my mid back. Again, the pain was unbearable, but I felt some mobility returning to my limbs, along with some energy and a burning rage about his plans for Seraphina.

"Which makes doing this to you even more satisfying. The girl is mine to take!" He spits the words like venom, twisting the spear into the flesh on my back. I grunt in pain, clenching my jaw. "The stuffy Archangels Council and their stupid rules. You know you could have joined me, brother, when I offered you the chance, but like a good self-righteous soldier, you chose to serve Michael. Now, look at you bending the rules by getting too involved with your human charge. Do you have feelings for her? Your feelings for her are making you weak." He rants. Oh, Bollocks, he loves to hear himself talk. "Razziel, I guess you want to pay back for that scar and your wings?" I scoff at Razziel with a self-satisfied half smile. I was enjoying goading them on purpose despite wanting to scream in pain.

"I will personally see to your accommodations in hell,

you arrogant soldier, I will have your golden wings as a trophy," Razziel seethes, his eyes blazing with white angel fire. Again, another stab in my mid back with the spear. "You're so busy watching over the human lass that you fail to notice that one of your squad leaders, Caleb, has been working for me. Razziel promises to return his vampire lover Alaria to him," Nathaniel says with a mocking laugh.

My rage about Caleb's treachery overshadowed the pain from my injuries. Jeb and I had stuck out our necks to save Caleb, one of the Powers, from the wrath of the Council of Archangels when he decided to take a female vampire as a lover. Vampires are unclean abominations, and liaisons between angels and them are strictly forbidden. They can get addicted to our blood, which enhances their abilities. We implored the Council of Archangels to be lenient with him for being so impulsive, and they did so by instructing one of the Powers to drive a stake through his Vampire lover's heart. He was devastated for a while but swore loyalty to Jeb and me, and we allowed him to be part of our faction on Earth.

I thought about Seraphina and how much I would fail to keep the promise to Zanael for not doing my duty to protect her if I got captured. And worse, rage simmers within me as I think about Nathaniel's plans for her. They can never find out her true identity. Resolve energizes me as I give Nathaniel a steely glare. "Always with the dramatics and petty grievances, Nathaniel. If you think a hexed magic spear is enough to subdue me, the Lord of the Powers, then you know nothing about me." I steady myself shakily to my full height despite the tortuous pain from my injuries. Nathaniel, Razziel, and the other Watchers advance upon me with their celestial weapons. I felt my eyes burning with gold angel fire as the Enochian runes Tattoos on my chest and back started pulsating underneath my bloodied and torn shirt. The Watchers and Razziel stop abruptly, shielding their eyes as the Enochian rune's tattoos glow with golden energy. I felt my body getting teleported involuntarily.

Nathaniel's faction is not the only one with a powerful High Witch. It's just that my High Witch is better than their High Witch. And much cleverer, too. Celeste had tattooed Enochian protection runes on my back and chest with celestial ink from the divine scribe, the angel Metatron. The Enochian runes act as a fail-safe that will teleport me to safety to the nearest place that has Enochian protection wards if I am seriously injured or about to be captured by the enemy. She did it because she knew it was a risk to Seraphina's safety and identity if I happened to get apprehended by opposing forces one day. It's good that the High Witch's magic on the hexed spear was weak, or my injuries would have been worse. I have to wait for the hex to wear off so my angelic healing can activate to heal my wounds. I also have to wait for the power blockage spell placed by the rogue High Witch to wear off for access to my celestial powers to return fully.

I landed unceremoniously on the front porch of a house. I immediately noticed where I was. It was Seraphina's house. Her place was the nearest safe house. Oh, bollocks!

This cannot be good at all. I mutter some swear words. The Enochian runes on her door and front porch were glowing. As the runes on my body stopped glowing, so did the ones on her house. I had this eerie feeling that someone was watching her house currently. I didn't have my angelic senses to sniff out who it was, but I could sense I was being watched. It seems like the Enochian protection wards are keeping whoever is watching the house at bay. I was grateful for that. I had to brace against her door to pull myself to my feet, and then I collapsed on her doormat in pain. Bollocks, I was a mess, I mutter to myself as I look at the stab wounds on my stomach, wincing in pain. I was too weak from my injuries to move away from her front door. My vision became hazy when I heard hasty footsteps approaching her front door. Ah, bloody hell! She heard me.

CHAPTER 7

SERAPHINA

"Gideon!" I woke up and started gasping Gideon's name. I was shaking and drenched in sweat. I had a nightmare that Gideon was seriously injured, lying in a pool of blood. I knew the loud thud at my front door was not a dream. Someone was at my door or, worse, trying to break in! I quickly threw the covers off and got out of bed. I glance at my alarm clock. It was around 3 a.m. I hastily dressed in my bathrobe to cover my pajamas, grabbed the taser gun that Jeb had gifted me for protection from my dresser, and walked cautiously to my front door. There was no more thumping noise, but I heard some low groans that sounded like someone was hurt. I cautiously opened the door to peek outside. I dropped the Taser gun and let out an audible gasp of horror as I saw Gideon lying on my front porch.

He was in the same clothing he was in earlier, but there were several bloodied stab wounds on his torso, staining his white shirt. His handsome face contorted in pain, and his matted dark hair glistened damply. I can tell he is in a lot of pain. My nightmare was a reality. He was seriously injured. Dread overcame me. "Gideon!" I shriek, collapsing near his body. He opens his eyes and grabs onto me, wincing in pain as he uses my body as a crutch to try to stand up. I was trembling as I tried to steady him. "Quick, let's get inside." He says in a strained voice, looking around the porch as if searching for onlookers. Trembling, I mutely comply, trying to help him walk inside. I was strong from being an athlete most of my life, but the sheer weight of his tall, imposing, well-muscled frame had me staggering to support him. His skin was warm and clammy. He was making most of the effort to walk, which took a lot out of him from the occasional grunts of pain. I was just a crutch he was holding on to support himself. We made it to the sofa bed in my living room, and he released me and collapsed on it.

"Gideon. What happened? Who did this to you?" I question frantically. "You need to get to a hospital. I should call 911 and inform Celeste and Jeb." Tears of worry were stinging my eyes. "No hospitals or Celeste and Jeb yet." He insists as he grabs my arm. "But you are seriously hurt!" I gesture at his bloodied torso with concern. The bleeding had stopped, but those stab wounds still looked very nasty. "Seraphina." He grimaces as he tries to sit up to look at me. "I will be fine. I won't die. I promise." He assures me as he pulls me closer, taking my hand and gazing into my face. I looked at him skeptically because I was finding that hard to believe. "I will explain everything later. But for now, don't contact anyone. It's not safe yet. It's a lot to ask, and I know you are worried, but you have to trust me on this." He pleads.

Again, with that cagey attitude. Is Gideon in some Mafia or organized crime, as Vicky had said? Or must this be some secret service mission that he got hurt on, and since people are after him, contacting anyone will endanger him?

All sorts of alarming scenarios were racing through my head. Everyone tells me that I reacted well in crisis and high-stress situations, but Gideon somewhat had me in a mess of nerves and panic mode. One moment, I was having a hot and heavy make-out session with this gorgeous specimen of a man, and now he was in my living room, all bloodied with nasty multiple stab wounds. I knew I needed to calm down if I was going to help. I could feel it in every fiber of my being that I could trust him and should do as he requests.

"OK, I trust you." I sigh with a nod. "I wouldn't call anyone, but those injuries need some first aid," I say to him, feeling slightly calmer. "Let me get the first aid kit to clean those wounds."

Gideon nods in agreement as he releases my hand, and I rush off to the bathroom. I grab the first aid kit from under my sink, filled a bucket with warm water, and gather some small towels and washcloths. I return with everything to the living room. Gideon was sprawled in a haze on the sofa bed but sat up all wobbly when he saw me approaching. His brow had pools of sweat, and his dazed eyes followed me as I brought the bucket of warm water closer.

"I will have to remove your shirt," I say to him as I reach for his shirt. He nods wordlessly and allows me to unbutton his shirt. His nice white shirt was torn and blood-stained. I cast it aside. I conceal my reaction and swallow as I examine his bronze torso. His body is like a well-sculpted work of art despite the present injuries. Dry blood stained the strange-looking tribal tattoos on his broad, well-chiseled chest. The few gaping gashes on his corded stomach muscles were trickling with some blood. I quickly soak a warm washcloth to wipe the blood from the deep gashes on his stomach. He sucks in his breath as I cleanse the wound. I noticed his upper back also had some strange-looking tribal tattoos. I gasp at the gaping gashes on his broad-muscular back. How he was still conscious and not writhing in constant pain was beyond me. Those stab wounds look like they might need stitches later on, but I will do the best I can to clean and dress them. Let's hope those injuries didn't damage vital organs, or he will probably have some internal bleeding. His injuries look like he had a wrestling match with an Iron Maiden torture device.

He flinches a bit in pain as I cleanse the gaping stab wounds on his back with warm water and a washcloth. "These stab wounds look like they might need stitches," I comment as I apply diluted hydrogen peroxide to one of the gashes on his back. "I will be fine. I need to rest." He reassures me, his words thick and slurred, still wincing as I apply sterile wound band-aids on all the gashes. All the adrenaline from this situation made me feel tired and sleepy. I glance at the clock displayed on my wall. It was 4:10 a.m..

"I have the guest bedroom you can sleep in," I offer as I examine my handiwork of the wound band-aids on his injuries. "I trust that you will explain what happened to you later unless that is classified information," I scold him as I stifle a yawn. I help him up on unsteady legs. "I will explain everything later, and I trust that you will not speak about this to anyone." He says in a raspy breath. Here we go with the cryptic responses. He drapes his arms around my shoulders, leaning on me as we walk toward the guest bedroom. It took a lot of effort for him to lie down on the queen bed. I prop his head on some pillows to keep his body upright. His jet-black hair, although matted, still feels so silky to the touch. I cover him with the comforter as he closes his eyes, and then he grabs my hand. "Seraphina," He murmurs. "Thank you." "You can thank me by not dying on me in your sleep." I switch the night lamp off. He gives a low chuckle. "I promise you I will not." "I will try to get some sleep and will check on you in a few hours," I say to him as I walk out of the bedroom.

I was still nervous, primarily worried about whether he would make it through until he could get further help. I resisted the temptation to contact Celeste and Jeb. He was very cryptic and adamant about not to contact anyone. Maybe contacting anyone might put them in danger? What sort of mess did he get himself into, and who gave him those stab wounds? What kind of mess did I get myself into being involved with him? I washed my hands and prepped for bed. I felt so much adrenaline earlier and now find myself very tired. With my mind still in a whirlwind of thoughts about Gideon, I doze off into a restless sleep.

Rays of sunlight filter through the curtains, waking me. Was it all a dream that happened to Gideon? As I wiped the sleep from my eyes, pieces of memories from earlier returned. I glance at the clock. It was 10 a.m. Goodness. Did I sleep that long? I threw off my comforter and got out of bed. I walk to the guest bedroom to check on Gideon. I had left the door slightly ajar just in case he needed me. I peeked inside, and Gideon was asleep. The comforter was on his waist, exposing his torso. His head was moving from side to side. I watch his chest heave. The tribal-looking tattoos on his chest had some dry blood. He was breathing heavily and whispering feverishly in an unknown language I had never heard. At least he doesn't look like he is in pain and is still alive. I sigh, feeling reassured as I watch his head stop moving, and the feverish whispers in the unknown language stop. His breathing was returning to normal. His sleeping form looks so peaceful. I was contemplating whether I should wake him up. The wound band-aids covering his injuries were not blood-soaked, which is a good sign, but I will need to change them when he wakes up. I let him sleep and returned to my room to freshen up.

I was itching to call Celeste and Jeb again but didn't want to break my promise to him not to. I went through the motions of my morning routine. I thought about what sort of trouble Gideon had gotten himself into. I checked my fridge to see what I had to make something to eat. He might be hungry when he wakes up. I didn't want to leave the house because what if he wakes up and I am not home? I decided to busy myself with my final research paper needed for graduation and internship applications. I saw several texts from Vicky. I had told her everything about my date with Gideon earlier. Many of her comments about my kissing session with Gideon would make a sailor blush. She was so excited that he wanted to invite me to his place for dinner. I told her I wanted to take things slow and not rush. I could feel my face flushing with embarrassment as I read some of her lewd text messages about what it would be like to have sex with Gideon. And then there was some gossip that Laurel's acolyte who saw us in the cafe was spreading around. Vicky is the most informed person I know. She is like a radio station tuned to all the latest gossip. I knew that I could not let it slip that Gideon was sleeping in my guest bedroom with several nasty stab wounds that I was not allowed to call anyone- not even 911 about.

It was not until the evening that I decided to take a chicken sandwich I had made for Gideon and a glass of orange juice and water. I watch his eyelids flutter then he sits up on the bed, fully awake. "I brought you something to eat. "I approach him with the tray of food. Despite those injuries, he looked well-rested and was a vision of vitality.

No haziness. His hair was tousled, with a few strands falling on his forehead. He blinks, looking perplexed, and then clarity seems to return as he focuses on me. "How long was I asleep for?" He inquires softly. "Pretty much all day. "I rest the tray of food on the nightstand. "How are you feeling?" I walk over to him to examine the wound band-aids on his stomach. He swiftly grabbed my hand before I could touch the wound band-aids on his stomach.

I watch in astonishment as the wound band-aids fall off his stomach. The skin beneath them was flawless. I blinked, hoping I was mistaken, but I wasn't. I stare at him in bewilderment, searching his face for answers. "What are you?" I stammer at a loss for words. I could feel my eyes widening in amazement because all the injuries on his back were completely healed. I must be going crazy. Was this all a bad dream or an illusion? No way could this be real. I knew there was something otherworldly and mysterious about him, but what was he? I immediately thought about some vampire movies and shows I had watched. "Are you a vampire?" I ask, backing away from him. I remembered the Twilight movies and Anne Rice books about vampires with healing abilities. "Please don't tell me that you sparkle," I blurt out with some sarcasm as I gazed at him in awe. He stared at me with raised eyebrows, an amusing smile playing on his lips before he spoke solemnly. "No, I am not one of those unclean abominations." He answers indignantly. He moves forward, and I stumble back, retreating cautiously from him. My mind was quickly trying to make sense of this. I didn't feel afraid of him for some reason, but I was in awe. "I was afraid it might come to this one day but not this soon. Don't be scared of me. I wouldn't harm you," He assures me, raising his hands, noticing my cautiousness. "Then what are you?" I croak, eyeing him warily. His beautiful eyes were pleading with me not to run. He looked relieved when he saw that I was not going to bolt. "I am an angel. One of the Powers, a warrior class if you want to get specific." He replies solemnly. I was floored. I was not religious or anything, but seriously! An angel? No way. When has my world become such a freak show? This situation makes me feel like I am in one big dream and will wake up soon. I pinch myself. Nope. I am awake, and this is real. He is real.

"An angel? Like from heaven? No way!" I blurt out, looking at him in awe. This time, I step closer to him. "But you look human, and you were hurt." My voice was shrill as I scrutinized him.

"I am incarnated in human form to blend in on Earth. Weapons hexed by High Witches can hurt us. That was what happened with my injuries, but I was able to heal and recover with some rest," He explains. My mind was spinning like a hamster wheel. I was trying to understand what he had just said to me. I have always been fascinated by myths, folklore, and legends, and now I feel like I am living in one of those mythological stories. I had so many questions swirling in my head. "You must have many questions, and how you found out about all this was... unexpected." He looks at me as if reading my mind. Wait, can he read minds? "Do you have wings... are you my

Guardian angel?" I ask, not caring if I sound silly. "Yes, I have wings, and I am your Guardian." "Guardian? Why do I need a Guardian?" I demand quizzically. "I will explain later." He responds curtly.

I watched him get up from the bed and reach for the glass of water I had brought. I cannot recall if I had ever seen him eating or drinking at the dinner with Celeste or drinking the coffee at the café. "So you can eat and drink human foods?" I inquire, watching him with fascination as he sips the water. "Being incarnated on Earth… yes, we can partake in human foods and other human pleasures too." He draws out the word "pleasure," giving me a sidelong glance with a hint of flirtatiousness. I felt my cheeks flush with heat when I remembered our make-out session. "Oh, so you are allowed to and can…?" "Yes, I am allowed to, and I already have." He answers for me with amusement on his face, knowing that I was going to ask if he can have sex being a celestial angel. And it looks like he already has done the deed. I was staring at him in fascination.

I study him intensely. I knew a face and body like his could only belong to something divine. I also remembered his friendly interactions with Celeste and Jeb; he seemed to know them well. "Wait, who are Celeste and Jeb…?" "Jeb is one of the Powers. A warrior angel like me. He is my right arm and my elite squad leader. Celeste is a High Witch." He finishes for me. Again, I was floored. Everyone has been keeping secrets from me, including my own adopted mother and Jeb, who is like an uncle to me. I knew Celeste was a psychic and a holistic psychologist; knowing she was part of the supernatural world was beyond me. And Jeb, I thought he was just a homicide detective who grew up on a Cherokee reservation, but he is an angel, too.

"Wait, so Celeste is a real witch… with *real* magic powers that are not just psychic Tarot readings?" "A very powerful High Witch too," he adds. "Her abilities helped save me from a grim fate last night." "Why didn't you contact her and Jeb when you were hurt? They could have helped!" My voice was high-pitched as I sat on the bed, feeling more comfortable beside him. "It was not safe to do so. Your house has Enochian runes that Celeste had put in place to block all supernatural access for your protection. I was attacked by rogue and unaligned angels last night, and your house's Enochian protection wards brought me here because it was the nearest safe place with those wards. My powers were also temporarily immobilized to make any communication. I didn't want the rogue and unaligned angels tracking Celeste and Jeb to come here for you if you had called them. Now that I am all healed and my powers have returned, it is safe to…" His voice trails off as he jumps abruptly to his feet and sniffs the air. I look at him in confusion. "Gideon? What's wrong?" I ask, feeling uneasy. I felt the prick of goosebumps. Something does not feel right. I saw his eyes widen.

"Seraphina! Duck now!" He yells. Instinctively, I drop to my stomach on the carpeted floor as a spike missile whizzes past me and pins itself to the wall. There was a flash of golden light, and I felt Gideon grabbing me as something like feathers enveloped my body. I raised my head to get a good look and squinted at the golden light emitting from him. I gape in awe at the golden wings protruding from his back. His usual hazel irises were now blazing golden orbs. He was wearing a dazzling golden armor with a golden flamed broadsword in his hand. I saw several spikes on the wall. His wings had shielded me from them. I was staring with my mouth open. He looks so regal and beautiful. "The Enochian protection wards have been breached. We are under attack. We have to leave now!" He commands in his deep baritone bass voice, which is now full of authority. Another shower of spikes came into the room.

A dazzling gold shield materializes in his hand to block the onslaught of spikes. "Hold tight!" He grabs me by the waist and pulls me to him. His gold armor was cold against my body. Golden fire engulfed us, which surprisingly was not burning my skin. Before I could react, we both went hurling toward the guest bedroom window, shattering the glass. Terrified, I clung to him as we propelled like a rocket missile glowing in golden fire into the night sky. We were flying! And we were moving so fast. I was awestruck watching his golden wings work. Then, like a falling meteorite, we hurled toward a huge mansion's courtyard. Gideon's mansion!

He touches down softly on the ground with me still in his arms clinging to him. Feeling a bit dizzy, I blink, taking in my surroundings. I saw Jeb in full black and grey color armor with a group of roughly seven men, all in dazzling copper-colored armor. Then I heard someone screaming my name, "Seraphina!" Celeste shrieks as she runs toward

Gideon and I. Gideon quickly sets me down as Celeste envelops me in a hug, and I cling to her, burying my face into her shoulder. "You sure do know how to make an entrance, my Lord," Jeb greets Gideon. I watch in awe as Gideon's golden armor and beautiful golden wings de-materialize, and he stands shirtless like he was in my bedroom. OK. That looks like something out of a superhero comic book movie.

"I was rallying for a search and rescue mission with the squad, then Celeste had a vision about what happened to you and that you were safe for the time being," He says as his armor de-materializes. He was back in his regular Detective work clothing with his badge. The others in the group all came over to Gideon to greet him. I noticed they were all young men. "Seraphina. I am glad you're OK." Jeb pulls me in a hug. "Thank you for taking care of her," Celeste says as she quickly hugs Gideon despite him being shirtless. The dazzling copper armor from the group of young men all de-materializes to reveal the jeans, sweats, and t-shirts they were wearing. They eye me wordlessly and curiously. "Leave us," Gideon commands them. There were some choruses of "Yes, my Lord" as they all seemed to disappear. Why is everyone, including Jeb, addressing Gideon as "my Lord?"

"Caleb. Where is he?" Gideon asks Jeb in a steely tone of voice. "In the dungeon awaiting trial by the Council of Archangels. Celeste's vision told us what happened to you and about his betrayal." He answers in a serious tone as he drapes an arm around Celeste. She drapes her other arm around me as I continue clinging to her, trying to process everything. Jeb looks at Gideon's torso, streaked with dried blood, his matted dark hair and smirks. "You look rough," He remarks with a low chuckle, clapping him on his bare shoulder. "I know. It was quite a night." Gideon agrees with a half-smile. "Can someone tell me if this is all real?" I ask, feeling overwhelmed as I search Celeste's face for answers. Before I could say anything else, I felt a sharp pain in my solar plexus area. I looked down and saw I was bleeding. I think one of those spike things got me. The courtyard felt like it was swimming. I felt myself collapsing, but Celeste and Jeb caught me. "Get Cael now!" I heard Gideon yell as everything went black.

CHAPTER 8

SERAPHINA

I woke up in a large, comfortable bed with the softest blue duvet covers. I had the same nightmare again, and then I had the most beautiful dream that Gideon was holding me in his arms. I blinked, then rubbed my eyes. I was in a vast, beautiful room decorated lavishly with Victorian-era decor. The events of everything that happened all came rushing back to me, hitting like a tidal wave of memories. I survey my surroundings, looking at Victorian-era furniture in the room. WTH? Please don't tell me I time-traveled. But judging by the luxurious modern Roman blinds and ceiling fan, I was definitely still in modern times despite the Victorian-era decor. No time travels. I blinked again, then was startled as an older man with streaks of grey sandy hair,a lined concerned face and kind grey eyes was staring at me in awe.

He was average-built and dressed in a preppy navy sweater and slacks. With a yelp, I backed away and was about to bolt from the bed. "My Lady. Please don't run. I do not mean to alarm you. I mean no harm." He assures in a British accent, raising his hands pleadingly. I relaxed a bit, eyeing him warily. His facial expression was begging me not to run. He does look too preppy even to harm a fly. "What happened? Where am I? Where is Celeste, Jeb, and Gideon?" Frantic questions poured out. "And who are you?" I ask, frowning at him in confusion. "Pardon my manners, my Lady. I am Cael. Gideon's personal manservant." He answers with a courteous bow. "You are in one of the chambers in the mansion. You fainted from the venom in your wound. Celeste administered a potion to draw the venom out to allow your body to heal. Celeste and Jeb are indisposed, but I will fetch my Lord Gideon. He told me to let him know when you are awake," He continues. "Are you an angel too, and why do you keep calling Gideon' my Lord'?" I question. "I am a Nephilim, and Gideon is the Lord of the Powers, warrior class of angels." He replies, beaming with pride. I remembered from mythology research that Nephilims are angel/human hybrids. WTH? Is Gideon royalty among angels??

"My Lady, I must make haste to fetch my Lord. I will be right back." He gives a quick bow as he bustles out the door. I was left stunned. He keeps calling me 'my Lady'. It must be a British thing. He sounds very refined and very British. One minute, I was just a typical college student worrying about research papers, internship applications, and how mundane my life was. Then I met this gorgeous man who turned out to be a warrior angel, and now my whole life seems to be in another reality with supernatural creatures like angels, Nephilim, and witches. Now, I am in a beautiful bedroom in a grand mansion owned by that gorgeous angel who happens to be the Lord of the Powers, a warrior class of angels. I look down at my solar plexus area where I had the injury. I felt the area with my hand, and there was no wound or pain. I was healed! I was also wearing a luxurious light blue silk pajama top and pants.

As I soaked in this revelation of being healed and ended up in these expensive silk pajamas, I heard the bedroom door opening. Gideon walks in, followed by Cael, carrying a silver tray with a glass of honey-colored liquid. He was wearing a black long-sleeved T-shirt and grey wool pants. No golden wings and armor. No blazing sword and eyes like golden orbs. He looked normal, but his demeanor still had that regal air of authority. His eyes were back to their beautiful golden-flecked hazel shade.

He sits on the bed beside me and takes my hand. "Seraphina. You're awake. How are you feeling?" He asks, his eyes full of concern. "I am feeling OK," I murmur, sitting up, and immediately start feeling light-headed. I press a hand to my forehead, feeling vertigo. "Here… drink this, my Lady." Cael presses the glass with the honey-colored liquid in it to my lips. I back away from it, eyeing it skeptically. "It's OK. Go on. Drink it. You will feel better after," Gideon reassures me, seeing my skepticism. I down the honey-colored liquid in a couple of gulps. Cael quickly took the glass. It had a tasty and light, refreshing, sweet citrus taste.

"That was healing nectar infused with the Archangel Raphael's healing energies," Gideon informs me. "Wait... you mean Raphael? The healing Archangel?" Another gasp of astonishment remembering some angel mythology from my studies. Both Gideon and Cael nod their heads. Just wow. Archangels are real, too. But he was right. The dizziness disappeared, and I immediately felt a sense of clarity that I had never had before. I felt rejuvenated and had a sense of tranquility. "Celeste was able to heal you, but the dizziness was a side effect of the potion. You should feel better now." He says, still staring at me. I look down at my silk pajamas and then at him. "Did you...?" I ask, feeling self-conscious, thinking that he was the one who dressed me, which meant he saw me naked. "Oh, no. Your modesty was safe. Celeste and two of my maidservants took care of you," He replies with an amused look, seeing my embarrassment. "Where are Jeb and Celeste?" I sit up straight on the bed. "Celeste is surveying the Enochian protection ward breach at your house, and Jeb is out patrolling. They will be joining us for dinner later." He moves closer to me in bed.

From the glimpse of the vintage clock on the wall, it was late afternoon. I was out almost all day. I thought about my place, and Gideon said returning there was no longer safe. He noted that Celeste and Jeb would get my things and bring them here, and his mansion was my only safe place now. I saw Cael still staring at me with wonder and awe. I ask Gideon why. He says that Cael had not met anyone of his kind since they were massacred thousands of years ago.

Cael was quick to add how he owed his life to Gideon. It is mind-blowing that Gideon was present at the Nephilim massacre thousands of years ago. But he looks barely thirty! I definitely didn't want to know how old Gideon was. All those historical events he explained to me before that made him sound like a human textbook; he was there for all of them. It blows my mind. He discusses some more details of his true identity, and I ask him if I had to address him as "my Lord" or something, and he smiles that addressing him as just "Gideon" was fine.

It turns out that I am a Nephilim disguised as a human, and my father, Professor Dr. Zane Abner, was an angel. He was the first immortal Earth angel named Zanael. He was a human before the blood seal of the seven Archangels altered his DNA to become the first created angel on Earth. He was the very first of his kind, and Gideon was assigned to be his Guardian. After his death, he passed on his Earth angel essences and the blood seal of the seven Archangels to me. My mother was a human archaeologist with whom he fell in love and had a forbidden Nephilim child. That child was me. I was not supposed to exist.

It was weird that Gideon knew my father and was the one who entrusted Celeste as my Guardian when I was an infant. Even weirder that he has been my Guardian since I was an infant and was supposed to keep his identity a secret from me unless told otherwise. I asked him if anything between us was real and if all our conversations and kissing me were part of his job. He seems taken aback by my accusation.

"Cael. Leave us." He dismisses Cael. With an understanding nod, Cael disappears out of the bedroom. Gideon explains that what happened between us was real—every moment. I felt my heart shattered when he told me that kissing me was very inappropriate and we could not be involved romantically. I am his charge; he is my Guardian, and it cannot happen again. I swallowed my disappointment, refusing to let him see the hurt. I nod my understanding. I was surprised by my composure. He says that he, Celeste, and Jeb would explain everything and answer all my questions at dinner and that Cael would bring some clothes and toiletries for me. As soon as he left, I let the floodgates open and burst into tears.

What made things worse was that discovering his true identity didn't change the feelings I was developing for him. I was trying not to be upset and angry at him but definitely upset about how complicated the situation was. Did I think I would ever have a normal romantic relationship with him? He is a celestial immortal angel who is Lord of the Powers, and I am a Nephilim who is not supposed to exist. It was too late to dismiss the feelings I had developed for him that had evolved beyond a simple crush. I knew I could never act on them. There was a knock on the door, and I quickly wiped my tears. I yelled for whoever it was to come in.

It was Cael carrying some bags. I must have looked like a dismal mess because Cael took one look at me, dropped the bags, and rushed over to me. He hugged me, which caught me off guard. I burst into tears again, crying on his shoulder. "It's OK, my Lady. I know all this must be quite overwhelming. Let it all out..." He soothes me by patting my back. I had just met Cael, but I felt I could trust him for some reason and found his presence comforting in my vulnerability. He gives me a silk handkerchief for my face. I stopped crying and just sat on the bed wiping my face.

I knew I was ugly crying. Cael takes a seat beside me, staring straight ahead, looking pensive. "If it is any comfort to say, I know my Lord Gideon for quite a few millennia, and I have never seen him upset over anyone in a while like he is right now," He simply says in a low, soothing voice. I look at him, perplexed by this revelation. "What do you mean? And how did you know about us?" I stare at him, quite surprised that he knows what transpired between us. There was so much wisdom in his grey eyes. Now I remembered he probably heard some details before Gideon dismissed him to give us privacy to talk.

"He left this room looking upset and went to the training room to work it off. He is your Guardian, but he also has feelings for you that are considered inappropriate, so he is feeling quite perplexed. He is hurting, too. He is a celestial warrior angel, but he does have some human emotions just like any virile young man." Cael looks at me wistfully, resting a comforting hand on my shoulder. I sigh, processing what I just heard. Gideon is just very confusing. He is upset, yet he was the one who said what happened between us was inappropriate.

"When you were in a coma from the demonic venom, my Lord Gideon was ever vigilant at your bedside. He didn't rest all night. He could have had someone else do that task to watch over you." Cael gives me a sidelong glance. Again, another revelation is that Gideon was so worried about me that he hardly slept but watched over me all night. "Promise me this, my Lady. Whatever I confide stays between us because my Lord Gideon will nail my wings to his wall like taxidermist decor if he ever finds out." He warns with a half-smile. That brought out an involuntary laugh from me. I think I like Cael. Talking to him made me feel better. "It's nice to hear you laugh, my Lady. Now, let's get you ready for dinner to meet the others." He claps his hands as he graciously helps me up from the bed. "My Lord Gideon has been good to me and has many fine qualities, but he can be quite pigheaded sometimes. Let's find you something fetching to wear. Such beauty as yours should be admired." He says, taking my hands and leading me toward the bags he brought in. "Us Nephilims have to stick together." He winks at me.

Cael chatted about his life with Gideon and the other angels who are part of his faction as he helped me prepare. It turns out that he was a culinary, fashion, hair, and makeup expert. He said he attended the best institutions to learn those trades to serve the faction better. He has the angelic gift of learning various skills at a genius pace and can speak any language like full-blooded angels can. I ask him about my father. He says that Gideon was better equipped to tell me more about him because they shared a close friendship. I asked him if he was also allowed to have a love life. He was allowed to, but his dedication to his duties makes it challenging to maintain any liaisons. He prefers the company of men as his lovers. He reluctantly had to leave to assist Gideon, but Celeste and Jeb came in to check on me. They were both worried that I would be upset at them for keeping the truth about my heritage, their identities, and my parents from me. But after my conversations with Cael, I was not upset with them. I was more upset about how much I still desired Gideon despite anything romantic with him being considered forbidden and appropriate.

CHAPTER 9

GIDEON

"Et, tu Brute Cael?" I ask mockingly with raised eyebrows as Cael rushes into my bedroom. I have been waiting for him to prepare my bath after a vigorous and intense training session in the training room. He is usually quite punctual, but this evening he wasn't. I watch him squirm uncomfortably under my scrutiny. "Apologies, my Lord, I was with… and it's just…" "I know where you were, and it's OK," I interrupt him, waving off his apologies. "I'm glad you're helping her get settled in. I know you were quite thrilled to be around another of your kin." I assure him as I watch him breathe an audible sigh of relief that I was not upset at him. Cael prepares the jacuzzi as I undress. He hastily removes my dirty workout clothes as I step naked into the warm, fragrant water. I submerged my body into the water and tried to relax, but my thoughts kept wandering to Seraphina. These past few days have been overwhelming for her. I traumatized her by showing up severely hurt and bleeding at her doorstep and revealing my true identity to her. Then she found out about Celeste and Jeb's identities, too. And worse, I told her that we could not have any romantic attachments after kissing her because it was inappropriate.

I saw the hurt in her eyes when I told her that whatever happened between us could not happen again, but she kept her composure. I was the one who had to leave because I couldn't let her see me lose my composure. I thought ending things before anything else could progress further with her would be easier, but I was wrong. It just made things more complicated because I desired her more than ever. I want to pleasure every inch of her body, and as much as I want to know the secrets of her soul.

I was in a haze from my earlier injuries, but I vividly remembered her gentle touch as she cleansed my wounds. Her beautiful face was tear-streaked with concern as she feared for my life, although I knew I was a far cry from dying. I knew my grave injuries were traumatic for her to see, but she kept her composure and took care of me in my state of vulnerability. When she removed my shirt, her gaze changed slightly from concern to a flicker any man would recognize. As she examined my torso, I knew that flicker was desire.

I could have compelled her to forget everything she saw, but I couldn't. She had seen too much, which would have put her in danger, given that someone was already watching her house. So, it was best to come clean and tell her the truth. I remembered the mixture of wonder and skepticism on her face when I revealed my true identity, and then we were attacked by spiker demons—nasty buggers with vicious, venomous spikes. Only a High Witch could have breached those Enochian wards at her house. It must be Nathaniel's faction, High Witch. Someone was watching Seraphina's house and knew I was there, so they worked on breaching the Enochian Wards. Jeb and Kafziel have been patrolling in stealth mode, and Celeste has been working with her coven of witches to track the identity of this rogue High Witch. The Council of Archangels will arrive in a few weeks for Caleb's trial. There is so much to prepare for their arrival.

I knew that Cael was comforting Seraphina. She tried to hide her disappointment and hurt under brave composure, but I knew she started crying after I left—preternatural hearing. I knew I was the cause of her hurt, so I went to exhaust myself with some simulated combat training. No amount of exhausting training sessions could take away the guilt of hurting her and the raging desire I still feel for her.

I usually don't go to human restaurants and cafes at all. As Lord, if I want any human food or drink, all I have to do is snap my fingers, and one of my servants will obtain what I want. Going to a human cafe and paying for coffee for Seraphina and myself felt strange because I am used to someone else doing all that for me. I find the experience enriching and enjoyed talking with her at the cafe. There were many human women in the cafe staring at me in awe. Flattering, but I had only cared for Seraphina's company.

I remembered how much I had enjoyed kissing her. The

logical part of me was conflicted that kissing her was very inappropriate and that I should walk away. But the primal part just took one look at her beautiful form, looking so confused as to why I stopped kissing her, which made me want to kiss her again with a raging desire. So, I did. The feel of her soft, full lips yielding under my own drove me wild with lust. Her taste, her smell, and her slender, toned, soft body against mine made me lose all semblance of self-control. I remembered the feel of her high rounded breasts filling my palms, and I wanted so badly to rip the bra off that was shielding them from me and take them in my mouth. I relished the feeling of her toned, slender legs wrapped around my hips and the feel of her firm buttocks. Her arousal as she traced her hands on my bare stomach fueled my ardor. If Kafziel had not called, I would have ripped every piece of clothing off her body and made passionate love to her against the wall. I knew she wanted me also. But I would have been in so much trouble since she is my charge. I know that she never slept with anyone, and it would have been so wrong to sleep with her and then tell her it was inappropriate and cannot happen again.

There have been many faes, witches, and other angels with tempting requests to service me in bed, especially from the beautiful fae sisters Lady Niahm and Lady Roisin, the daughters of fae Duchess Riona. I recently had both of them in my bed. Unlike many other faes I have had in my bed, they usually keep our arrangements very discreet. Lady Niahm and Lady Roisin were to be married off to two other fae nobilities, but they rejected their grooms and chose to be my lovers instead. I took both of their virtues the night of their engagement parties. I remembered Niahm's body emitting a beautiful dazzling light from her light fae abilities as she climaxed in ecstasy on top of me with her long golden blonde hair whipping my face. Her fiery copper-haired sister, Lady Roisin's body, erupted in flames with her fire fae abilities when she climaxed in ecstasy as I pounded into her. If it were not for invulnerability, she would have burnt my body. My beddings were not so lucky, though. I remembered Cael shaking his head in dismay as the servants changed the charred beddings. That was not the first time the bedding got burned and destroyed during one of my sexual encounters. The two fae sisters just stood there grinning at Cael and the two maidservants with satisfied looks on their faces as they clutched a sheet around their naked bodies. Those were some fun times, but now I feel that my forbidden desire for Seraphina, my charge, Zanael's daughter, is neutralizing all desires for anyone else. It is unlikely for me to desire one female this much that I ignore the others. She is not the type I usually go for anyway. I tend to leave chaste women alone. I knew I had to end things because kissing her again would make me lose all self-control.

All these lustful thoughts about Seraphina gave me the most uncomfortable erection. Oh, bollocks! This is precisely why I had to end things with her. These carnal thoughts about her are so wrong. I held her as an infant and watched her grow into an adult, for goodness' sake! A lovely adult that I have inappropriate thoughts about. What is wrong with me? I look down at my throbbing erect cock sitting in the jacuzzi. I was very aroused. Oh, *you betray me!* I scold inwardly. Maybe I should contact Lady Niahm and Lady Roisin after dinner to satiate my lust, but I lost all desire to have them. These inappropriate thoughts for Seraphina need to go away and cool off.

I remembered how I hardly rested because I was worried about her well-being after the spiker demon's venom had her in a coma. I sat vigilant by her bedside, watching her sleep. The venom exiting her body had taken a toll on her. She was tossing and turning, breathing heavily, and whimpering as if having a bad dream. I held her to comfort her until her breathing returned to normal, and she was sleeping peacefully again with all her nightmares chased away. She clung to me but remained asleep. Her body felt so frail in my arms, but I knew she was resilient, had a courageous resolve, and a fierce spirit. I held her in my arms, her head resting on my chest, listening to the rhythm of her breathing for as long as possible, even dozing off a bit until Cael knocked. That was the first time I held a female, whether supernatural or human, in my arms, just holding her, watching her sleep without partaking in any carnal pleasures. That's when I knew I could not hurt her by letting her hope there could be more between us.

Cael brought me out of my thoughts by letting me know my clothes were ready for dinner. I decided to take a cold shower and pleasure myself to release all the aroused thoughts.

CHAPTER 10

FAE PRINCESS LAURELIANA

"You allowed Gideon to escape with your petty thirst for vengeance!" I scold Nathaniel, glaring accusingly at him. "You already know it will take more than a hexed spear to subdue the most powerful of the Powers, your Highness," Nathaniel shrugs. His dismissive manner only fuels my anger. "But you had him on his knees, and you wasted time just toying with him like a pin cushion instead of bringing him to me bound in celestial chains!" I yelled as I raised a hand to smack him, but with preternatural speed, he grabbed both of my arms and pinned me to the wall. I tried to wiggle free, but he was stronger than me.

Although fae folk shares similar gifts of supernatural speed, healing, stamina, strength, and some invulnerability levels, many species of angels are naturally stronger than us. He looks at me with desire glistening in his eyes as my squirming only fuels his arousal. "Your temper tantrums are quite the turn on, your Highness." He says in a husky tone as he licks my hand and sucks on one of my fingers. "Lord Gideon is quite clever, more than you gave him credit for, hence why it will be a difficult task to subdue him. I was not counting on the fact that he had Enochian protection runes tattooed on him with celestial ink from Metatron," Nathaniel reasons. "But now we have leverage and know his weakness." He grins with triumph in his icy blue eyes. "The human prude he has been protecting," I scoff, rolling my eyes at him. "Caleb says she is a Nephilim. I knew there was more to the lass, but the question remains: Why did the Archangels allow her to live, and why is the Lord of the Powers watching over her? She must be a lot more than just a forbidden Nephilim. The High Witch is working on it. We will find out what she is." He loosens the towel from around his waist and allows it to fall to the floor, giving me a full frontal of his hard erection. We already had sex three times, and it looks like he is ready to go again. *Damn Angels and their sexual libido in overdrive.* That is another reason why the fae women covet them as lovers.

Nathaniel is a great lover who is more than willing to try to fill the chasm in my heart and soul that Gideon left, but he is not Gideon. We have been having a sexual relationship for years, but I still would prefer it if he was Gideon. I have had many lovers from different supernatural species, including human males, and none could match Gideon's sexual prowess and the carnal pleasures he gave me that one midsummer night of passion at Queen Mab's midsummer festival. I remembered how we were both buzzing from so much fae ambrosia. We indulged in sexual pleasures all night well into dawn. I remembered his passionate kisses and how his mouth and hands brought out pleasures I never knew existed within me.

I remembered how much he had filled me. I remembered how I felt my insides stretching to accommodate his huge cock, and every thrust was the most pleasure I had ever felt. I have had many from supernatural and human males, but none brought me as much pleasure as his. His chiseled, muscular body looked like a sexual god designed it. I remember riding him, which was the most exhilarating feeling. But when I woke up in the morning after a night of passionate sex with him multiple times, he was gone. I knew I was hooked on him like a drug and needed an encore. I had to have him as my lover.

I have tried every love spell, ritual, and enchantment to make myself more appealing to him and seduce him, knowing that as a warrior angel, he is impervious to those frivolous magic, so I had to do those on myself. Nothing worked except that my longing for him turned into obsession. I was starting to feel so aroused by the memories of our passionate affair. Nathaniel senses my arousal and kisses me. "Come back to bed, my love." He whispers as he nibbles my lips. He presses his lean, muscular body against mine, pinning me to the wall, lifts my silk camisole dress, wraps both of my legs around his hips, and thrusts roughly into me. I moan in pleasure and pain at his rough thrusts clawing his back. He knows how much I like it rough. With preternatural speed, he carried me to his bed, and we continued our rough carnal session. Moments later,

Nathaniel got up to shower, and I just chose to lay there with the sheets tangled around my legs.

I thought about how close I was to having Gideon beg me to be his lover again. I saw how he looked at Seraphina when he dropped her off at my sorority house for my birthday party, and I was outraged. Worse, he didn't even acknowledge my presence. He never looked at me the way he looked at her. I even had a reputable fae mage prepare a seduction ritual bath with some costly blood from a Cupid Cherub angel to make me desirable to him. The Cupid Cherub demanded a high price of rare fae jewels for just a few vials of his blood, which had to be given willingly for the seduction potion.

I was in Gideon's chambers in all my tempting glory, and he looked at me with annoyance and still rejected me. I couldn't read his feelings with my clairsentient abilities, but I could tell he cared for the Nephilim prude because of his furious reaction when I insulted her virtue. Nathaniel also confirmed my suspicions about his feelings for her because he threatened to run him through with his sword if he ever touched her again. Nathaniel was supposed to seduce her so we could lure her to the faction to find out her true identity, but she didn't want him. He got a swift kick for his troubles. I may not be able to read Gideon's feelings, but I can certainly read hers, and she wants Gideon.

When one of my maidservants reported that Gideon was at the popular college cafe with Seraphina on a coffee date; I decided to follow them after the cafe as they went back to her house. I saw her hugging him goodnight, and then he was kissing her with such desire and passion. I saw him backing her into her house, still kissing her. I was so enraged that I went back to my room at the sorority house and created such a mess, breaking the bottles of all the love, seduction, and passion potions I had amassed over the years.

My father, the Fae King Aodhan, would be furious with me if he ever found out that I was the one who risked the lives of his two best fae portal Guardians, Lachlan and Floriana, for my self-serving plan to lure Gideon into an ambush. The Fallen Throne Razziel sent the Soul Suckers demons to cause some commotion at the fae portal. Lachlan and Floriana did put up a good fight but were subdued. I knew that Caleb would ensure that Kafziel was on patrol around that area and would be alerted of the demonic activity at the fae portal, and then he would immediately contact Gideon. It was a brilliant plan.

Caleb bargained with the fallen Throne Razziel to lure Gideon into an ambush so they could capture him if he promised to resurrect his vampire lover Alaria, whom one of the Powers had staked. I made a bargain with Razziel to hand over Gideon to me after they capture him, and if he doesn't agree to be my lover, he can torture him in hell all he wants. Razziel was happy to do so because he had a massive grudge against Gideon. Nathaniel got the High Witch to hex a spear to incapacitate Gideon and block access to his angelic powers. Still, the spell was insufficient to render Enochian runes protection tattoos useless. I hate to admit that Nathaniel was correct, that we didn't see that one coming.

The Watcher angel that Nathaniel had watching Seraphina's house saw Gideon landing on her porch. He couldn't get past the Enochian protection wards, and it took the High Witch hours even to breach the wards. We hoped to catch Gideon in his still vulnerable condition, but we were too late. He had recovered and escaped with Seraphina in a golden blaze of celestial glory to his compound. I watched him in his dazzling gold celestial armor and beautiful golden wings as he flew away with her in his arms.

I was so enraged with Nathaniel for messing up this brilliant mission by toying with Gideon for too long. Now they have Caleb in their dungeons. I tried to direct my rage toward Nathaniel, but we just ended up having rough, angry sex. There was one upcoming silver lining when I saw Gideon again, though. My parents have an upcoming audience with him about the attack. Lachlan and Floriana get rescued by him and Kafziel, but they are still in a coma.

I knew my father would indulge my whims and have me accompany him as part of the royal entourage. Although I have several brothers and sisters, I was the eldest one he chose as his heir and crowned princess. He still hopes for a union between Gideon and me to secure an alliance with the angels. Still, he knows that Powers are warriors, and they rarely take liaisons with fae or any female seriously. But one can still hope, right? My father allowed me to infiltrate human society by indulging my desire to gallivant on Earth and attend college in the city where Gideon was staying.

I knew I was not too fond of Seraphina when I first saw her. Still, I was also curious about her because her energies differed from an average, mundane human. I had to know more about her. I was jealous that Nathaniel found her attractive and wanted her in his bed. The only reason he wants her is that he wants her virginity and how much it will displease Gideon that he got there first. I knew Nathaniel well enough to know that he would discard her out of boredom when she was no longer a virgin. He was furious when he found out that Gideon was making out with her, and they both went into her house, and no one knew what had happened.

After Gideon flew away with her, I immediately went and surveyed the scene in her house now that Nathaniel's High Witch had breached the Enochian Protection wards. I smelled some of her blood on the carpet in the room she and Gideon were in. It looks like she got injured by one of the nasty spikes from the spiker demon. I tasted some of her blood. She is still a virgin. I had to tell Nathaniel that her virtue was safe for now. I took a sample of her blood because our High Witch would find it beneficial for her spell to decipher Seraphina's true identity. I quickly left when the Homicide detective elite squad leader and the High Witch, who is Seraphina's adopted mother, came to the house.

CHAPTER 11
SERAPHINA

"My dad was a human King before he became the first Earth angel? So that will make a..." My voice trails off at that mind-blowing revelation. "Royalty, my Lady, among us mere warrior angels," Kemuel finishes for me with a wink as he sips his wine. I was having dinner with Gideon, Jeb, and the small group of Powers, warrior angels that were present on the night my parents were murdered. My mind was reeling from everything I learned about my true heritage and my parents. I found myself digesting all these supernatural revelations more quickly than I expected. My mind was reeling that Nathan Beckett is Nathaniel, an unaligned Gregori Watcher angel. He is in cahoots with a fallen Throne angel, Razziel, who wants to find out my true identity. I knew there was something off about him. He has angelic good looks but is just vile. I also learned about the fae folk in the supernatural community. Laurel Sanders is the daughter of the fae King Aodhan. Her true identity is the crowned Princess Laureliana.

All her sorority acolytes at her party were fae glamoured as humans, too. Mind-blowing. The other Powers acted like college boys joking and teasing each other. It was mind-blowing that they were all celestial warrior angels. They only look a few years older than me, except for Jeb and Gideon. Surprisingly, the dinner felt like a typical family dinner. Jeb even slapped one of the Powers named Ezekiel behind his head like an elder brother would chastise him to stop throwing food at another quiet one named Kafziel and mind his table manners in the presence of a lady. The others snicker at him. They all look like a handsome team of athletes at the top of their fitness game. But none are as gorgeous as Gideon.

I watch Gideon casting me a few glances as Kemuel, one of his lieutenants was trying to engage me in conversation. Where Gideon had jet black hair that fell in waves, slightly brushing his shoulders, Kemuel had long, straight, light blond hair down his back secured in a ponytail. Gideon's complexion was a bronze hue while Kemuel's was a light sun-kissed tan. He had bright, deep blue eyes to Gideon's hazel golden flecked eyes. Kemuel was tall, lean, and broad-shouldered but slightly shorter than Gideon and gorgeous, too, with the cutest dimples. He was still in tight black leather pants and a moto biker jacket from the motorcycle ride he was on earlier. He looks like the charming, self-assured bad-boy type that probably has a trail of broken hearts. Vicky would die a sweet death if she were in this dining room with all these gorgeous warrior angels.

Kemuel's charm was endearing, and I found myself enjoying our conversation. I couldn't help but steal furtive glances at Gideon, who was nodding his head at something Jeb was saying to him about a homicide case he was working on that had supernatural elements to it. Our eyes keep connecting briefly. Why did he have to look so damn sexy in that dark red silk buttoned-down shirt and black pants? I kept a poker face as I gave him a curt nod, and he returned to sipping his wine.

My thoughts wandered as I half listened to Kemuel recounts the events of an encounter he had with a nasty demon that devoured the skin of both supernatural and humans while he was out on patrol. He gave me a crash course about celestial weaponry and how the Powers warrior's armor, shield, and weapons are part of their soul, like their wings. They all manifest from the ether when needed because of celestial magic. I learned that Kemuel had the rare ability to split his celestial weapon into two short swords for combat and that Gideon had the most coveted ability, the Lord of the Powers.

The Archangel Michael had bestowed upon Gideon the coveted ability to transform his celestial angel weapon into any weapon he wished for combat. The warrior Archangel Michael is the only other angel that has that ability. Kemuel scoffs that Gideon prefers the uninteresting broad sword as his preferred celestial weapon, which is a nod to the medieval and Renaissance era he enjoyed. Gideon scowls at him for mocking his weapon but joins in our conversation when I ask about Nephilim and Earth angel abilities. He said that we wouldn't know about my angelic abilities and what celestial weapon I would manifest unless the Archangels unbind my celestial powers that Celeste had bound when I was an infant. Gideon did tell me about my father, Zanael's abilities, though. He could heal other supernatural folks and humans from grave injuries and regenerate himself from injuries much faster than regular angels. Zanael also had silvery white wings; his celestial weapon was a scimitar. As an Earth angel, he did not have celestial battle armor. I might not be similar to my father since I am both a Nephilim and an Earth angel.

I watch as the seven elite Powers, Jeb and Gideon, all laugh and joke with each other. It was hard to believe this youthful group of gorgeous young men helped rescue me as an infant. Celeste was telling the truth when she told me that angels rescued me. I thought she meant it metaphorically to describe the people who rescued me, but now I know they were angels. It was Gideon himself that took me to Celeste as an infant. Oh goodness. It's wrong to want to date Gideon because he held me as an infant and watched me grow up.

Kemuel offers to give me a grand tour of the mansion, the next day and flirted blatantly with me all evening. He ceases his flirtations when Celeste arrives and gives him an irritated look for flirting with me. Jeb and Gideon were scowling at him also, but he charms them by making them laugh with some jokes about the pet peeves of the

Archangels to prepare for their impending visit. Cael winks at me as he refills drinks, watching the other Powers try to outdo each other to impress me. Celeste wanted to know how her Enochian rune tattoos and protection wards worked to help Gideon. It was experimental, and she wasn't sure it would work, but Gideon was willing to get the Enochian runes tattooed on his body anyway. So that's what those tribal-looking tattoos on his chest and back are. Enochian runes. The other Powers looked at me with admiration when Gideon told them I kept my composure when he showed up on my front porch, all bloodied with severe injuries, and that I helped tend to his wounds until the hex wore off and his healing powers kicked in. Kemuel was incredibly impressed with my composure after I discovered Gideon's true identity. I saw Gideon scowling when Kemuel offered to escort me to my room, but he didn't say anything to stop him.

Kemuel was quite a gentleman and kissed my hand good night. He curtsied with a dazzling dimpled smile that he would see me at breakfast. I shut the bedroom door in his face with a laugh at his antics. I quickly changed into silk pajamas and combed my hair to prep for bed when there was a light knock on the door. I quickly throw on a robe to cover the silk camisole and open the door. Gideon was standing there gazing at me with such intensity. He was wearing the same clothes he wore to dinner earlier. He asks to come in, and I nod, closing the door behind him.

"Is there something you need, Gideon?" I ask as neutrally as possible. I watch him as he walks over and sits on one of the chaise lounges so he can face me. "Us together is inappropriate because I am your Guardian," He says in a low voice. "Tell me something else that you didn't mention before." I pull the robe closer to my body, eyeing him, folding my arms. "The Council of Archangels will never allow a union between us. I am responsible for you as your Guardian, and that's all. How should I say this? I also don't do this whole what you humans like to call "dating." I don't want you to get the wrong idea that there could be more between us." He says as he stands up from the chaise lounge and approaches me. He is very confusing. I get it that he doesn't do dating. But he had an entire make-out session with me and now says he doesn't want me to get the wrong idea! The paradox and contradiction of it all. I backed away from him toward the bedroom wall, bracing myself against it to face him. He hadn't mentioned this earlier.

"Then why did you kiss me knowing the council would forbid anything between us? You don't want me to get the wrong idea that there could be more between us, but you kissed me. You are very contradictory, you know that, right?" I snap between clenched teeth, glaring at him. I was livid at his confusing signals demeanor. He sighs in frustration, then returns his gaze to me. "The more I got to know you, the more I feel that I am losing my self-control around you," He answers, his voice husky. I stare at him, stunned, as he grabs my forearms and pulls me to him. "I don't want to hurt you, but all I can think about is how badly I want to kiss you." He stares at my lips, and that warm flutter he tends to cause in my chest quickens. "Then what should we do, Gideon? What happened between us cannot happen again." "Yes, because it will be inappropriate..." He raises a hand to my face, tenderly caressing my cheek. His fingers felt warm on my skin, and I saw desire shining in his eyes. "Inappropriate because you are my Guardian? What do you want from me, Gideon?" I ask, mesmerized by his eyes as I stare at his handsome face.

His lips claim mine in a hungry kiss as he pulls me to his body. I moan as his tongue parts my lips, and the robe I was holding together over my silk camisole falls to the ground. He pins me against the wall, still kissing me as his hands caress my shoulders. His smell and taste made me giddy once again. He made low groans deep in his throat as he trailed kisses down my neck to my shoulders. I entangle my fingers in his silky dark hair as his teeth toy with the thin straps of my camisole. His hands caress my breasts through the thin fabric, and I let out a moan as his mouth captures a hardened nipple through the fabric and suckles on it. He slips the straps of my camisole down on my shoulders to expose my breasts. My knees felt weak as his tongue teased, and his mouth sucked on the exposed hardened nipple of one of my breasts while his hand caressed the other. "This is me losing self-control." He murmurs between ragged breaths as he trails kisses back to my neck, his hands roaming my body. He groans as his hands caress my thighs and squeeze my buttocks. I let out a moan as he pressed his hard erection against my groin area. I felt all semblance of self-control slipping from me.

"What I want is to take you right here against this wall. Is this how you want your first time to be?" He asks huskily, his breath hot against my skin. I froze, feeling the heat of embarrassment on my face. "How did you...? Is it a supernatural sense?" I frown at him, feeling embarrassed as I pull the traps of my camisole back on my shoulders, shrinking away from him. I quickly pick up the robe and wrap it around my body. Gideon watches me, his eyes dancing with some amusement at my embarrassment, and then it softens. "Your virginity is nothing to be embarrassed about. And yes, some supernatural folks can sense your virginity by the smell or taste of your blood or by your aura." He walks over and sits on the chaise lounge. "Wait... so you knew all this time?" I gulp as realization dawns on me. He nods. So, he knew that I had never slept with anyone. A bit embarrassing. I went and sat next to him on the chaise lounge.

"So, what happens now?" I ask, glancing at him. "We will keep you safe here. You will learn more about your heritage and the supernatural world, and if you decide to continue your college studies, I will assign one of the elite squad lieutenants to guard you on campus. You are not a prisoner here, but you have to be protected. The ones after you will not risk attacking you among humans. What happens after you graduate college is up to the Council of Archangels. Remember that many things will never be normal again for you," He says.

I thought about Vicky and how I would keep all this from her. "As for us?" His eyes did not break his gaze from me. "I already told you I don't date or try to get romantically involved with anyone," He reiterates. I nod in agreement as I clasp my hands on my lap. A bit of silence fell between us, and then he broke it. "It will be best for us not to be alone like this again. Because I might not be able to stop myself again from ripping every clothing off your body and pleasure every inch of your body with my mouth and hands."He smirked a bit, and I could see devilish thoughts running through his mind as he glanced at my silk pajamas, his eyes making his desire known. He was shamelessly staring at my hardened nipples poking through the silk fabric. I wanted him to lose all restraint and kiss me again, but reality gave me a quick slap to remind me that we could not let it get to that. Feeling self-conscious, I quickly pull the robe closer. I agree that we should not be together like this again. "There has been a lot of information to digest for you these past few days and many more to learn. Get some rest, and I will see you at breakfast." He rests a hand briefly on my shoulder and gives me a quick kiss on the forehead, then makes his exit.

I settled into my bed as soon as he left. My thoughts were trying to decipher Gideon's confusing persona. I knew he was definitely attracted to me, but the physical attraction was all there was because he made it clear that was all he wanted. He does not date or get involved in romance. He only prefers casual sexual encounters. As Lord of the Powers and being as gorgeous as he is, I am sure he has several women who want him without him having to date them. I know I was thinking about what happens with dating and romance in human society. Still, I am discovering how supernatural communities operate concerning those things differently.

As a former gymnast and ballet dancer, I was used to rejection and disappointment. I got rejected for many lead ballet parts I wanted because the instructors gave them to someone who did not do as much hard work. But when it came to men, it was mostly me who often rejected them. Gideon made it clear that he was only interested in sex from me and nothing more. Even sex is off-limits for us because he is my Guardian. Somehow, with all this insanity, I still yearn for him. Not just sex, but I want more from him. I must be losing a few marbles. The logic of all this is quite insane. The chemistry between us is pretty insane and amazing. Who would have thought the first guy I ever had this amount of chemistry with would have been an immortal celestial angel? I will lose all my common sense trying to make sense of that one. I am still trying to make sense that I was a half-angel, too, and I carry this powerful blood seal that my dad transferred to me before he died, saving my life.

I felt myself dozing off as I thought about how much I enjoyed Gideon's searing kisses and his hands caressing my body. His muscular body pressing against mine made me lose all semblance of self-control. His warm mouth kissing and sucking on my breasts made me wet with arousal and weak in the knees. I would have allowed him to take things further until he mentioned he knew I had never slept with anyone before. That question dampened my desires out of embarrassment. I knew I didn't want my first time to be against a wall and with someone off limits.

"I beg you to stop stealing the sausages before the pancakes are ready!" Cael rebukes Abdiel, one of the Powers, a warrior angel, and smacks his hand with his spatula. Cael was wearing an apron as he busied himself making breakfast. Celeste and Jeb returned to her house, so I was having breakfast with the rest of the group. Gideon was absent. The mansion's central kitchen was spacious and luxurious, with high-end appliances and a huge butler's pantry. Light filters through a beautiful bay window. The seven elite Powers were all sitting around a huge breakfast table in sweatpants and T-shirts. They all seem close-knit and operate as a team, doing most activities together. Each possesses unique gifts, which I am learning about as I get to know them.

Both Kemuel and Ezekiel gave a low chuckle at Abdiel as they continued playing with their cell phones. I watch them all with a smile and how they behave and act like human college boys. Texting on cellphones, joking, and teasing each other. I learned that the eight Powers Jebediah, Kemuel, Ezekiel, Kafziel, Abdiel, Zerachiel, Yael, and Danael from dinner last night is Gideon's elite task force squad of hand-picked best warriors for special missions. According to Kemuel, besides immortality, the Powers enjoy the perks of invulnerability, heightened senses, accelerated healing, preternatural speed, enhanced stamina, enhanced reflexes, teleportation, and immunity to many forms of magic, enchantments, and human ailments. They also can turn translucent for short periods, called 'phasing.' Their main kryptonite is weapons hexed by High Witches because it can render them vulnerable to injuries.

Jeb, Gideon's second in command, is their squad leader; hence, the black and grey of his celestial armor denoting his status. I learned that Jeb's celestial weapon is a Tomahawk axe, and his angelic unique gift is his brute strength, which is more enhanced than that of the other warrior angels and supernatural folks. I can definitely see that given that Jeb's build is like a burly, well-muscled statue of Hercules. His massive size, military haircut, and a perpetual scowl that always seems plastered on his face have scared away many potential dates from me whenever he was around as I was growing up.

Kemuel is considered the charming jock in the group. His angelic, unique gift is that his agility and reflexes are more enhanced than other warrior angels and supernatural folks. He is considered the best fighter in the squad. Kafziel, the quiet nerdy one, had curly red hair, the color of sunset, and his celestial weapon was the Halberd. His unique angelic gift is that he can turn transparent with his phasing and stay phased for longer than the other warrior angels. He is very effective with espionage and intelligence. Kemuel playfully calls Kafziel the Ninja Turtle Donatello. It feels like the United Nations being around them because each of them looks different, yet they are brothers created from the same celestial matter.

Yael and Danael are twins that look Japanese. Their celestial weapon is the Katana. Their angelic, unique gifts are very remarkable indeed. As twins, they share a unique bond where they can combine their invulnerability to make themselves twice as invulnerable, which is more enhanced than other warrior angels and supernatural folks. Their combined invulnerability can withstand most High Witch-hexed weaponry. They are like the perfect human shields.

Zerachiel looks Middle Eastern, and his celestial weapon is the Turkish scimitar. He also likes to carry several dwarf-forged knives and other sharp-throwing weaponry. He explained that he could set those ablaze with his angel-fire and use them as throwing missiles for long-range attacks. His angelic, unique gift is that his enhanced eyesight is better than that of many supernatural folks and other angels, which makes him an excellent marksman.

Abdiel looks like he is from India, and his celestial weapon is the Urumi whip sword, which he was very excited to let me know how it works. His angelic, unique special gift is enhanced speed, which is far more advanced than the levels of other supernatural folks and angels.

Ezekiel looks Black African, and his celestial weapon is the Shotel's double-edged sword, which looks like a scythe. He says it originated from Eritrea and Ethiopia and was happy that this celestial weapon chose him. His angelic, unique gift is his advanced telekinesis, which he likes to levitate and juggle fruits at the dinner and breakfast table. I also learned that there were no female Powers, only males. There are other Powers, divided by squads with an appointed squad leader at different outposts worldwide. They usually have to brief Gideon on their operations. The seven Powers, with their squad leader Jeb, are the only ones that live in the mansion with Gideon since they are his elite task force. They all treat Cael like a father figure, and he treats them like his sons.

"Forgive my brothers, Seraphina. They forget their manners around a lady sometimes and act like they were raised by wolves." Kemuel says graciously with a dimpled smile, taking me out of my thoughts. Kafziel, the quiet demeanor one, rolls his eyes and scoffs at him, then returns to the book he was engrossed in. "Donatello over there is always engrossed at breakfast with his books or laptop," Kemuel smirks, throwing a grape at Kafziel, who catches it with preternatural reflexes and frowns at him.

"He is trying to impress you since he has not been around any female as intelligent as you. Given that the fickle fae women he usually dates tend to fry his brain cells with their simpering vapid chatter, and he has regained a few of them back since talking to you," Kafziel quips, resting his book on his lap and grinning smugly, at Kemuel. Cael stifles a laugh as the other Powers howl with laughter. "Oh, you got jokes, Donatello," Kemuel teases, rolling his eyes and throwing an apple this time at Kafziel, who catches it and bites it with a chuckle. I shake my head, smiling at them all. Who would ever know that these are fierce celestial warriors?

Kemuel told me that Gideon was probably on a conference call with the Fae King Aodhan in preparation for a meeting with him and his entourage later today. "I bet Lord Gideon's stalker will probably be in the royal entourage since she is the crowned princess. I think you know her by her alias, Laurel Sanders. She goes to your college." Kemuel's lips quirk in a sarcastic half-smile, glancing at me. I was immediately intrigued by this bit of news. "Wait...Is Laurel stalking Gideon? Why?" I ask quizzically with a pique of interest in this juicy news. He chuckles, a hint of mischief dancing in his deep blue eyes. "Oh, they had what you humans like to call a one-night stand a few centuries ago at the fae deity Queen Mab's Midsummer festivities, and she has been obsessed with him ever since." He answers nonchalantly with a dismissive wave of his hand. "Why doesn't he want her again?" I raise my eyebrows at him. "The Venus fly trap is hot but has the personality of a barracuda," Ezekiel joins in our conversation, shaking his head. "Dumb as a box of rocks, and that is insulting to those rocks," Zerachiel adds, rolling his eyes. I glance back and forth between them, listening to their comments about Laurel. The twins Danael and Yael only smirk, nodding their heads in agreement. Kafziel smiles and shakes his head.

"Lord Gideon had too much Fae ambrosia with Zanael that night of the festivities, and it must have clouded his judgment a bit," Kemuel remarks mockingly, looking quite sure of himself. I turn my attention to Kemuel. "Let me get this straight... so Gideon got angel wasted with my dad and hooked up with a fae princess bimbo who is now stalking him for more?" I cross my arms over my chest, looking at them all. There were some snickers and murmurs.

I should not be jealous that Gideon slept with Laurel. He probably saw more butts than several church pews, given the fact that he is an immortal warrior angel that is quite a few millennia old. I didn't need to or want to know who he had been with. "Yep, pretty much," Kemuel shrugs. "Fae women act like our groupies, and many can be 'fatal attraction'. I heard she was a good lay because they broke all the bed posts, and those posts were sturdy dwarf wood. The brick walls had several dents too. Supernatural stamina will do that." Abdiel snickers, wagging his eyebrows. I made an audible gasp, covering my mouth as I felt heat rising to my face. Laurel and Gideon broke beds and had dents in the brick walls when they had sex. That was TMI. Cael noticed my reaction. "Gentlemen! Refrain from lewd talk around the lady. How crass!" He chastises, glaring at each one of them. They all went quiet as Gideon walked into the kitchen and casually grabbed a glass of orange juice from Cael. I wonder if he heard what they were all saying about him. They all murmured greetings at him.

I tried to get up to help Cael prepare breakfast, but he insisted I was a guest and should sit. I keep forgetting that I was in a kitchen full of sexual libido in overdrive and youthful, handsome male warriors with celestial superpowers who act like college boys, so I should expect to hear some inappropriate jokes and comments. I keep thinking about what they said about Gideon and Laurel. No wonder she acted as she did when she saw him that night at her party. That definitely makes sense how offended she was when he ignored her. But now I know why. Would he treat me that way if we slept with each other? I wonder. There was nothing to worry about since that was a far-fetched idea. It looks like the seven elite think that Gideon's one-night stand with Laurel was a poor judgment on his part.

I listen to their boisterous banter and how they admire and respect Gideon, who smiles occasionally at Kemuel and Kafziel's constant bickering. His eyes would often meet mine as he listened to their conversations. They have been very accepting toward me and made sure I didn't feel left out of their discussions, and they will often ask for my opinions on many things. I thought about Gideon's passionate kisses. How much I had enjoyed kissing him, and the pleasures of his hands on my body awoke within me. Now I see why she is obsessed with him. Okay, I must admit I feel jealous of what transpired between him and Laurel.

CHAPTER 12

SERAPHINA

"They want to meet her right now, my Lord," Cael insists. Gideon let out a huge breath as he paced with his hands on his hips. "What do you mean right now? Their arrival is not until a couple of days." He looks at Cael, who looks like he is about to panic. "This was unexpected, my Lord, but they are all in the foyer waiting," Cael adds. "Wait, what is going on?" I ask quizzically as they both turn and look at me.

These past couple of weeks have been a blur. I spent it learning a lot about the supernatural world. Kafziel discussed that each supernatural community has its own governing body. The angels have the Council of Archangels. The faes have their King, queen, and other royal members as part of their governing body. The Dwarves have a group of seven Lords as their councilors. The Witches and Mages have the Council of High Witches and the Council of High Mages, consisting of seven members each. Celeste is a council member of the Council of High Witches. The vampires mostly keep their distance from other supernatural folks and have their King and Queen. The Shifters have their Alphas, but they also keep their distance from other supernatural folks. I learned that only High Witches and High Mages are immortal, and their immortality comes at a terrible price. Regular Witches and Mages have longevity but not enough powers for immortality. Kafziel has been extremely helpful with reading materials to get me up to speed, while Kemuel gave me grand tours of the mansion compound. He took pride in showing me around and amusing me with his playful antics. I find myself always laughing in his company. My head was reeling from how grand it was.

Because I restarted classes, I hardly saw Gideon, but he always ate dinner and breakfast with us. Vicky told me that she is taking a break from college to go on a vacation. I was surprised, but knowing Vicky, it was expected of her to do something unpredictable like that. I do miss her company and seeing her around campus. Kemuel was happy to volunteer to be my angelic bodyguard whenever I left the mansion for campus and would take me home after classes on his motorcycle. I had never been on a bike before and was skittish at first. He reassured me that I should trust him because he will always ensure I stay safe. His arrival on campus on his motorcycle usually causes quite a commotion among the college girls. They flirted shamelessly with him and acted like they wanted to throw their underwear at him at any time if he even looked in their direction. He seemed to enjoy some of the attention from the college girls but mostly responded to them with polite greetings rather than flirting. I remember how muscular his body always felt whenever I held onto him during these motorcycle rides.

Sometimes, it would be Kafziel as a substitute, but never Gideon. Kemuel said he is busy with supernatural world politics and prepping for the Council of Archangels' arrival. There were times when Gideon and the other Powers would walk in drenched in blood, grime, and gooey substances from demon hunting, talking, and laughing like it was another typical day on the job. They would discuss the demons they killed. It sounded like they had fun, although it was usually dangerous. Cael usually has a fit at the mess they were tracking all over the beautiful floors. Many of the servants were other supernatural creatures like brownies, gnomes, and dwarves that helped maintain the compound. Most of them seem to avoid talking to me and make themselves scarce.

"The Council of Archangels are here, and they want to meet you right now," Gideon replies, turning his attention to me. I felt my eyes widening. "What? Now?" I blurt out, gesturing at my pajamas. "You need to be presented in proper attire right now, my Lady. Let's make haste." Cael grabs my hand and ushers me to my bedroom. "I will be waiting outside to escort you." Gideon nods at me. I quickly freshened up and got dressed in a pair of jeans and a sweater. There was no time to look for anything else fancy. I was nervous when Gideon offered his arm to escort me to the foyer. He noticed my nervousness and reassured me that I was not in trouble. Then, he gave me a quick crash course on the descriptions of each of the Archangels.

As soon as we enter the foyer, seven pairs of eyes turn to scrutinize me. Gideon gives me an encouraging nod to step forward. It felt like I had just walked into a top business CEO board meeting because all seven Archangels were dressed in expensive-looking business attire by top designers. Two of them were females dressed in prim skirt suits, and they both stared at me and smiled. They must be Ariel and Chamuel. "Whatever happened to Archangels being in tunics and robes?" I ask with a nervous smile. Gideon glances at me, furrowing his brows. A look that says, 'You didn't just speak to my bosses like that'. They all stared at me with grave looks, then broke out in chuckles, smiles of amusement, and murmurs. I let out a breath of relief, and so did Gideon.

One of the Archangels, the tallest in the group, stood up, straightens his black suit coat and clears his throat, and the murmurs and chuckles stop. He had such an authoritative and confident presence. He approaches us while the others remain seated. He looks like an almost seven-foot-tall Persian prince in his early forties with curly dark hair and an impeccable Armani suit. He was absolutely gorgeous, regal, and very intimidating. "We do wear ceremonial robes," he replies in a deep baritone bass voice, a hint of amusement playing on his lips. "But only for special occasions and rituals. We have evolved as humans did with modern times and will improvise in proper human attire whenever we visit Earth." He says, then turns his attention to Gideon. I can only stare at him, feeling star-struck because his dignified demeanor oozes confidence. "Lord Gideon. You look well." He greets him with a smile, clasps Gideon's hand, and gives him a quick embrace. "That suit becomes you, Lord Michael," Gideon compliments with a smile and nod of approval at his suit. Another mind-blowing moment. I was in the presence of Archangel Michael. The Michael. The famous Archangel of kicking asses and taking names. No wonder his presence was so intimidating. "And this must be your charge, Zanael's daughter." Michael regards me with light grey eyes, scrutinizing me from head to toe.

There were murmurs among the other Archangels as they approached us, each greeting Gideon with smiles and hugs. Then, they all turned their attention to me. "Come, child. Let's have a look at you." One of the Archangels with kind, deep green eyes beckons to me. He must be Raphael. I glanced nervously at Gideon, and he gave me a reassuring nod. I slowly approached the other Archangels. They all circle, studying me. "I thought she would be taller." Raphael frowns as he surveys me from head to toe. What? I am five feet eight inches! I huff indignantly inwardly. But compared to all of them, yes, I was short. They were at least well over six feet four inches, even the females Ariel and Chamuel. "She is lovely, though." One of the female Archangels with ash blonde hair adds, eyeing me with interest. She must be Ariel. I just stood there feeling stupefy, shifting timidly under their scrutiny." A bit on the thin side but lovely regardless." A dark-skinned male with a booming voice comment. He must be Gabriel. Gideon did mention he had quite the voice. The one named Azrael, dressed in a dark blue suit, stood solemnly a distance away, eyeing me curiously. "Has Gideon informed you of our customs and formalities, my child?" Michael asks, gazing down at me. I swallowed, shifting timidly under his gaze, clearly intimidated, and glanced at Gideon for answers to what he meant. Gideon shakes his head. "Ah, give it a rest, brother." One of the female Archangels with bright red hair waves a dismissive hand at Michael. "You are scaring the poor child. She barely just discovered our world," Chamuel scolds. Michael gave Chamuel an irritable look. She rolls her eyes at him. "Point taken sister. I forgot she was raised human in their community." He concedes with a nod of understanding. I would love to be a fly on the wall at their dinner table to hear their sibling's banter.

"No need to be nervous, child. You have our blood in your veins," Raphael says in a soothing voice. "And your father was a noble warrior King before he became the first Earth angel. You are royalty, my dear," Ariel adds, smiling at me. "Lord Gideon," Michael rests a hand on Gideon's shoulder. "Ensure she is presented in proper attire befitting her station for the banquet in two days." He gave the jeans and sweater I wore a condescending, disapproving look. "Escort her out, and then we must convene shortly for Caleb's trial. We also need to discuss the events that led to you revealing your true identity to Zanael's Nephilim daughter." He continues glancing at me. "Her name is

Seraphina," Gideon quickly reminds him. "I know." Michael gave a dismissive wave. "And tell Cael to fetch me his best bourbon whiskey and have it ready in my chambers," He adds. I guess being the head honcho for cans of whoop asses comes with the territory of being a condescending ass too.

Gideon escorted me out of the foyer to where Cael was waiting. "I know the Council of Archangels can be intimidating, especially since you are still new to everything, but you did well in there." He commends me with an approving nod. "Are you in trouble for revealing your true identity to me?" I asked him, very curious, why Michael mentioned that. A smile plays on his lips. "No." He shakes his head. "Because I think they like you." "Really? Because, according to Michael, I lack decorum. What am I going to wear to this banquet anyway? That is proper attire befitting my station?" I call after him as he walks away. "I will arrange that very soon." He answers with a wave of his hand as he keeps walking.

"Is he always like that?" I asked Kemuel, who was sprawled on a recliner playing with his cell phone. We were in one of the entertainment rooms with a giant flat-screen TV. The other six were in the training room, while Kemuel was with me in the entertainment room after the training he did earlier. He just wanted to be around me, although I was working on some homework. Gideon was in a meeting with the Fae King Aodhan and his consort, Queen Aoibheann. Kemuel wanted to know about my meeting with the Council of Archangels. I told him how condescending Michael was. He turns his attention to me with a half-smile. "Yes. And it gets worse if anyone accidentally spills wine on his favorite Armani suit. Oh, you should hear the banter at their social gatherings." He replies with a chuckle. "When someone is a head honcho like him, that comes with a certain level of arrogance. But the fact that he addressed you directly and did not let Lord Gideon be your mouthpiece means you definitely piqued his interest, my Lady." "Oh, not you too with my Lady thing too." I playfully slap his arm, rolling my eyes at him. "You are technically a princess with royal blood and the blood of the seven most powerful Archangels in your veins and I will address you as such." His voice had a serious tone. "We will render you the same honor as your father, Zanael." He rests his hands behind his head, staring with those unusually bright, deep blue eyes of his. He then started telling me some stories about my father. It was weird to acknowledge that he had known my father for quite a few millennia, although he barely looked a few years older than my twenty-one years old. I heard someone entering the room, and it was Gideon.

He scowled at him when he saw Kemuel lying down next to me on the recliner. "My Lord," Kemuel quickly greets him as he sits up. "Kemuel, leave us," Gideon orders as he turns his attention to me. Kemuel nods wordlessly, then quickly makes his exit. "There is someone here to see you. She goes by the human name "Vicky," Gideon says. My mouth drops open. "What???" I shrieked quickly, standing up and looking at him in confusion. Another bombshell dropped. "Vicky is not human? What is she?" I ask him, still in shock. The only friend I have known for years is also part of the supernatural world. "And you failed to mention this to me?" I scowl at him. "It was not my place to tell you. Now that you are part of the supernatural community, I brought her in to tell you who she is herself." He explains. Everyone has kept secrets from me, including my own best friend. Worse, she knew who Gideon was all this time. "Did she know who you were or who I was?" I question as I fold my arms and search his face for answers. "No, but she could have sensed your Nephilim aura like any other supernatural, but she wasn't sure since your human glamour is strong. And she never met me until today," He answers, and his eyes and facial features soften. "She is still your best friend. A true one, too, because she made a bargain with the fae King Aodhan and begged me to see you," He reasons, his voice tone softening. I gasp, remembering how the fae folk usually operate based on what the seven elite and Gideon told me. The fae can be very transactional. What trouble has Vicky gotten herself into with them?

"Why don't you ask her?" He glances toward the entrance. "Come in, Lady Victoria. I knew you were eavesdropping." He says, still looking at the entrance. I watch with widened eyes as Vicky slowly appears at the entrance of the entertainment room. She looks like the regular college girl Vicky in her usual jeans and long-sleeve top. She stares at me wordlessly and then smiles. "I will leave you two to get reacquainted," Gideon says, signaling his cue to leave. "Thank you again, Lord Gideon," Vicky thanked him fervently, grinning her silly grin at him. It was unfair that I could not stay mad at her for long. With a nod at both of us, Gideon makes his exit. I approach Vicky and hug her long and hard. "It's best we sit down because you have much explaining to do," I scolded her. "Then you better ask someone to fetch us wine because we need it." She laughs.

CHAPTER 13
GIDEON

The past couple of weeks with Seraphina staying in my mansion went by in a blur. We have not been alone since that night we kissed again in her room, but that doesn't mean I have forgotten. I have been thinking about how much I had enjoyed every minute of that moment with her as I lay resting every night. Sometimes, I will doze off thinking about her in my arms and then wake up very aroused. Many fae women, witches, and female angels have been contacting me, offering to serve me in bed, but I rebuffed all their advances. The fae sisters, Lady Niahm and Lady Roisin have been distraught with me because they were hoping to be my regular lovers. My new behavior has caused quite a commotion, especially among the fae women, and there have been all sorts of gossip and speculations that I took a human lover. I ignore them all because I have more pressing matters.

Celeste and Jeb confronted me in my office, inquiring if

there was something inappropriate between Seraphina and me. She gave me a scalding look like she wanted to burn my wings with her witch fire when I confessed that we had a few inappropriate moments. Her voice rose a few octaves when she said I am supposed to be Seraphina's Guardian and not try to sleep with her. I reassured her that I ended things before they could progress further. She said she could see that Seraphina was infatuated with me, and I better not take advantage of that and sleep with her. She went on in a lecture about how I showed up at her doorstep with Seraphina as an infant for her to take care of, and now that she is a young woman, the type of attraction I feel for her is inappropriate and not supposed to happen. That is what I kept telling myself, too, but one has to be blind not to notice that Seraphina is lovely. She said she is pretty aware of my reputation among the female supernatural population and doesn't want Seraphina to get her feelings hurt. I asked her since when has my sex life become a hot topic for gossip. Jeb laughed and said that it is because I am a Lord, and half of the supernatural female population is complaining that I have been rejecting their advances for my human charge. Celeste did not think he was funny with that comment and gave him a scathing look. She warned me again to keep it zipped up around Seraphina and not to make out with her again to encourage her infatuation before she and Jeb left my office.

King Aodhan has been pushing for an alliance with my faction since demons and fallen angels have attacked the fae folks. The fae kingdom usually stays neutral concerning many angels' affairs, but now they are under attack by our enemies. So, this alliance is definitely self-preservation for King Aodhan. The Council of Archangels has invited him and his royal attendants to the banquet to discuss this further.

My squads have been busy on their patrols because attacks on humans have also increased. Jeb's homicide division has reported many murder cases of gruesome ritual sacrifice types of murders and missing people. The Council of High Witches also wants to discuss matters with the Council of Archangels because there have been kidnappings of witches, especially the ones with seer abilities, by fallen angels. Fallen angels also target High Witches because they can hex weapons that can harm angels. They have a better chance of defending themselves than regular witches, but many have gone into hiding out of self-preservation. For her protection, Celeste has temporarily moved in with Jeb in his cottage in my compound. Her coven is under my protection. She and her coven have been working diligently to discover the identity of the mysterious rogue High Witch working with Nathaniel's faction. There have been no sightings of Nathaniel, but I know he is plotting something sinister.

All of the council members and representatives for each supernatural faction will be present at the banquet. They will all be curious about Seraphina since she is a Nephilim who was allowed to live beside Cael. It will cause quite a controversy. Michael and the rest of the council suggest that she has to learn the Powers combat style to defend herself, as her father, Zanael, was taught. Michael and the council agreed to unbind her Nephilim powers but thought it too risky to unbind her Earth angel powers. That part of her identity has to remain hidden.

Sometimes, I miss having Seraphina for myself. I do miss our banter about numerous topics. Kemuel seemed quite taken with her and had quickly volunteered himself to be her temporary Guardian in my place since I had other matters to take care of as Lord. I do want her to move on from me and find someone else who can give her more than I can. But there is also a part of me that is selfish and doesn't want her to move on with anyone else. I have never had to fight to not lose self-control with my desires around any female like how I had to with her.

I watched how she laughed frequently in Kemuel's company and how he flirted with her. He has not made any moves on her because of Celeste's threats. Celeste is quite familiar with Kemuel, who does have a reputation for leaving a trail of broken hearts and wants to protect Seraphina. I envy him sometimes because he gets to be in her company quite often. I know she misses her best friend, Lady Victoria or Vicky; she calls herself, hence why I agreed for her to visit.

Lady Victoria belongs to the Fae realm because of her high-born Mother, Princess Aoiffe, and her uncle, fae King Aodhan. She has agreed to work part-time as one of King Aodhan's treasurers in exchange for visiting Seraphina. Lady Victoria's father is one of the Dwarf Lords, Lord Ronan, who owns a vast treasure mine, and her mother, Princess Aoiffe, is the Chief of King Aodhan's fae healers and his sister. King Aodhan had wanted Lady Victoria to work as one of his treasurers for a while due to her abilities to manage finances and identify the essences of any magical treasures and their properties. But she preferred to go to a human college instead. I knew it would make Seraphina happy to see her and have someone else around who is another female.

My elite squad have all been charmed by her beauty and personality and treated her with the utmost respect. They all tried to outdo each other to impress her. They were very excited when they found out she would have to learn combat training and exercise regimens with them.

As I sorted through some paperwork, my thoughts wandered to Caleb. Thankfully, he doesn't know Seraphina's true identity because he was not part of my elite squad, but he knows she is a Nephilim. He claims no knowledge of the rogue High Witch Nathaniel works with during the interrogations. He revealed that Nathaniel is also working with a fae but does not know which fae he is working with. That will be tough to find out which fae since many will work for anyone if it serves their purpose. Caleb's betrayal saddens me, and the Council of Archangels had no choice but to sentence him to a celestial prison. He swore vengeance as he was bound in celestial chains. Cael took me out of my thoughts with a summon from Archangel Michael, who requested my presence in his private quarters.

Michael was staring out the window at the picturesque view of the city with a glass of bourbon. His room had one of the best views of the city. He was wearing a luxurious white linen tunic shirt and black pants and looked regal as usual. "You may enter, Gideon," He says without turning around. I walk into his grand room and watch him still staring outside. "Do you think humans are aware of the supernatural wars around them? The things we do to protect them?" He asks solemnly. "Some of them are aware, hence why they have images of us everywhere in their religious texts as their interpretation of what they think is going on," I answer, staring at his pensive form. Michael turns to face me, walks over, and pours some bourbon into another glass. "Come, son. Sit and have a drink with me." He hands me the glass of bourbon whiskey he poured and gestures for me to sit opposite him on the luxurious cushioned chair. I sip the bourbon. Hmm. Cael did find the finest one indeed.

"I was there at your birth from celestial matter, and then when you were just a boy, I saw the potential of what you would become. I remember overseeing your combat training myself. Besides, Lucifer, I have never seen anyone who was a prodigy like you," Michael sips his drink. "You are like a son to me." He continues staring at me with his light grey eyes with a hint of softness. I wonder where he is going with this. I thought. It sounds like I am about to get one of his lectures. "Which means I can read you quite well,

Gideon. I know about you and Zanael's daughter." He says with a stern gaze. I almost spit my drink out. "Do the rest of the council know?" I ask him in a low, neutral voice. I was fearing the worst but trying to keep my composure. "Yes. But I told them I would talk with you and address the matter." He replies between sips of his drink.

"I have given you so much leniency over the years, Gideon. Spare you from the council's wrath for certain questionable decisions you made. Her scent was all over you, and I saw how you looked at each other with longing and desire," He lectures, almost spitting the words. "She is your charge, Gideon. Your job is to protect and train her like you did her father, Zanael. These human feelings for her are a liability and will compromise your duties. Any liaison that is more than just her being in your charge cannot happen. We already lost Zanael because he fell in love with a human, and now his Nephilim daughter is the new Earth angel. I assigned you as her Guardian because I know you will put duty above all else, and you are my best warrior for the mission." He chastises his facial features darkening. "I ended things with her before they could progress further," I say to him feeling his words starting to sink in. Michael sighed, eyeing me. "I know she is lovely for a Nephilim. But you have been with more beautiful than her. You have your pick of eligible supernatural females who are more than willing to be with you. If you want a bond mate to rule by your side, choose someone of your station. "Lady Anael has always been infatuated with you," he suggests. His features soften as his mouth quirks with a hint of an amused smile.

Lady Anael is a Dominion angel and quite a gifted warrior. She always thought we were meant for each other given that we are both warriors and, as humans, call it a "Power couple." She is six feet tall, slender, and beautiful, with hair like woven flax and light blue eyes. She looks like one of the Pagan Gods Odin's Valkyrie. But more beautiful and ruthless. She is the faction leader of the Dominions and will be at the banquet. Michael always thought we would make a good match. Lady Anael and I had a brief sexual liaison when we both first came to Earth. Although Lady Anael is beautiful, I cannot see her as anything else beyond our friendship. Michael probably saw my scowling expression when he suggested her as my bond mate.

"You can speak freely, son." He says, raising his glass. I let out a breath of relief. "Lady Anael is lovely. Our existing relationship has always been one of friendship only. She is what humans will describe as the definition of an "ice queen," I remarked with a short, sarcastic laugh. Michael looks at me and then laughs. His demeanor is usually very military, so it was a bit weird to hear him laugh. "Thought you might say that. You've got a point. She is a piece of work." He admits. We sipped our drinks silently, and then Michael looked at me curiously. "So... tell me more about Zanael's daughter, Seraphina. What is it about her that has the Lord of the Powers and my most fierce warrior infatuated with her? I understand that you showed up at her doorstep in a bloody pulp, and she didn't panic like many humans would have but helped you heal, rest, and recover. Then she found out your true identity and is now adjusting quite well to our world. She is intriguing for sure." He admits, still looking at me with a curious expression. I let out another huge breath. "I think we will need more bourbon if I am going to discuss her." I look at the empty bourbon bottle. With a smile, I summoned Cael for another bottle of bourbon and then discussed Seraphina more with him.

CHAPTER 14
SERAPHINA

"So, your dad Ronan is one of the Dwarf Lords of a vast treasure mine, and your mum is one of King Aodhan's sisters and his royal healer? Which makes Laurel your..." "Cousins, unfortunately," Vicky finishes for me, rolling her eyes at the mention of Laurel's name. We went through a bottle of fine wine catching up on everything last night, but that was not enough for her. Now she arrived early in the morning again to seek my company. It was the day of the big banquet, and everyone was busy. Gideon and the others were nowhere to be seen. She waltzed into my bedroom dressed in a light green fae nobility kaftan dress outfit.

Gideon told me that my Earth angel identity should remain a secret. She was in awe when I recounted the events that led me to where I was now living with Gideon and his elite squad. As I had predicted, Vicky would die a sweet death of happiness if she were bunking with such gorgeous men, and she was jealous of my luck. She said she would like to have one of them. Anyone of them. She knows Laurel's obsession with Gideon and finds it very embarrassing.

On the other hand, Laurel finds Vicky's Dwarf heritage demeaning even though she gets many of her trinkets from Vicky's dad's treasure mine. She mentions that Laurel cannot shut up about Gideon's prowess in bed even though they slept together centuries ago, and she needs to move on already. We laugh about how the seven elite described Laurel's personality and what they thought of her.

I asked her if she knew who Nathaniel was. She said that she knew Nathaniel was a Gregori Watcher angel but didn't know he was unaligned and was so sinister, especially after she heard what he did to Gideon. She knew he was bad news after the inappropriate way he acted with me, hence why she was glad I kept my distance from him.

She had heard of Gideon because he is legendary in the supernatural community. But she had never seen him or his appearance until he dropped me off at Laurel's party that night. According to Vicky, Laurel was drooling when she said that the hot guy who dropped me off in the expensive Mercedes was the legendary Lord Gideon, Lord of the Powers, and she wondered why he was with me that night. Laurel also told Vicky that I was living with Gideon as his charge. Vicky then begged and bargained with her uncle, King Aodhan, to contact Gideon so she could request to see me. Vicky was speechless that Gideon agreed and teleported in to meet her to escort her to his compound. She was star-struck at first to be in his presence, but he made her feel at ease by being courteous and cordial. He insisted on addressing her as "Lady Victoria," although she told him that calling her "Vicky" was OK. He gave her a quick explanation about me and encouraged her to tell me her true identity. She said that many in the supernatural community think he is arrogant and condescending, but they know him, and his faction represents protection for them. She believes he has a sweet side besides being a hot, broody warrior angel. Despite having a complex enigma of uncertainty about his personality, he has a sweet side. We both agreed that the mysteriousness of his persona is what makes him so much more attractive.

It was nice to be able to have some girl talk. She teased me relentlessly about my infatuation with Gideon and Kemuel's infatuation with me. She thinks Kemuel is gorgeous in a bad boy sort of way since he has a reputation for leaving trails of broken hearts. I told her Kemuel had been a perfect gentleman and had not made any moves on me. But Gideon has shoved his tongue twice in my mouth, leaving me longing for more than dropping the bombshell that we cannot be together. Vicky said she is giving it a few months before we can't keep our hands off each other. She noted Gideon and I have been the talk of the supernatural community. Just as I was about to tell her I didn't have an outfit for the banquet, there was a knock at the door. It was Kemuel.

He says at the request of Lord Gideon, he is to be our escort to the fae Kingdom to see Madam Deirdre, who will assist me with proper attire befitting my station. Vicky looks at him with her mouth agape, then squeals in excitement. I asked her what was so special about Madam Deirdre. Between her hyperventilating words, I could decipher that Madam Deirdre is the supernatural world's royal stylist. She is like Chanel, Gucci, Yves Saint Laurent, and Hermes of the supernatural world. She is very picky with her clients, and making appointments at her boutique is highly sought after. But somehow, Gideon was able to get an appointment for me.

I roll my eyes at Vicky, ogling at Kemuel and flirting blatantly with him. I asked him why he chose to be our escort to go clothes shopping, and he said it gave him something else to do besides lots of patrolling. Besides, Gideon asked him specifically since he has been my bodyguard. We will be traveling to the Fae Kingdom via the portal. Kemuel informed me that newbies to portal travel would react differently until our bodies get used to it. Teleportation, on the other hand, feels like everything is spinning for a brief moment. Kemuel teleported Vicky and me to a fae portal by a preserved park. The two tall and beautiful but solemn fae Guardians greeted us and quickly opened the portal because they recognized Vicky and Kemuel. A colossal oak door covered in vines and briars materialized. I was not too surprised by this. Kemuel opens the door for us and gestures for us to walk through. After meeting the Council of Archangels and many other supernatural phenomena, I wouldn't be surprised if we have to wear ruby slippers and click their heels to travel.

As we stepped through the portal door, there was a series of multicolored flashes of lights blurring my vision, so I closed my eyes, which didn't improve it. The lights looked similar to disco lights. My insides felt a bit queasy as I held on to Kemuel and Vicky. Within a few minutes, I felt solid ground on my feet. I opened my eyes to see a picturesque brick building that looked like a modernized luxury store, but this one seemed very elegant. There was a massive sign in fancy italics that said, Madam Deirdre.

Vicky couldn't stop smiling, and I also found myself smiling excitedly. "Here we are, ladies," Kemuel gestures at the store door. We all walk toward it, and a teenage-looking female fae in a yellow flowing dress with pointy ears, blue eyes, and hair the color of ripe corn opens the door. She looks like a human-size Tinkerbell. She smiled widely at Kemuel, especially when she greeted us and said Madam Deirdre was expecting us. I saw Kemuel giving her a flirty wink as she giggled.

As we walk in, the smell of honeysuckle and jasmine greets our nostrils. I gaze in awe at the paraphernalia of beautiful displays of dresses, coats, capes, and accessories. The inside of the store looks like something out of a fairy storybook. A melodious voice greets us from behind a velvet curtain. I turn around to see a tall, statuesque face that looks like it is in her early forties. She has copper-colored hair in a tight chignon bun and bright green eyes, smiling at us like a Cheshire cat. She was in an elaborate lime green silk kaftan dress that brought out the green in her eyes. She looks very elegant and eccentric. "So, who is the young lady Lord Gideon says I will be dressing today?" She asks, still smiling at us. Kemuel and Vicky both gesture at me.

In a flurry of fabric, she bustles over, directing her attention at me. She frowns, scrutinizing me like a piece of lab specimen as she circles me rapidly, talking, "Let's have a look at you and see what I can do-A bit on the thin side. Athletic with a decent body shape. Good posture though." She grabs my chin, forcing me to look at her. She furrows her brows, still scrutinizing me. "Hmmm Pretty face, good skin tone; I definitely have a dress that Lord Gideon will be pleased with." She releases my chin and then turns her attention to Vicky and Kemuel barking orders. "The two of you wait here. My attendants will bring you refreshments. As for you, dear, come with me. "She grabbed me by the crook of my elbow and led me to an exquisite-looking dressing room. Her grip was firm. I walk along in awe at her and how opulent everything looks. She gestures to a dark blue velvet platform that has huge antique-looking mirrors. She orders me to undress, put the silk robe on from the cushioned stool, and disappear behind some curtains. I could tell she was the no-nonsense type, so I quickly did as she instructed. She reappears shortly in the most beautiful-looking gold dress. "Close your eyes, my dear," she orders. I quickly close my eyes. A brilliant flash of light lasted only a few seconds, and then she told me to open my eyes. She clasps her hands, looking at me in awe. I look at myself in one of the mirrors and nearly pass out from sheer shock.

I stare agape at the floor-length gold metallic gown with

a Mandarin collar that opens into a plunging v-neckline and cinch waist. Tiny shimmering citrine crystals on a base of gold glitter and tulle-like fabric decorated the gown. It features dramatic shoulder detailing with an embellished cape. It fits like a glove and feels extremely airy and lightweight. I barely recognize myself. I look so regal and avant-garde. "No alterations needed. It looks perfect. You are one of my best works of art. You look like a goddess." She compliments me. I saw her wipe a tear from her eyes with a handkerchief. "You are one lucky young lady. Lord Gideon has never bought any of my rare collection pieces for anyone before." She smiles at me. I was floored once again. Gideon was the one who selected this dress for me. She opens the dressing room and beckons Vicky and Kemuel to enter. They both stare at me in awe. Vicky whistles while Kemuel chokes and sputters on the fae beverage he is sipping. Vicky arches questionable eyebrows at him. He blinks a few times, staring at me with something I noticed for the first time in his eyes. Desire. He was checking me out.

She told them to leave the room so I could get dressed. As she boxes up the dress, I ask her if I will turn into a pumpkin at midnight, and she laughs. She says Gideon owes her one for booking this last-minute appointment for me by purchasing one of her most expensive designs. She then mentioned that Gideon already paid for the dress and that his maidservants had my accessories and would know the instructions for putting them on me. Besides Celeste, I have never had anyone pay for something this expensive looking for me.

"My Lord Gideon, you can come in," Cael says as he pats my hair, then gives me a final once-over look. Getting ready for the banquet was a blur. When I returned to the mansion, I was ushered into a spa-like room by two tall, dark complexion females. They were twins named Erella and Elaina. I discovered they were angel third-class Cherubs and part of the servants at the mansion. They were very bubbly, laughing and giggling as they administered spa treatments to me.

I stared at myself in the mirror and saw my hair was up in an elaborate updo with gold accessories. I was wearing gold jewelry and matching gold color pumps. At least they kept the makeup light. I look ready for a masquerade ball. The Cherub twins quickly exited the bedroom with giggles, and so did Cael. I turned around and saw Gideon staring at me. I found myself staring at him, stunned. He looks so regal, dignified, and handsome. My eyes take in the long metallic gold color form fitted at the torso of the ceremonial jacket he was wearing. Its slightly open Mandarin collar went down in a slight V, exposing a glimpse of his muscular chest—decorative raised etchings in an intricate design all over it. I can tell from my studies that they look like celestial runes. He had matching warrior's forearm guards and black pants with intricate designs at the waist. His dark hair was styled loose in silky, shiny waves. He looks like a royal warrior prince. He walks over to me, still staring, "Deirdre has outdone herself. You look every bit as lovely as the princess you are," he remarks. I saw a hint of desire in his eyes. "And you look like a handsome Lord." I smile at him. He offers me his arm with a smile. As my Guardian, he was my escort to the banquet. He gives me a quick briefing on the protocols.

As we walked into the opulent banquet hall, there were many murmurs and stares. I felt a bit nervous and found comfort in being on Gideon's arm. Servants of different supernatural species were busy serving drinks and exotic-looking finger foods on beautiful gleaming splatters. The Council of Archangels was seated at a grand table, looking as majestic as ever. Archangel Michael was engrossed in a conversation with Archangel Raphael, but he quickly turned his attention to us. His light grey eyes survey me from head to toe as we approach the tables. He was dressed in a similar outfit to Gideon's, except his was dazzling silver. He gives me a curt nod, then returns to his conversation with Archangel Raphael. Was that his nod of approval that I was in proper attire? Archangel Chamuel, dressed in a beautiful floor-length reddish color Mandarin collar dress, smiled at me and greeted Gideon. Archangel Ariel, seated next to Archangel Azrael, also smiles at us. She was in an ivory floor-length dress similar to Chamuel's. Archangel Azrael, dressed in a navy hue outfit similar to the other male Archangels, stared at us with a solemn expression on his face.

Gideon escorts me to where Jeb and the seven elite are

seated, then leaves to take his seat among the different faction leaders. Jeb and the seven elite all greeted me. They were dressed in similar outfits as Gideon, except Jeb's jacket was black and grey, and the seven elite jackets were copper colored. Celeste was seated among the Council of High Witches, and when she saw me, she quickly came over to greet me. She looks beautiful in a dazzling cream color floor-length dress with exaggerated long sleeves. Her long, bushy brown hair was in an intricate updo. "I will need to have a few choice words with Gideon about this dress, which is stirring up quite a commotion. You look beautiful, my dear." She smiles and hugs me. "I saw the dirty looks every supernatural female gave you when you walked in, escorted by Gideon. How much do you want to bet that they are probably plotting how to spill fae wine to ruin your dress?" She whispers in my ears with a giggle. I had to cover my mouth from laughing loudly. Everyone was eating and talking while a few supernatural folks, especially females in exquisite dresses, gave me furtive and curious glances. They were primarily fae and other angels.

There was one particular blonde in an exquisite silver dress with light blue eyes seated at the table of the faction leaders. She was staring daggers occasionally at me. She was gorgeous, tall, and willowy, like an international supermodel. She had a very intimidating vibe. I will have to ask the seven elite about her. Laurel sat with her parents, the fae King and Queen, and her other royal siblings. Vicky was at their table next to her parents. Laurel looks like a fairy princess in an exquisite circlet, with crystal flowers in her long blonde hair and a beautiful light blue dress. She was looking at me like she had dung under her nose. Who knew being Gideon's charge and living with him would open up a can of worms where every supernatural female wants my head delivered to them on a silver platter? I don't think I should be a threat because Gideon and I are not together, and he is still on the market.

After Celeste returned to her council table, the seven elite started briefing me on who was who at the different council tables. I learned that the Valkyrie-looking blonde staring daggers is Lady Anael, the warrior leader of the Dominions angel faction, and she wants to be Gideon's official bond mate. Even Michael and the Council of Archangels approve of them being together. Is this another one of his former lovers? It turns out that she and Gideon have always had a close relationship that goes back to when he was under the tutelage of Archangel Michael. They had a brief fling when they first came to Earth but chose to remain friends after that. No one knows many details about why the fling ended. Someone alive for as long as Gideon is bound to pile up a few exes and lovers. Jeb said Gideon is very private about what transpired between him and Lady Anael. I glance at Gideon. He looks engrossed in discussions with Michael, the Council of Archangels, and the other Lords and Ladies.

The seven elite told me that Lady Anael would be helping to supervise my training so that when my dormant angelic abilities get activated, I will be ready. My excitement about training dimmed a little after hearing that she would be part of my training. I can already tell she despises me. There is also talk of her and Gideon officially bonding to unite the factions. That put another knife in my heart, but I kept my composure. Vicky came over to get me because the fae king and his Queen wanted to meet me, so I allowed her to guide me to their table.

The fae King Aodhan looks like a man in his forties dressed in a white regal fae tunic with a bejeweled circlet crown around his Ash blond hair. He was tall, lean, and handsome with sparkling blue-green eyes. His eyes look like Laurel's. He had a very arrogant face. Queen Aoibheann looks like the spitting image of Laurel, except her eyes are the color of blue skies. Her sparkling sapphire blue dress brought out the blue in her eyes, and her curly golden blonde hair was in an elaborate hairstyle crowned by a dazzling diadem. She looks like she is in her early thirties. Her beauty was ethereal, except she looked at me with a slight scowl and forced a smile.

"Do you speak, girl?" King Aodhan asks, spitting out the words. Both he and Queen Aoibheann gaze condescendingly at me. Laurel stifles a giggle. "Yes, your majesties. And my name is Seraphina." I respond politely with a quick curtsy. "So, you must be the human that is Lord Gideon's concubine. I heard you might be a Nephilim abomination, but I sense no angelic powers from you," He says haughtily, scrutinizing me. "She is pretty, though-could be prettier. My regards to Madam Deirdre for that beautiful dress," Queen Aoibheann comments in a low, melodious voice, eyeing me from head to toe. A few onlookers of other fae and angels turn in our direction. They probably heard King Aodhan refer to me as Gideon's concubine. I remember my studies about the fae and how things have to be worded carefully with them.

Lord Gideon's concubine? OK. I have had it with their insufferable, condescending attitudes. Laurel was looking at me quite smugly. "Your majesties. You both wanted to see me. Well, here I am. Is it to give me backhanded compliments? If so, I must politely take my leave from your presence." I say to them with a courteous smile. Laurel stops smiling. Vicky's eyes widened like saucers. The Fae King and Queen looked like I had slapped and poured cold drinks on them. "How dare a human speak to us like that? Such brazen audacity! The insolence!" King Aodhan rebukes in a low, scathing voice. Queen Aoibheann glares daggers at me. More supernatural folks turned their attention to us, and now we somewhat had an audience. I refused to let King Tinker Bell and

his just as condescending Queen insult me like this. "The last time I checked, both of you wanted to see me, but then you blatantly insulted me. Any complaints concerning me? Take them up with Lord Gideon. Queen Aoibheann, as for my dress, my regards to Madam Deirdre and Lord Gideon. It was his idea for the dress. After all, a human concubine must look presentable on his arm, your majesties." I scoff in my sweetest voice, give them a smug smile and a quick curtsy, and walk away. I need to get out of this banquet hall. I left them all looking stunned at my retreating form.

I saw Gideon watching me as I tried to make my exit out

of the banquet hall. Some faes and angels were eyeing me and whispering to each other. It felt like the supernatural version of Mean Girls. I kept walking until I made it back to my room. I was fuming a bit—those pompous fae pricks. I need to get out of this dress and relax because tomorrow will be a long day. The Cherub twins knocked on my door to help me get out of the dress. I knew it was them because there was so much giggling. After they left, I prepped for bed, and just when I was about to pull the covers over my body and go to sleep, there was another knock. Ugh, who could it be this time?

I reluctantly got up and opened the door. It was Gideon still in his banquet outfit. "I thought we agreed not to be alone like this anymore," I remind him, eyeing him warily. "I know. I promise I will make it quick. I saw you leaving the banquet early. I came to check on you," He says, letting himself in. He seats himself in one of the chaise lounges while I decide to sit on my bed. "If you are here to scold me for standing up for myself against King Tinker Bell and his Queen of Shade throwing, then step in line because I am sure the whole room heard him call me your"concubine." I give a short, scornful laugh. Gideon glances at me, and his lips quirked in an amused smile. "I heard everything. The fae can be quite prejudiced in their beliefs." He mutters, shaking his head. "You're not my concubine. He knows I don't have concubines, unlike him. He will apologize to you. The Fae Kingdom wants an alliance with my faction for protection against rising demonic threats. I am sorry he insulted you, and they probably deserve it whatever you told them." He says as he stands up. "So, I heard Lady Anael is your pending bond mate, and she will be helping with my training. Why her?" I inquire, staring at him. He furrows his brows and turns his attention to me. "Lady Anael is not my pending bond mate," He responds dismissively. "She will be helping with your training. That is not up for debate. Your training begins after breakfast. Get as much rest as you can." He says in a firm tone as he walks toward the door. I knew I would not have a say regarding my upcoming training. But why does my instructor have to be one of Gideon's exes, who I already sense does not like me? "Tomorrow, the ritual will be performed by Celeste's coven to unlock your Nephilim powers. The Council of Archangels has granted their permission. "He gave me one last look before he left.

CHAPTER 15
SERAPHINA

"I still feel very human. Everything hurts. Am I not supposed to have healing abilities or something?" I whine to Cael as I throw myself on my bed after today's conditioning exercises and obstacle courses. Being a former ballet dancer and gymnast didn't help because Lady Anael was quite sadistic and creative with her training methods. She will make a fine dominatrix.

With her coven and the Council of Archangels, Celeste performed the ritual to unbind my Nephilim powers. They did everything right, but it will take a bit to manifest since my abilities were bound for too long. The Council of Archangels believes that training sessions will help my abilities to manifest as well as help me to be prepared for whenever they do. They said that I am still very much human for the time being. Cael had prepared a nice healing bath with herbs that Celeste recommended. It helped, but every muscle still aches. And then I will be doing it all over again tomorrow.

Rigorous ballet and gymnastics conditioning regimes had already conditioned my body, but Lady Anael's training sessions felt overkill for my body. I had zero social life between college classes, supernatural studies, and training sessions.

The fae King and Queen did send a formal apology for their rude behavior toward me, though, by allowing Vicky to visit me whenever with no restrictions. Once again, that apology was self-preservation to save face because they still need that alliance with Gideon's faction due to the increased attacks on fae folks. The seven elite and Jeb have been busy on patrols, many working with Lady Anael's faction of dominions.

Lady Anael made no qualms about hiding her disdain for me. Gideon insists she was the best person to help with my training. If Gideon were observing my training sessions, she would tone down the insults, but after he leaves, she will revert to being a relentless drill sergeant. I do feel I am making immense progress, though, with the conditioning sessions. My muscle tone, strength, stamina, and agility have progressed to levels where I don't feel too tired and overly sore after each day. I felt back to my fitness level when I competed in gymnastics and trained in ballet.

On the last day of my final class, Kemuel was waiting on the campus grounds, but he was not in his usual leather pants and biker jacket. He was in a blue buttoned-down silk shirt that brought out the deep blue in his eyes, tucked into black slacks. His long blond hair styled neatly in a ponytail down his back. He looks very handsome and ready for a formal event. When he saw me, he gave me a dimpled smile, and I asked what the occasion was. He says I was since it was the last day of my final class as he takes my backpack and books and leads me toward a black Audi car. No motorcycles today. I ask him where we are going, and he says we are going to this supernatural fine dining fae restaurant. I started complaining that I was not in proper attire for that. He insisted that my jeans and long-sleeved top were fine. I chastised him, saying he should have given me a heads-up, but he kept smiling his dimpled smile with that mischievous glint in his eyes.

We stop at the same fae portal we had taken previously to visit Madam Deirdre's boutique, step through it, and arrive at a beautiful medieval-era-looking building that looks like a place out of a storybook. Kemuel explains that it is owned and run by Brownie Fae. The chef cooks the most delectable delicacies. Getting a reservation is exclusive to the supernatural community's higher echelon. The short, prim hostess dressed in a light brown tweed skirt suit with pointy ears eyed us as we walked in. I am guessing she is a Brownie Fae. "What brings one of the Powers to our establishment this evening? Do you have a reservation?" She inquires shrewdly, then turns her attention to me and blanches. "She is a..." She gasps, pointing at me. I look at Kemuel, clearly confused, mouthing, "Wth?" "She is Lord Gideon's charge, and yes, we have a reservation." Kemuel finishes for her with a smile. The hostess's demeanor changes when Lord Gideon's name is mentioned, and then she checks her ledger. "Ah, Lord Gideon. Yes. Yes. That's right. You're one of his lieutenants." She shakes her head and then smiles widely at us. "Right this way. We have your booth." She gestures for us to follow her. Kemuel offers me his arm as we follow the hostess. "Is this where you bring all your fae women on dates?" I whisper to him. "No, just you." He winks at me.

The restaurant was unlike any other I have been to. Fae decor and the fae lanterns gave it a romantic ambiance. Soft, exotic violin music was playing, but I didn't know the source or where it originated. Instead of an open floor with tables and chairs and patrons dining, there were several opulent private booths. Kemuel explains that each booth has a private chef and waitstaff service. This restaurant was beyond luxurious. I can tell by the murmurs and chatter of voices I was hearing that many of the booths had customers dining.

"Your waitstaff will be right with you." She gestures for us to enter our booth, then disappears with a smile. I can only stare agape at the luxurious and elegant decor. Instead of traditional chairs, there was an exotic-looking marble table with comfy lounge recliners. Fae lanterns dimly lit the booth, which was very intimate and romantic. I took a seat on the recliner, and Kemuel joined me.He asked if the restaurant was too overwhelming, and if so, we could go to a human establishment where I would feel more comfortable. I was curious about this dining experience and told him I was fine.

"You have to try this one here." Kemuel scoops a spoonful from a dish that looks like a chocolate lava cake and offers it to me. I took a bite and was impressed by how delicious it was. It tasted like fine dining chocolate cake that melted in my mouth. We had already eaten various exotic dishes, each tasting better than the other, and now we were enjoying desserts and fae wine. We toast to my upcoming college graduation. The fae wine was delicious, and I relaxed as we conversed about my upcoming combat training, which Gideon will be supervising himself. He also discusses some of the supernatural society politics and how much he misses my father, Zanael. Kemuel mentions some more stories about their adventures with Gideon. He was sitting close to me, and our bodies were slightly touching. It felt like a date with a regular human male, although Kemuel was not a human male. He is an immortal warrior angel who looks like a young human male but is quite a few millennia old. I couldn't help but think about whether Gideon would like this restaurant or if he had tried it already. I need to move on from Gideon because we cannot be together. I do like Kemuel and find him quite attractive. And I am allowed to date him without the Council of Archangels frowning upon it. Well, Celeste might think otherwise. Is it wrong to think he can help me move on from Gideon?

"A scoop for your thoughts?" Kemuel asks as he hovers a scoop of chocolate lava cake at my lips. I smile at him and eat the scoop of chocolate lava cake. He watches me with amusement as I wipe the chocolate from my mouth. I told him I still felt underdressed for such a beautiful restaurant, but he brushed my complaints off that my outfit was just fine. "You don't need much to look beautiful. You're already beautiful." His hand reaches up and caresses my cheek. "Do you say that to all the ladies?" I gaze at him with a smile. He gives a low chuckle. "No, just you." His handsome face moved closer to mine, desire shining in those deep blue eyes. He kisses me, his lips softly caressing mine. He tastes of chocolate dessert and fae wine.

Before he could eagerly deepen the kiss, an image of Gideon kissing me passionately in my room flashes in my mind, and I froze. Kemuel senses the change and stops kissing me—his facial features change from desire to confusion. I guess I am not over Gideon yet.

"Kemuel… I can't. It's just that I am not…" I mumble, turning away from him. "Over Lord Gideon… I know," he finishes for me with a sigh. It was my turn to look confused. "How did you know?" I ask softly. His lips quirk in a smirk. "I think everyone knows. You're his charge, but the way he looks at you sometimes, any male can recognize it more than just him caring for you as his charge," He answers, giving me a sidelong glance. "You look at him the same way, too. You light up like a fae lantern at the mere mention of his name. No one is blind to your infatuation with him. You know Lord Gideon doesn't do the whole love thing, and any bond mate of his has to be approved by the Council of Archangels, right? So, he has to be with someone mostly for political alliances." He says, his voice switching to a serious tone. "I know," I sigh with a nod. I already knew where I stood with Gideon and the council. "The Council wants him and Lady Anael together because they are of the same station. But I am still not over him yet." "I know. But a guy can try. This is Lord Gideon, and we are talking about it here. It's hard to compete with him. But I had to try. Not even Laurel is over him, and it has been centuries." He gave me a wry smile. "It's OK. There are no hard feelings here. I can wait until you're ready to move on. Meanwhile, I will still be your friend. I hope our moment earlier doesn't change that." He rests a reassuring hand on my shoulder. I sigh, wondering if I will ever be over Gideon. "Let's get you back to the compound before he sends a search party, then shears my wings if he finds out where we are." He brightens as he helps me to my feet. I laughed as I let him lead me out of the booth.

When we returned to the compound, Gideon saw us as we walked into the foyer laughing. He looked at how dressy Kemuel's outfit was while he was with me and scowled at him. That look means we are in trouble. "You were assigned as her bodyguard, Kemuel. Not to take her on dates." Gideon chastises Kemuel coldly. "It's the last day of her final class. I wanted her to celebrate a bit," Kemuel said to him. "Yes, he is right. I wanted to celebrate too," I add, glancing at Kemuel. Gideon stares at both of us, still scowling. "Tomorrow, your combat training begins. If I were you, I would get some rest." He says brusquely to me, then turns to Kemuel. "A word in my office now, Kemuel," He says in a steely, cold voice to him. Kemuel nods in agreement, and they walk off.

I immediately called Vicky, fuming over FaceTime with her. I complain about how jealous Gideon was acting. How dare he be jealous of me and another I am allowed to date when he doesn't want me? I told her with the way Gideon was behaving with any guy who showed interest in me, I would probably remain a spinster virgin. She says that means he hasn't moved on from me as well. I told her he should because he has Lady Anael now. I told her about the date with Kemuel and how Gideon came into my thoughts when he kissed me. I couldn't even get Gideon out of my mind, even when I was trying to move on. I hope Kemuel is not in trouble for our date. If so, I will have some words of choice for Gideon.

Vicky shook her head at me, laughing. I scolded her that the situation was not funny, but she said she was laughing at the fact that Gideon and I were falling deeply in love with each other. I opened my mouth to speak, but she shushed me, and told me the queasy feeling in my stomach and him grating on my nerves was love. She says that, as a half-fae of the nobility class, she is clairsentient and can feel that I am in love with him, and she can feel that he is falling in love with me, too. She says his feelings are difficult to read because he usually has psychic wards up to shield them, but there was a rare moment when it was not as shielded, and that was when she sensed his feelings for me.

I told her it did not matter because it was not like we could be together and that whatever feelings I had for him had to be buried. She sighed, called me a pessimist, and told me all that might change soon. I told her I had an early day tomorrow and we would talk later.

I wanted to be alone with my thoughts because Vicky's assumption about me falling in love with Gideon started sinking in. As I lay on my bed, I thought about the weird, queasy flutter I usually feel in my stomach whenever I was around Gideon. The type of queasiness that makes me giddy, and it's worse whenever he touches me. I had questioned my feelings for him several times to decipher if it was just infatuation because I couldn't have him. But Vicky knew that it was more than just infatuation. What started as an infatuation was blossoming into a full-blown, messy, and terrifying feeling of falling in love with someone I could not be with. I knew that I would have to compartmentalize these feelings in a box somewhere because I would have to be trained and mentored by him starting in the morning.

CHAPTER 16

SERAPHINA

"Seraphina! Focus! Your left is wide open!" Gideon barks as he whacks me on my left side with his wooden fighting staff. Ow! That hurts. I grimace at the pain and try to whack him with my wooden staff, but he easily sidesteps and parries the blow with his own. "Too much telegraphing of your offense blows," He scolds. He agreed not to use any superhuman abilities for sparring. We were alone in the training room because Lady Anael left for the day to tend to some duties for her faction. Even without him using superhuman abilities, I couldn't have gotten one blow-in with Gideon. He evaded and blocked everything. He seems to predict every one of my moves. I was a hot mess of sweat with hair looking like a bird's nest, while Gideon looked like he hadn't broken a sweat with not one strand of hair out of place. We have been training with various weaponry within the past weeks, and today is staff fighting, my favorite melee combat weapon. Unlike Lady

Anael, he has been like a drill Sergeant, minus the insults. His attitude during our training sessions was that of an intense mentor I sometimes despise, but I know I was learning from the best. He wouldn't even indulge me in playing workout music during our training sessions. He says it was a big distraction. I tried to have some fun by keeping things light-hearted. I would playfully hit him or make some jokes, and he would scold me to quit it, but there was a hint of an amused smile sometimes that would play on his lips for a brief moment.

Sometimes, I wonder where the hot angel I made out with twice and used to have light-hearted banter with went. Because the one training me had zero chills during our training sessions. Jeb and the seven elite encouraged me to listen to his instructions because he knew what he was doing. And he always has zero chills like that with training because he is trying to prep me for the harsh realities of the powerful evil forces after me. I know he wants me to be able to protect myself, too—he certainly is no Mister Miyagi.

He hasn't mentioned anything about my date with Kemuel, and Kemuel hasn't tried to invite me to other places since that night when Gideon scolded him. We still talk and tease each other, and he is still my assigned Guardian, but he has toned down his flirtations. "You're distracted," Gideon's voice was annoyed as he brought me out of my thoughts and then swept me off my feet with his staff. I went sprawling on my back, feeling the wind knocked out of me. I groan at the impact. Of course, I am distracted. Why did he have to look so hot in that form-fitting sleeveless workout shirt that had his bulging biceps on full display? Arms like those should be illegal. "Get up!" he commands as he peers at me, still sprawling on the rubber floor. With a groan, I reluctantly pull myself into a sitting position. My body was feeling bruised all over. I give him an irritated look as I watch him walk over to a table, grab a water bottle, and throw it at me. I almost didn't catch it. "Take a break," He suggests as he takes a water bottle. He glances at me as he drinks his water. "What's on your mind today? You're more distracted than usual. Please don't tell me it's Kemuel, isn't it?" He inquires with a hint of sarcasm when he mentions Kemuel's name.

"Jealous?" I ask him with half a smile as I drag myself to my feet and walk over to sit on a gym bench. "Of you and Kemuel?" He raises his eyebrows mockingly. "No. I don't do jealousy." He scoffs as he walks over and sits beside me on the bench. I knew he was slightly jealous of the way he was currently reacting. "You are jealous!" I laugh and swat his arm playfully with my gym towel. He scowls at me. "He took you to that Brownie fae restaurant when he was supposed to bring you back to the compound. Those were my orders, given that Nathaniel's faction and a pissy fallen Throne have a bounty on your pretty head." "How did you know we went there? Did he-?" "No. Word gets around, especially when dealing with the fae kind. They will spread rumors if a Nephilim glamoured as a human enters an exclusive restaurant like that and then mentions that she is my charge." He says in a grave voice tone. Please leave it to the fae folk to spread gossip. We sat in silence for a bit, sipping our water.

"I wanted to take you to that fae restaurant before he did but we both know that wouldn't be appropriate," He says, glancing at me. I didn't need a reminder of our forbidden situation. I told him about the recurring dreams I usually get of celestial battles. He asks why I hadn't previously mentioned those dreams to him or Celeste. I told him I didn't think they were that serious. He says Zanael used to get those recurring dreams, and he must have passed those on to me. Those dreams are some of the memories of the seven Archangels since their blood now flows in my veins. I also mentioned that I had a vision of him severely injured that woke me up that same night when he teleported to my front porch. That got his attention. He asked if I had visions of other events, and I told him if visions of landing a punch in Lady Anael's face counted. That brought a chuckle from him as he told me break time was over and we should spar again.

"You were there at my gymnastics meets?" I inquire. I was panting as I climbed down the ropes from the obstacle course outside. This obstacle course looks like American ninja warriors or American gladiators. "Every one of them. I even saw when you injured your hamstring on the vault," Gideon answers. He watches me trying to balance on some logs as I walk toward the massive wall. I smile. It was nice knowing he was there to see me perform. Celeste and sometimes Jeb, when he wasn't on detective duty, usually were there to support me at my gymnastics meets. Vicky was always there with huge gaudy signs. I remembered how painful that hamstring injury was from that Tsukahara vault. I was out of gymnastics for a while and stopped competing altogether.

"I was also there to see you perform as *Andromeda in the ballet Perseus and Medea in Jason and the Argonauts*. Your dance performances were beautiful to watch." His eyes follow me as he paces alongside the obstacle course with his arms folded. I remembered that neither Celeste nor Jeb could make it to those performances, but it was nice knowing he was there to see those dance performances. Those were the only two major lead roles I had ever had since I had been dancing ballet.

I wonder what else he has been watching with my life. But he swears that he has never infringed on my private moments. I discovered many of the gifts Celeste and Jeb gifted me growing up were from him. He also gave Celeste a large sum of money to assist with my extracurricular expenses for gymnastics and ballet. Those were expensive activities. All those history, mythology, and Archaeology books were from him. I was feeling extra motivated and finish the course in record time. We went back into the indoor training room for hand-to-hand combat. Jeb and the seven elite were all sparring outside, and they waved at me as we walked by.

According to Kemuel, Gideon was quite the prodigy for

combat training since he was trained by Archangel Michael in private lessons more than the other warrior angels. He has taught me various hand-to-hand combat styles since he started overseeing my training, while Lady Anael primarily oversees my conditioning. Despite my anticipation, there have been no signs yet of any of my angelic abilities manifesting. I've been hoping for them in each training session, but they remain elusive. Gideon, in his attempts to help, even tried guiding me through meditation and grounding techniques. However, my inability to focus and tendency to goof around only seemed to irritate him. I even overheard him mutter that his job would be so much easier if I were a boy.

Gideon temporarily tones down his invulnerability with a handy magic spell Celeste gave him for training so I wouldn't shatter a limb if I hit him. He easily counters and blocks every blow, kick, punch, and swipe from me. Somehow, we ended up on the rubber mats doing some jiu-jitsu moves, and Gideon subdued me by wedging himself in between my thighs and locking my legs in place with his muscular thighs. He pins my arms above my head with his hands. I tried to wiggle free, but he pressed his body against mine, his chest pressing down on my breasts. His muscular body was so warm on top of mine, and it was eliciting involuntary sensations in my body. He was staring down at my face, his ethereal hazel gold fleck eyes showing hints of yearning.

"Stop squirming. You're not making this any easier." He murmurs. "I will if you let me go," I manage to say in between breaths as I try to move my legs and hips. Now I know why he wanted me to stop squirming because I was feeling his erection lengthening against my thighs. Trying to wiggle free from beneath him was making him very aroused. "I told you to stop." He whispers close to my lips. "I thought we had an agreement about not letting moments like this happen," I remind him, feeling my body betray me as his now rock-hard erection presses on my groin area. "I know. But you're irresistible." He kisses me softly and deeply but stops at the sound of approaching footsteps. He abruptly let go of me and got to his feet. It was Lady Anael. She was in workout leggings and a tank top, with her long blonde hair in a neat crown braid. She looks at us with a slight scowl. I leave you two to it." Gideon nods at her, then gives me an encouraging wave before quickly exiting.

Judging by the look on her face, I didn't have to wonder how much she had seen what had transpired between Gideon and me. She ignores me, walks to the weapons stash, and brings out two staff. She throws one at me and says I will be sparring with her. "It's already bad enough that you're not supposed to exist as a Nephilim abomination, but I have to tolerate you trying to seduce my betrothed bond mate," she says icily as she strikes at me with precision and speed. "The Council of Archangels will never allow an official union between you and him. The only union will be his clandestine concubine." She taunts. I was getting riled up at mentioning that I was Gideon's concubine. I have had it with this Valkyrie Komodo dragon and her insults for weeks. My body instinctively reacted, and I sidestepped and blocked her strike. I have had many staff fighting training sessions with Gideon that were enough to hold my own.

"I know our union is forbidden. But as for you and him, Lady Anael, does he even want you the way you want him? -Even as his *clandestine concubine*," I retort, taunting her with a smug smile. Her beautiful face contorted with rage as her light blue eyes blazed with fury. "You don't know your place, little Nephilim. How dare you speak to me like that?" She grates as she slashes at me, using more strength than what was allowed to spar with me. I went flying toward the wall from the sheer force of her blow, but instead of hitting the wall in an unceremonious splat, I used her momentum to do a back layout flip with my body and anchor myself to the ground with the staff skidding to a halt. "You cannot be the only one hurling insults," I growl, looking at her. I almost saw a hint of admiration at my agility move in her eyes. "Not ba,d little Nephilim. Gideon has been teaching you a few tricks." She nods curtly. "If my ears deceive me, that is almost a compliment." I gave her a half smile. "Don't push it, little Nephilim." She sneered, but there was a hint of amusement. "Let's see what he taught you about sword fighting."

"I can sense this is the handiwork of a High Witch," Kemuel says grimly as his deep blue irises change to copper orbs and his celestial copper armor manifests from the ether on his body. We were leaving campus after I had turned in my final thesis. Vicky was with us. Then we found ourselves in a magical ward surrounded by three demonic-looking faes. "The Witch is clever enough to glamour this from humans," He remarks in a hollow voice as his celestial double short swords materialize in both hands and his body starts glowing with copper angel-fire. Vicky's face was a horror mask as she stared at the demonic faces. I am sure my face was reflecting the same, too, as I stared at them aghast.

They look like they were once beautiful, but now their faces and bodies look like ghastly twisted versions of their former selves. Dry blood and dirt caked their matted hair, and their faces and skin looked mutilated with weird, discolored, swarthy lumps. They opened their mouths, revealing rows of sharp teeth. They were brandishing various weapons and making high-pitched howls. "I know them," Vicky manages to say, still horrified. "They are Sidhes that went missing a few weeks ago." She grabs my arm, trembling a little. "Ladies, stay behind me!" Kemuel instructs, his voice full of authority, as he twirls his double swords at the advancing demonic faes.

I felt a gush of wind as Vicky started activating her fae elemental powers of air manipulation. She had the elemental powers of air manipulation as a half-fae but not as strong as full-blooded faes. Kemuel's body and his double swords erupt in copper angel-fire as he charges toward the demonic faes with supernatural speed. I felt useless without a weapon or powers. Even Vicky had remarkable powers. Her face was scrunched solemnly in concentration as she fashioned balls of air energy and directed them toward the demonic faes to assist Kemuel.

I watch Kemuel propel himself in the air, hurling himself at the demonic faes in a blur of copper angel-fire and twirling double swords. His enhanced agility and reflexes were a wonder to watch in combat. I could not have asked for a better substitute as my Guardian besides Gideon. One demonic fae hurls a spiked ball on a chain at him, but he easily dodges it as Vicky directs the weapon with her air powers to hit the fae instead. She beams at me with a self-satisfied smile, then returns to creating more air energy balls. She and Kemuel make a good fighting team.

I heard Celeste screaming my name, and then I turned around and saw her standing a distance away, looking frantic. I started running toward her, feeling relieved to see her. Then danger alarm bells began to scream at my instincts, making me stop abruptly in front of Celeste. I started feeling prickly goosebumps as I took a good look at her. She wore clothing similar to Celeste's and looked exactly like her, but her vibes were off. "You're not Celeste!" I snap and back away from her. Kemuel and Vicky immediately divert their attention toward me as Celeste's doppelgänger demeanor changes from frantic to a sinister smile. She quickly pulls me toward her with her telekinetic abilities. "No, I am not Celeste, but a much better version of her." She answers coldly with a sinister grin as she grabs me with supernatural strength in an iron grip.

My whole body was starting to feel numb, but I quickly released a ring and my bracelet off my hand and let them fall to the ground. Shortly after, her spell worked its mojo and immobilized my entire body. She had hexed me, and as a Nephilim, I am susceptible to spells and enchantments. The demonic faes were all on the ground, probably dead, as Kemuel and Vicky advanced toward us. The demonic faces were just a distraction to keep Kemuel and Vicky occupied so that Celeste's doppelgänger could get to me. The High Witch raises a hand, and Kemuel and Vicky halt as if trying to push against an invisible wall. They both watch me helplessly in horror.

"So, you're the new Earth angel parading as a weak human. Clever of the Council of Archangels to hide you away like this," She remarks as she eyes me from head to toe. "Nathaniel and Razziel will be pleased. You're coming with me, girl." She tightens her grip on my arm. I know we were helpless to fight her. I turned to Kemuel and Vicky. "Tell Gideon and Celeste to find me!" I called out to them, and then everything went dark.

CHAPTER 17

GIDEON

"Again, she looks exactly like Celeste," Kemuel insists as Celeste, Jeb, and the others rush into the foyer. "Yes, she did." Vicky nods her head vigorously, supporting Kemuel's report. I quickly dispatched Vicky to get her uncle, King Aodhan, because this matter also concerned him with the demonic fae. I was enraged and worried after Kemuel and Vicky teleported in to report what had happened to Seraphina. "Who looks like me?" Celeste asks quizzically, furrowing her brows in confusion. "Nathaniel's High Witch and it was not a glamour. She looks exactly like you," Kemuel replies gravely as Celeste's face blanches, and she lets out an inaudible gasp. Jeb put a supportive arm on her. I turn to Celeste, scowling at her reaction. "Celeste? Who is she, and what do you know of her?" I demand harshly. Celeste looks at me, her eyes pleading for me not to be upset with her. "It can't be. She was in our dungeons for rogue witches, mages, and warlocks. The prison is in another dimension parallel to this plane but was created specifically as a prison for the worst of our kind by one of the first High Witches and High Mage. She is my twin sister… Cerinda." Her voice falters as she looks down at her hands. Everyone stares at Celeste in astonishment.

"And now you're telling us this news about a rogue High Witch twin sister??" I snap, between clenched teeth glowering at her. I can feel my eyes flaring with gold angel-fire. "Lord Gideon. She was unaware that her sister had escaped her prison and was working with Nathaniel. We want Seraphina back as much as you do. She is like a daughter to Celeste and me." Jeb reasons in a slightly raised tone of voice, giving me a look of disapproval as he comforts Celeste, who looks at me with a glint of hurt. It was the first time Jeb had ever raised his voice at me. There was also a glint of hurt in his dark eyes. I knew I shouldn't have yelled at Celeste like that. "Celeste, forgive me for my outburst. It is not your fault." I say to her apologetically, seeing the hurt in her eyes from yelling at her. "Gideon, before I met you and Jeb, Cerinda was imprisoned and wiped clean from our records and history books. Her name is not even spoken of anymore. The council apprehended her for conducting horrific experiments on both humans and supernaturals using extremely dark and forbidden magic. And now she took Seraphina." Celeste burst into tears as Jeb hugged her. I sympathize with her because it was not her fault. She is as worried as I am about Seraphina and wants her back safely as much as I do. Seraphina is her daughter, after all. "She knows that Seraphina is the Earth angel," Kemuel interjects solemnly, then hands Celeste Seraphina's bracelet and ring she dropped before her abduction. Celeste quickly dries her eyes, and then her face brightens a bit. "Clever girl. She knows I can use these to track her even if a shielding ward is up." She smiles, grasping the ring and bracelet on her chest. "She has been paying attention to her lessons." She looks at me wistfully. "I don't know how Cerinda escaped from prison, but the Council of the High Witches needs to be informed immediately. She is dangerous and unhinged. I will summon them, and they will help me with the tracking spell to locate Seraphina. We will find her location, Gideon." She rests a reassuring hand on my shoulder. "And then I will set Nathaniel's wings ablaze with witch-fire." She declares with resolve in her voice and eyes ablaze with determination.

While Celeste went to summon the High Witches for the tracking spell, the other Powers gathered around me in our war room as we planned how to attack Nathaniel and Razziel's forces. I contacted Lady Anael in angelical, and she teleported in immediately. Her faction of Dominions agreed to help. She requests to speak privately with me. I dismissed the others so we had some privacy. "I don't know what is so special about this little Nephilim of yours, Gideon, but you look ready to watch the world burn just to find her." She remarks in a grave voice tone. "We both know you haven't even taken her as a lover. Why is she so important to you, Gideon? Even the Council of Archangels wanted to meet her. Is she Zanael's forbidden Nephilim daughter with that human scientist he was dating? I see some resemblance. And don't lie to me, Gideon." She stares at me, her face searching mine for answers. I nod at her, and then she raises her eyebrows at me in disbelief, realization dawning on her features. "So little Nephilim is the new Earth angel. Who would have thought? Why did you keep this from me, Gideon?" She inquires, crossing her arms over her chest, still staring at me with a glint of hurt.

"The ones who were there that night when Zanael died swore secrecy not to reveal that Zanael had a Nephilim child whom he passed on his celestial essences and the blood seal of the seven Archangels," I answered gravely. She nods her head in understanding, her features softening a bit. She was familiar with Zanael and the importance of the blood seal of the seven Archangels. It's not too often that her features will soften over anything. I watch her pacing the room with her arms still folded. "Do you have feelings for her? Is that why you declined the bond mate ceremony with me?" She asks softly, looking earnestly at me. I turned away from her because I didn't want to answer her. I was struggling to accept the revelation of falling in love. I spent many nights trying to understand my growing feelings for Seraphina logically. Lady Anael scrutinizes me and then laughs as realization dawns on her. "Of course! It's worse! You are falling in love with her! I swear you are even blushing right now!" She exclaims, looking at me with her beautiful face, a mixture of amazement and mockery. I couldn't even deny it. Lady Anael has always been able to read me well. "The Council of Archangels will have a field day when they find out about this juicy revelation. Especially Michael." She says, shaking her head in amazement. "He knows and told me not to let anything develop further. He chose to discuss the matter with me privately and didn't get the council involved," I quickly informed her. "Michael always has a soft spot for you somehow not to allow the council to be involved." She rolls her eyes mockingly at me, shaking her head. "So, Lord Gideon is in love with Zanael's daughter. Zanael was your former charge and friend. It is quite poetic. I thought love and romance were not your thing." She teases sarcastically. "I thought so, too." I give her a half smile. We sat in silence for a bit. "We will get her back safely." She squeezes my hand reassuringly. "What can I say, Gideon? The little Nephilim is quite resilient and growing on me." She confesses with a slight smirk. "They won't harm her yet. For now, she is safe. I will rally my forces." She says as she stands up. "Good, I promised Nathaniel I would run him through with my sword if he touched her. He didn't take the warning before." I say to her as we walk out of the war room. I told the others to come in. I was glad to have Lady Anael by my side with this. She is a formidable warrior and a great battle strategist.

It felt like a High Witch hexed weapon stabbed my heart when I found out Seraphina got abducted. I felt distracted and anxious all afternoon about her for no apparent reason. Usually, I am very grounded, and anxiety never affects me. I knew something had happened to her as soon as Kemuel and Vicky teleported in. I was so livid that Nathaniel's High

Witch took her. I commended Kemuel and Vicky for fighting to protect her. Kemuel was hard on himself and felt that he had failed her. I told him he did well by bringing her ring and bracelet for Celeste's tracking spell. The other Powers and even Cael are beside themselves with worry. They have all grown to love and accept her as part of them.

After our moment in the training room when I kissed her again, I have been avoiding being alone with her. I broke our agreement about that happening again. I lost self-control again, became aroused, and kissed her when she tried writhing to free herself from my grasp during that combat session. Her warm and toned body felt so inviting beneath mine. I knew I wanted her more than ever.

We have been spending many hours training together, and I enjoyed being her mentor for each training session and being in her company. I enjoyed our conversations and banter as much as I loved watching her training progress. Zanael would have been proud of her progress. She was very resilient and a fast learner. I was very jealous that Kemuel took her on a date. He confessed that he had a crush on her. I wanted to punch him when he said he kissed her. Then, being the smooth talker, he saved himself by saying she didn't kiss him back because she was not over me. And he could tell I was not over her, too, given that my eyes flared with gold angel-fire in anger when he mentioned he kissed her. That was a revelation that made me realize that Lady Anael was right.

My feelings for her were beyond lust and longing. She has been the only one to put dents and cracks in my defenses to make me feel something more than the exhilarating lust for battle as a warrior. I was falling deeply in love with her, and it's terrifying now that they took her from me. And worse, they know her true identity. I promised Zanael I would look after her, and when I find her, I will never let her go. And I will scour this Earth to find her.

I was taken out of my thoughts when Archangel Michael started speaking to me in angelical language telepathically. He sounds agitated. *"You need to get Zanael's daughter back, Gideon. Your feelings for her have blinded you from doing what was best for her. You allowed her too much freedom, knowing that an unaligned Watcher and rogue fallen angels were after her. And now they have a powerful High Witch working for them."* He chastises. *"If I had restricted her freedom, she would have hated me for it and gladly joined Nathaniel's faction. Then Razziel would have handed her over to Lucifer,"* I respond in an angelical tongue. *"Celeste is working on a tracking spell to locate her. We know she is no longer on Earth, but we will find her,"* I assure him. I heard Michael sigh. *"Lucifer knows her true identity now and will come for her. You have to get her back before they extract the blood seal from her. Lucifer will use your feelings for her against you, so thread carefully, Gideon."*

CHAPTER 18

SERAPHINA

I open my eyes and blink several times, taking in my surroundings. I was in a luxurious bed with dark red sheets in an opulent bedroom. I rubbed my eyes as pieces of memories of what happened started coming back to me. I can move my body again. The High Witch spell must have worn off. I quickly push the covers off, sitting up. I was still wearing yesterday's clothes of jeans and a fitted sweater. Where was I?

I remembered being abducted by Celeste's evil doppelgänger. "Ah, sleeping beauty is awake," Nathaniel's voice drawls as he walks into the bedroom. He was in jeans and a shirt. His icy light blue scrutinizes me with a smile. I back away from him, eyeing him warily. I guess this must be his bedroom. "Relax. I wouldn't hurt you." He raises both of his hands in a truce to reassure me. "And don't even try to attempt to escape. I have this place warded," He warns as he sees me looking frantically at the door and windows.

"We both know your Nephilim and Earth Angel powers are inactive. So, you're just a helpless human right now." He says as he walks over and sits in a chair, his eyes still on me. I remained in my corner against the wall, as far away as possible from him. He was still staring at me, and his lips suddenly curved in a grin. I look at him, puzzled at what he could be grinning at.

"So, it was you all along that is the new Earth angel? I knew there was something different about you. Very different than the mighty Lord Gideon himself was assigned to watch over you," He remarks with hints of sarcasm. "Clever of the stuffy Archangels hiding you in plain sight as a human, though. Gideon must have the most amazing self-control because you have been living with him for months, and he hasn't taken you to his bed yet." He gives me a leering half-smile. I didn't need to wonder how he knew, too, that I had never slept with anyone. "You know he will come for me, right?" I retort as I hug myself with my arms, glaring at him. "Let him. If he can find you," Nathaniel said, looking quite self-assured as he put his hands behind his head and reclined in the chair.

I smile inwardly, remembering the ring and bracelet I deliberately dropped, knowing Celeste and her coven would be able to perform a tracking spell to find me. I knew Vicky and Kemuel would retrieve them and give them to her. I cannot reveal my wild card. Kafziel was the one who mentioned how many tracking spells work during my lessons about the supernatural world and what to do if I ever find myself in danger. He said it was easier for accuracy to do a tracking spell if the item from the person was from the exact place they got abducted.

"Who is the High Witch that brought me here? Celeste's evil twin?" I ask him. "Hmm, pretty much. She is Cerinda, and yes, her twin sister. She pledged her loyalty after I helped her escape from prison. I guess you didn't know everything about your adopted mother after all." He answers as he gets up and walks over to me. I wedged myself in the corner. He circles me like a predator stalking its prey. I stopped backing away and decided to hold my ground.

"Gideon is a fool to have not tasted such beauty." He murmurs as he brushes strands of my hair from my shoulders.

"You know the Council of stuffy Archangels will not approve of your union with him, right? But with me, you don't have to worry about all that. Join my faction. Come to my bed willingly, and I will make you my bond mate." He whispers close to my ear as he traces a finger on my cheek down to my neck. I flinch away from his touch as if his finger was burning me. "If you come willingly to my bed, you will find me a pleasing lover who will pleasure you. I don't want to force you," He coaxes as he kisses my neck. "Your touch makes my skin crawl, Nathaniel. I will always choose Gideon," I snap at him as I elbow him, but he catches my arm with supernatural reflexes. He shoves me against the wall and pins both of my arms with supernatural strength. His eyes were cold and furious. "Gideon cannot offer you what you want. I offered you to be my bond mate, and you still chose him. If you don't come willingly to my bed, I will have to make you comply." He grates as he presses his body against mine. I kick him hard, but he catches my legs laughing mockingly. "Oh no. You already got me once with that. Not again." He holds on to the leg I kicked him with. I try to wiggle my leg free and swipe at his face with my hands. He dodges but has to let go of my leg to do so. I may be a weak human, but I was going to put up a fight as much as possible. He was getting infuriated. "Feisty, aren't you?" He lunges at me again, but I quickly move out of the way. Reflexes got activated from all my training. Nathaniel's eyes started glowing with blue angel-fire as he glared at me. The door opens, and to my surprise, Laurel walks in. He turned to her with an annoying look. I quickly composed myself.

"Go away, Laureliana. Don't you see I am busy here?" He yells at her. She rolls her eyes at him. "The High Witch wants to see you now. It's about the ritual. She sent me to babysit her," Laurel huffs as she gestures toward me. Nathaniel turns toward me with a quick smile. "We will finish where we left off later, love." He gives me one last lecherous look as he walks out the door. As soon as he left, Laurel turned her attention to me.

"So, you are the new Earth angel? Who would have thought it was you all along glamoured as a human? Zanael's Nephilim daughter. You know I have met your dad a few times. He was hot" " she comments with a half-smile. Ewww much? She thought my dad was hot? I hope she didn't have sex with him, too. That would be quite a disturbing revelation. I would rather have her watching me than Nathaniel, though. I move away from the wall and decide to sit in a chair that was by it. My eyes quickly scanned Nathaniel's room, and I saw pink silk lingerie and thong underwear by the bedside that I knew didn't belong to him. I put it all together and started to feel nausea and bile in my throat. "Oh god. I was in that bed where you and Nathaniel did the nasty." I made a face of disgust, looking at the bed I had woken up in now, feeling nauseous. The two of them conspiring together. Who would have thought?

She smiles a very catty grin. "Nathaniel is not as good as a lover like Gideon," she sweetly responds as she sits in the other chair. "Rubbing your past one-night stand with Gideon would not work, Laurel. I heard about it all." I scoff as I watch her smile disappear, and she frowns at me. Laurel is not too bright, although she has a few centuries of experience compared to my few years of existence. I will have to make her my pawn on this chessboard. She is probably my only means of escaping from this place.

"I thought your obsession was with Gideon. Why are you with Nathaniel?" I ask her. "Nathaniel is a means to an end. Same as how you are a means to an end." She answers irritably. "Gideon is the one I want." "Well, he will come for me so that you can tell him then. Why him? Because it's not like he can be with you or me. The Council of Archangels has to approve his choice of a bond mate." I watched her as she twiddled her fingers, looking bored. "Silly girl. I know I wouldn't be able to be his bond mate, but being his lover is allowed. When the High Witch extracts your Earth angel essence and the Archangel blood seal, there will not be much left of you for Gideon." She gives me a smile of mockery. I would die if they extracted the Archangel blood seal-it is linked to my soul, life force, and Earth angel essence. I don't want to die. I need to think fast about how to get out of here. Laurel has light powers as a light fairy and has enhanced strength and speed over me, and there was not anything in the bedroom I could use as a weapon. I saw Laurel suddenly get up and walk toward the window. My eyes follow her as she opens the window.

The sky looked reddish brown with twin suns that were setting. Evening time was approaching, but it looked like we were not on Earth anymore. "Where are we?" I ask her, gazing in awe at the twin suns and the weird-looking sky. "A High Witch dimension that is parallel to the Earth plane. That is why Gideon wouldn't be able to find..." Her voice trails off. Several humanoid flying figures dotted the sky. I smile as the flying figures approach closer and see their wings flapping. Angels! My heart and stomach start somersaulting as I recognize a distinct pair of gold wings and gleaming gold armor streaking like a meteorite across the sky in gold angel fire.

"Gideon," I whisper his name with a smile. I knew it was him despite the gold helm. I recognize Jeb's black and grey armor and grayish black wings, the copper color armor and copper wings of the seven elites. About two dozen other angels were in grey steel armor with white wings. As they approached closer, I saw other flying figures that didn't look like angels. I immediately recognized they were warrior fae, led by King Aodhan, in full battle armor. I saw Laurel's face blanching as she recognized her dad. She is in big trouble if he discovers what she has been up to. "Laurel, if you care about your dad, let me out of here. If they extract the Archangel blood seal from me, your dimension will be in danger too." I gaze at her, hoping she would listen to reason. She turns away from the window to look at me. She sighs as if processing what I just informed her. Her face had a grave look.

"Promise me that you will ask Gideon to look out for my Dad with this battle. And that you wouldn't speak to him about Nathaniel and me, and I will let you walk out of here," She finally says. Everything about faes always has to be transactional and bargains. "The door is unguarded, and I cannot guarantee you will be able to get out of here without being caught. As soon as you walk out of here you are on your own. Now, promise me about my dad!" "Yes. I promise I will ask Gideon to look out for your dad," I reassure her. She nods her head, satisfied with my answer. "Now go before I change my mind." She gestures at the door. I give her a quick nod and cautiously open the bedroom door.

My heart was pounding as I quickly surveyed my surroundings. It looks like I was in a house or building. Judging from the height I was looking at through the bedroom window earlier, I am at the very top floor. The dim lights were modern-looking, and the hallway looked empty. I quickly made my way to a door with an exit label and saw some spiraling stairs several flights long. I didn't know where it led, but I had to try and find out. I cautiously descend the stairs, staying close to the wall. The stairs seem to go on forever but finally end at a foyer with a window and a huge tree not far from it. It looks like I am not on the ground floor yet. Everything was quiet. Too quiet, I thought, until I heard some shuffling of feet and voices. I ran toward the window as three men walked into the foyer. They seem surprised to see me as their eyes flare a glowing blue. Judging by their glowing blue eyes, they were Gregori Watchers.

Before they could run toward me with supernatural speed, I leaped out the window in a dive roll toward the tree. I quickly grab a branch, but it breaks, and I feel myself falling as other branches scrape at my skin. My reflexes kick in, and I grab another sturdier branch. I maneuver my body on it and stay momentarily to catch my breath. I realized the twin suns were soft glows in the reddish-brown sky, and it was getting dark. I looked down to see if those Watchers were following me, but no one was around. It seems like I was in an unfenced yard. I gaze in wonder at the building I had leaped from. It looks like a modern fortress. I decide to climb down the tree. As soon as my feet touched the ground, I felt a pair of hands grabbed me.

I scream and lash out with my arms. "Seraphina. It's Kafziel!" Kafziel tries to calm me in his usual low voice as his body materializes into its solid form. I have never been so happy to see him. I hug him hard, feeling relief. "We need to get you away from here." He grabs me by my waist, picks me up, and takes off running with supernatural speed with me.

As soon as we were out of the yard, we saw several streaks of angel-fire hurling toward us. Kafziel stops and sets me down as a giant meteorite of gold angel-fire halts before us. Gideon's tall frame materializes, and he lands on his feet on the ground in front of us with golden wings outstretched, looking imposing and regal in his full golden celestial armor. The other meteorite balls of angel-fire materialize into Jeb and the others with their wings outstretched. Gideon's golden wings and helm quickly de-materialize as he stares at me. His irises were golden orbs. "Gideon!" I yell, running toward him like a mad woman. I have never been so happy to see him. Gideon crushes me in his arms and hugs me. "Did Nathaniel and his High Witch hurt you?" He asks in a soft voice tone as he looks at the bruises on my face and arms with worry etched on his face. "No. Those are from the tree branches." I quickly assure him. "I am fine; it's just I…" My words were cut off by his mouth covering mine in a passionate kiss. A kiss I was not expecting in front of everyone. The taste of his mouth and being in his arms drove all my anxiety and fears away. The escape from the bedroom prison, the building, and Laurel letting me go felt too easy and too good to be true. But I am not going to question it. Being in Gideon's arms feels safe, and I kiss him passionately to match his own. For a moment, I forgot all about being abducted to a different dimension, and it was just us exploring each other's mouths. There were several murmurs, low whistles, and even a few comments of "It's about time."

Then someone clears their throat loudly, and a fit of fake coughing at us as the kiss drags on. "The two of you are making me blush," Jeb remarks, shaking his head with an amused grin. Gideon breaks the kiss as he presses his forehead against mine. We momentarily locked our gazes, and he gave me a quick kiss on my forehead and put an arm around me. I felt heat rising to my face with embarrassment as the seven elite and Jeb all stared at us with smiles of amusement. After that kiss, I guess everyone knows how Gideon and I feel about each other.

The seven elite and Jeb all surround us, asking me how I escaped. I told them they would never believe me if I told them. I told them it was Laurel, but I didn't mention that she was working with and sleeping with Nathaniel as promised. They were all surprised and wondered what she was doing here. I told Gideon that she requests that he look out for his father, King Aodhan. Gideon thinks she is the fae that Caleb confesses that Nathaniel is working with, and it is not a coincidence that she is here. I noticed it was just us, Jeb, and the seven elite. I ask where the others I saw earlier are. Jeb says they are doing recon around the heavily warded building. "We need to get you to safety," Gideon suggests, his arm still around my waist.

Suddenly, there were several bright lights as multiple orbs of blue angel-fires erupted around us. "Stay behind me," Gideon commands as his helm and celestial broad sword materialize. Jeb and the others follow suit. I watch as a white and blue angel-fire orb materializes into Nathaniel and the fallen Throne Razziel.

"You really think it will be that easy, Gideon?" Nathaniel scoffs. I watch as the other blue orbs materialize into unaligned Watcher angels. Razziel was staring daggers at Gideon. "I was hoping it wouldn't be," Gideon responds as his irises flare in gold angel-fire, and his broad sword erupts in gold angel fire. "I was counting on it not being easy." "This is my turf, Gideon. The High Witch has blocked all exits for teleportation and flight out of here, so you are outnumbered," Nathaniel smugly informs us. "Hand over the Earth, angel, and you might walk out of here still intact." "What can I say, Nathaniel? I owe you a rematch. And as for you, Razziel. I wouldn't leave another scar. I wouldn't miss this time," Gideon taunts as his eyes scan the other Watchers. Nathaniel seethes his eyes, blazing with blue fury, as Razziel's eyes blaze with white fury. They advance toward us.

"Keep her safe!" Gideon says quickly to the seven elite. He gives me one last look and nods at the twins, Yael and Danael. They both immediately activate their enhanced invulnerability, shielding me with their bodies, their katanas ablaze with copper angel-fire. Razziel and Nathaniel start attacking Gideon, and the other Watchers start attacking Jeb and the squad. Gideon was magnificent to watch as he blocked and parried every blow from Razziel and Nathaniel while giving them many of his own. They were all moving in a blur that my eyes couldn't keep up with. Those two are so going to lose to him.

I watch in horror as several demonic creatures and demonic faes materialize, brandishing weapons-now it seems we are outnumbered. As soon as I began to fear the worst, a human-sized silver orb materialized into Lady Anael in full silver armor with outstretched silver wings. Her eyes were blazing silvery angel-fire like the Calvary sword she was wielding. She was looking like a magnificent Valkyrie. Other silver orbs materialize into angels in grey steel armor and white wings, all brandishing celestial weaponry. Orbs of green materialize into King Aodhan and his fae warriors. I heard distant thunder as the sky flashes with lightning. The winds howl as some of his fae warriors activate their elemental powers. King Aodhan's hands were ablaze with fiery balls of energy. He was a fire elemental fae, after all.

Lady Anael's silver wings de-materializes as she approaches me. "Here, little Nephilim. Make yourself useful." She throws a sword at me. I gave her a quick smile and picked up the sword. I observed the weapons the demonic fae and rogue Watchers were using must have been hexed by High Witch Cerinda because some of the angels were getting hurt and some were bleeding. I watch Zerachiel levitate in the air as he throws knives and shooting stars ablaze with a copper angel fire at the demons with his impeccably enhanced marksman skills. Abdiel was zooming in, blazing copper angel-fire between the ranks of demons with his enhanced speed. Ezekiel snatches many of the High Witch's hexed weapons away with his enhanced telekinesis. Kemuel was slashing relentlessly with his double swords, twirling his body in ways I didn't know were possible with his enhanced agility while his sharp reflexes dodged any blows. Jeb was bulldozing through a group of demons like an angry juggernaut, easily flinging many of them away with his enhanced brute strength.

I watch as Lady Anael, with her cavalry sword ablaze in silver angel-fire yelling rapid-fire commands at her warriors as she joins the fight. I told the twins Danael and Yael to help out the others and that they didn't have to stick around to babysit me. Before they left, they set my sword ablaze with copper angel-fire as I saw a Demonic-looking creature galloping on all fours toward me. I told them I had got this one.

The creature looks like a mutated demonic wolf and raccoon combo. Its eyes were red lumps of coal as its mouth opened, and long snake-like tentacles shot out, aiming at me. I quickly dodge out of the way, but the tentacles follow me. They had little circular sharp razor teeth in the suction holes at their ends. I don't want to know what those suction tentacles will do if they latch on to me. With my sword, I slashed at the tentacles, and a few of them went flying. With a shriek, the rest of the tentacles retract into the creature. It pounces on me, but I quickly maneuver out of the way. More tentacles shoot out, this time several more than before. What is this creature? The Hydra or something? I thought in frustration. "Here... you can use some more of this," Kemuel says as he quickly appears beside me.

I watch as he touches my sword, setting it ablaze with more copper angel-fire. "Go for its head!" He urges encouragingly at me. The creature pounced at me with its tentacles, but I leaped out of the way. The tentacles missed my feet by a few inches. I swipe at its tentacles, and the creature screeches as angel-fire from the sword burns its tentacles. I leaped toward it with the sword and swiped its head clean off its body. My first demon kill. I smile and pat myself. "Not bad for your first kill." Kemuel smiles at me and pats my back. My eyes scan the area, searching for Gideon. He was locked in a duel with Razziel using a celestial Halberd instead of his typical broad sword. I saw Nathaniel running toward us with preternatural speed as Kemuels attacked him with his double swords.

Cerinda suddenly materializes with a few other women-witches, probably. They were dressed in robes and chanting in a strange, unknown language. Cerinda had a spear with wisps of black smoke surrounding it. She uses her telekinesis powers, chanting in a strange language to levitate the spear. I watch in horror as she directs the spear straight at Gideon. I broke into a run, screaming Gideon's name. I knew if Gideon got seriously injured, the battle morale would swiftly decline. This battle was because of me. Razziel saw the spear whizzing through the air in his direction and quickly moved out of the way. "Gideon! Look out!" I shrieked as I leaped at him. Gideon moved both of us away from Razziel with preternatural reflexes as I felt a burning sensation in the middle of my back. It was the spear sticking out of my back. "Seraphina!" Gideon shouts in a pained voice as he pulls the spear gently out of my back. I was feeling numb all over, and I knew I was dying.

Gideon's wings materialize as he gathers me in his arms and takes off, flying with me away from the rest of the battle.

He lands on a grassy clearing and rests me gently on the grass as he stoops down next to my body. "You silly girl. This spear would not have killed me. Stay with me. Please don't die..." He pleads in desperation, caressing my face. I was seeing something I had never seen in his eyes before. Fear and despair. Love. I have to tell him how I feel before I die. "Gideon... I love you..." I murmur, feeling drained, staring into his beautiful gold flecked hazel eyes. Gideon gathers me in his arms, pulling me close to his body. "Seraphina. Please don't die on me- I love you." His helm de-materializes as he cups my face and kisses me. I could see his love for me in his eyes. It was beautiful. It was pure. It was fierce. It was passionate. I felt his love as he held me, as his gold angel fire engulfed our bodies. "Gideon. It's OK...It doesn't hurt anymore..." I smiled weakly at him as I felt tears on my face. His tears. I heard Celeste screaming my name as everything went dark.

CHAPTER 19

SERAPHINA

I cover my eyes from a brilliant flash of light that almost blinds me as a luxurious-looking room materializes. A tall, handsome man with an olive skin tone, dark curly hair, and brown eyes stares at me. Eyes like mine. Standing beside him was a tall, statuesque woman with long, kinky hair and a flawless dark brown skin tone. She looks like a mirror image of me. I know who these two were! My father, the Earth Angel Zanael, and my mother, Dr. Athania. "Mom? Dad?" I run toward them, and they both hug me. "Wait… am I dead?" I ask them as I look down at my body. "No. You're in a place called the 'in-between'. We were sent here temporarily to tell you it's not your time. You need to go back," My dad, Zanael, responds. "It's your destiny to be the new Earth angel." He rests his hands on my shoulders. "Look at how lovely you are. Our daughter is so grown up." Mom remarks as she takes my hands into hers, smiling. "We have been watching you and we couldn't be prouder of what you have become. You have the blood of the most powerful Archangels flowing in your veins. You are stronger than you think," Dad says, squeezing my arm.

"We will always be with you, watching over you." Mom smiles a brilliant smile at me. It was a smile that looked like mine. "Tell Lord Gideon I forgive him," My dad says. "For what?" I inquire curiously. My dad sighs. "I will let him tell you. "He gives me a pensive look and then smiles. "Oh, and tell him that he owes me a pitcher of fae ambrosia," Dad says with a smirk, his brown eyes twinkling with mirth. "For what?" I asked quizzically. "For falling in love." He gives me an amusing smile. "He wagered me a pitcher of fae ambrosia that he would never fall in love, but we both know he did. Now go back to your Lord Gideon, " he teases as he hugs me and kisses my forehead. Before I could say anything else, there was another flash of white light, and I opened my eyes and quickly stood up.

My body didn't feel numb and drained anymore, and I was glowing in gold angel-fire. "Seraphina…" Celeste looks at me with her tear-streaked face in awe. I felt wings materialize on my back. I turned around to look, and they were golden. A golden bow glowing with gold angel-fire appeared in my hand. It felt made for me. "It cannot be… the celestial bow," I heard Kafziel say as the seven elite, Jeb and Gideon, quickly approached me. "Seraphina, "He says softly, looking at me with relief and wonder. I felt my wings and the golden bow de-materialize as he hugged me. "Your Earth angel powers have been activated." He smiles at me. We both suddenly saw a burning flash of fire and heard a blood-curdling scream. It was Nathaniel, and his wings were on fire. The source of the fire was from Celeste. It was witch-fire she was using. His wings will regenerate, but it will take a while.

Cerinda moves in to attack, but Celeste deflects her energy balls with telekinesis. Seeing that Celeste was holding her own, Gideon turned his attention back to me. "You didn't die on me." He grabs me by my waist, pulls me to him, and kisses me. "You two love birds are making me gag," Lady Anael scoffs. We turned and saw her looking at us with a look of disgust on her face. "Good to see you alive." She nods curtly at me. I smile at her. "We have several of the rogue Watchers bound in celestial chains," Lady Anael reports as we watch Celeste subdue her twin sister Cerinda with a spell that had her writhing to break free from invisible chains.

Several body parts of different demonic creatures littered the ground. King Aodhan's forces had subdued the demonic faes. Gideon detaches from me as his broad sword materializes, and he advances toward Nathaniel with supernatural speed, who is preparing to launch his sword at Celeste. I watch in horror as Razziel seizes the opportunity to launch his weapon, Gideon. In my fear, I felt my hands erupt in gold angel fire as the golden celestial bow materialized in my hands with a golden arrow bathed in gold angel fire. I can get used to this. I aim the bow at Razziel and let the arrow fly. Before he could react, the arrow hits home squarely in his back, and he topples to his knees with a grunt. His sword was already flying toward

Gideon, who heard Razziel's grunt, turned around quickly, materialized his shield, and easily evaded Razziel's sword. Razziel's sword de-materializes as soon as it hits Gideon's shield. The seven elite quickly pounce on Razziel with celestial chains. Gideon advances on Nathaniel in a blur, dodges his slashing sword, and stabs him in the gut. "You should have listened when I warned you the first time not to touch Seraphina," He says to Nathaniel in a steely voice between clenched teeth as the Watcher falls to his knees, looking stunned. Celestial chains materialize in Gideon's hands, and he binds them around Nathaniel.

I took out a few more demons with my angel-fire arrows as Cerinda wiggled free from the invisible chains Celeste had bound her with and threw a crackling energy ball at Celeste. The energy ball hits her, and she falters from it. I let an arrow loose toward Cerinda but quickly re-direct it away from her. She gives me a sinister smile as she raises a vial of blood and chants in an unknown language. I started feeling the wound from the previous spear injury in my back re-open, and the pain was unbearable. I realized that the vial of blood she was holding was mine. I scream and drop to my knees in excruciating pain. Gideon was by my side in an instant after hearing my cry as he saw Cerinda chanting with the vial of blood. His eyes were ablaze in gold angel-fire. "I have her blood and will extract the blood seal from her. Your celestial weapons cannot harm me, Lord Gideon." She laughs mockingly. I watch, still in pain, as Gideon quickly sends a burst of gold angel-fire toward Cerinda's hands, which shatters the vial of blood from her hands.

"Clever spell to ward yourself off from getting harmed by angels, Witch. I may not be able to harm you, but she can," Gideon says, gesturing to Celeste, who wipes some blood from her lips as her entire body erupts in earthy orange witch-fire. "There is the reason you got excluded from family dinners, sister," Celeste taunts Cerinda as balls of crackling energy whirl in her hands. The last thing I heard was Gideon screaming my name as my vision went dark.

I heard voices, one of them I recognized as Archangel Raphael insisting to Gideon that he had done all he could to heal me, and it was up to my angelic healing powers to kick in to heal me. I open my eyes and blink to see Cael staring at me. "This feels like deja vu. Meeting you like this again. I think I have had enough with comas." I smile groggily at him, rubbing my eyes. I was feeling achy all over as I tried to sit up. "My Lady, you are awake." He quickly rushes over and hugs me. "You need to stop scaring me like this, my Lady." He scolds me, still hugging me. "I must go fetch Lord Gideon." He detaches from me and runs out the door. I was in my bedroom in Gideon's mansion, and the horrors of the past events seemed like a nightmare. I hope that being here all safe means we won. Someone had dressed me in my silk pajamas.

I heard footsteps approaching as Gideon walked in, followed by Archangel Raphael, Michael, and Chamuel. They were dressed casually in jeans and button-down shirts. Even Chamuel was in a flowing maxi dress, not a business casual skirt suit. When Gideon saw me awake and sitting up, he rushed over to me, pulling me into a crushing hug. He presses feverish kisses on my lips, not caring if the three Archangels are watching. Michael clears his throat loudly to interrupt us. Gideon stops kissing me, and we turn our attention to the Archangels. "Have some decorum, Lord Gideon. She just woke up," Raphael chides, frowning at Gideon. Then he turns his attention to me, surveying me with softness in his green eyes. "I second that." Michael nods his head in agreement. He had a slight look of disgust on his face. Chamuel stared at me with amused wonder as she walked over to me with her bright red hair in a prim French twist. She touches my face and tips my chin to look into my eyes. Her touch felt extremely warm. Both Gideon and I watch her with intense curiosity as she continues her examination of me. "It couldn't be, but it is. It is true." She turns to Michael and Raphael with a nod. I look at them in confusion. "What is it, Chamuel?" Gideon asks Chamuel with a look of anticipation in his eyes. Chamuel smiles serenely at him. "She is your true soulmate. Your souls share some similar angelic essences. Her gold angel fire is from yours due to the soul mate bond." She answers, still smiling. I looked at Gideon, wondering what she meant about him being my true soulmate, but all he had was this silly grin.

"How is that even possible?" Michael asks, looking very skeptical at Chamuel. "It's a rare phenomenon, but it can happen. You know I am well versed in these matters,

Brother. This bond is something we cannot interfere with." Chamuel emphasizes smiling at both Gideon and me. "And the seal?" Michael inquires. "Still intact within her, but due to the potent blood hex from that High Witch, her angelic powers will need some time to return fully," Raphael answers. Michael's eyes narrow as he scrutinizes Gideon and me. "This is still inappropriate, Gideon because she is your charge but not forbidden anymore. As long as this doesn't interfere with you being her Guardian and your duties, the rest of the Council and I will convene to discuss a formal bonding ceremony." He says to us in a formal tone. "We shall take our leave so you can properly rest and recover, Seraphina," Raphael says graciously. "And restrain your excitement a bit, Lord Gideon, and let her get some rest." Chamuel gave Gideon an admonishing look and smiled at me as she, Michael, and Raphael exited.

As soon as they were gone, Gideon pulled me into his arms. "So, this means we can be together without being considered inappropriate?" I ask him with eager excitement. "You nearly died trying to save me from a fatal blow. I couldn't ask for a better soulmate by my side. Even the Council of Archangels is convinced." He caresses my face. I asked him questions about the soul mate bond, and he said it's rare for his class of warrior angels to experience that phenomenon, but he has no complaints. He told me that I was in a coma for a few days after Archangel Raphael came to heal me. Celeste subdued her evil twin, Cerinda, who is back in the High Witch prison, and the rogue angels are awaiting judgment from the Council of Archangels.

King Aodhan's forces were able to subdue the demonic faes, and the Council of High Witches and fae healers are working to undo the evil magic horrors Cerinda inflicted on them. Laurel was back at her father's court and had a cover story about how Nathaniel kidnapped her. As promised, I didn't tell anyone the truth.

I told Gideon that I saw my parents when I was dying and what my dad said about what he owed to him. "That is only something Zanael would say." He shakes his head and laughs, then kisses me again. I told him my dad said he forgave him, and I asked him what he meant. Gideon's body immediately went rigid as his mood went pensive. He tips my chin up to look at him. His gold-fleck hazel eyes were solemn. "Seraphina...what I am about to tell you is something I have been carrying since Zanael's death like a constant weight on my shoulders," He says in a grave voice tone.

"When things started to get too serious between Zanael and your mother, I told him to end the relationship before the Council finds out. She was human, and he was immortal, and there was only one way it would have ended- in heartbreak. But he was already in love and secretly married her. Although we were close friends, he feared I would inform the Council of his growing relationship with your mother, hence why he went on the run with her when he found out she was pregnant with you. I was disappointed that he didn't trust me enough to ask for my help because I had told him to end things with her or I would have to inform the Council. I have not forgiven myself for saying that to him. I will just have to carry that guilt that I failed him as a friend and Guardian," He confesses in a soft voice with hints of sadness. I stare at him, feeling stunned by his confession.

I knew he did care for my father with brotherly love, and his death devastated him. I could tell he had been carrying the weight of that guilt of failing my dad for a while now. But if not for him rescuing me, I wouldn't be alive. "I understand if you see me in a different light after what I just told you," He says as he turns away. "Gideon, my dad says he forgives you. Now you need to forgive yourself," I told him, turning his face to look at me. I kiss him softly, then rest my head on his chest. There was a momentary silence between us.

I asked him if my parents were in Heaven. He says that Zanael had been rewarded for his service as an Earth angel and currently resides in Heaven with his human wife, my mother. He doesn't have access to where their souls currently reside, but Archangel Azrael does. He mentioned that the place I saw them when I lost consciousness was the in-between since my soul was not one of the dead yet. He confirms that Archangel Azrael sent them to me to encourage me to return to the world of the living. I will have to thank Archangel Azrael when I see the Council again. I thought about my parents and how at peace and happy they were. My dad, Zanael, was so handsome, and my mom was so beautiful. I asked Gideon if Archangel Azrael would allow me to see them again. He says that would be a challenging request because Azrael prefers the dead to stay at peace. Him sending them to me when I was dying was a dire emergency request by Archangel Michael. I rest my head on Gideon's chest as he holds my hand. There was another silence between us as I thought about my parents. How different would things be if they were both alive?

As a forbidden Nephilim, I knew there was no way the Council of Archangels would have allowed me to live. My dad transferring the blood seal of the seven Archangels to me which made me into the new Earth angel was the only reason they allowed me to live. I asked Gideon if he would have allowed the Council to kill me if I was not the Earth angel after my dad's death. He went pensive for a bit, then said he would have tried everything he could to ensure that I was safe, even if my human mother had to go into hiding with me. He says Zanael would have never forgiven him if he had allowed something terrible to happen to me. He would not have ever forgiven himself, too. He drapes his arm around me as Celeste, Jeb, and the seven elite barge into the room.

Celeste scolded him for not letting her know I was awake and that the only way she knew was from Cael. The seven elite stared at us, cuddling with amused grins, jokingly inquiring if they were interrupting more make-out sessions. Celeste was not amused and stared daggers at Gideon. They all crowd around my bedside. Jeb had to silence them because they all started asking questions about why Archangel Michael and Chamuel visited me besides Archangel Raphael, who healed me. I was beginning to feel tired and started yawning. Celeste, noticing my tiredness, told everyone to leave so I could get some rest and that they could speak to me later. Gideon also told them all to leave. There were whines of disappointment, but they all left. Celeste gives Gideon a scathing look and tells him he should let me rest before she leaves with Jeb and the others.

After they were gone, After they were gone, Gideon kissed me and told me to get some rest and he would see me later after I wake up. As soon as he was gone, I fell into a deep sleep.

"The two of you need to get a room already, geez." Vicky rolls her eyes at me as she watches me making flirtatious eyes at Gideon all evening. At the mansion, Gideon, Jeb, Celeste, the seven elite, and Vicky were all having my college graduation celebration dinner. Gideon was looking polished in a navy silk shirt and black slacks. When he showed up at my graduation ceremony dressed in formal business attire, it felt like every female in attendance wanted to throw their underwear at him. The flirtatious stares Gideon received from other women, both young and elderly, didn't bother me. I knew he was mine and was there to support only me. There were many jealous glances when he picked me up by the waist and kissed me long and hard after the ceremony.

He was also giving me lustful looks throughout the dinner at the mansion, with eyes showing promises of sensual pleasures to come later on. I saw Jeb rolling his eyes in exasperation at Gideon when he saw him keep glancing at me, distracted during their conversation. The others were all laughing and conversing while drinking fae wine. Cael came over to refill Vicky's wine glass. "Lord Gideon says to meet him in the hallway," He whispers. Then he bustles away with a smile. "Just go to him." Vicky gives me a mischievous grin, wagging her eyebrows and making a lewd signal for sex. I quickly got up and made my way toward the hallway.

As soon as I got to the hallway, Gideon grabbed me by the waist spun me around to face him, and kissed me savagely, his tongue searching the deep recesses in my mouth, making me ache to my core. I press my body to his, winding my arms around his neck and kissing him back passionately, craving more of the sweet ache. "Come with me!" He whispers against my lips. He picks me up and starts moving with me at a preternatural speed. The intense look in his eyes said all about what he wanted from me tonight, and I was excited and nervous because I wanted him just as much. Archangel Rafael finally gave me a clean bill of health to resume all physical activities this morning. The sexual tension over the one week we had to wait for his decision about my physical health was starting to get unbearable for both of us.

He stops with me at his bedroom door. "Lead the way, my Lord Gideon," I say to him with a flirty giggle. It was the first time I addressed him as "my Lord." He looks at me with wonder and playful amusement. "Say that again," He murmurs with a smile, cupping my face and kissing me again. "My Lord Gideon," I murmur flirtatiously against his lips. "It has a nice ring to it, doesn't it?" He says with a wicked grin as he opens his bedroom door and pulls me inside.

His bedroom was very grand and opulent with Renaissance-era decor. The dimly lit lights illuminated a beautiful, large four-poster bed decorated with dark blue and gold velvet drapes that looked very comfy with matching bedding. His bedroom was fitting for a Lord, and this was my first time in it. I was excited about what was going to happen between us.

"I have been thinking of this moment with you for a while now." He murmurs as he kisses me with unrestrained passion, his hands unzipping my dress. When the zipper got stuck, he quickly ripped the dress, and it fell to the floor. He saw my concerned face as I looked at the torn dress. It was an expensive dress Celeste bought for me for my graduation celebrations. "You're the Lady of my faction now. There will be plenty of dresses at your disposal." His golden flecked hazel eyes shone with desire as he watched me step out of my shoes. He takes out the clips that held up my hair and lets it fall free, then he kisses my shoulders as his deft fingers unhook my bra and toss it aside, exposing my breasts. "You're beautiful." He murmurs as his large hands cover my breasts. I felt my nipples harden under his touch. His devouring gaze was making me feel like the most priceless treasure. I let out a soft gasp at the heat and gentleness his touch was arousing within me. He kisses me again, his tongue spearing into my mouth, creating swirling desires. He was breathing raggedly as he kissed his way down my neck and stopped at my breasts. He made a primal sound deep in his throat as his warm mouth sucked and nibbled on my nipples switching from one breast to the other, feasting hungrily.

I arch with a gasp of pleasure so he could take more of my breast into his mouth. With a growl, he lifts both of my legs around him and presses himself against me. I could feel the hardness of his erection, straining for release from his pants. He carries me toward his bed and gently lays me on my back. He detaches from me, unbuttons his shirt urgently, and tosses it aside. I watch him feeling sensations of arousal as I admire his well-chiseled muscular physique. He kicks his shoes off and quickly removes his pants. My eyes widen at his fully naked body. Botticelli's *statue of David* looks like a cheap hardware store statue compared to Gideon's naked body. I gape at his huge hard erect cock and instantly felt very nervous. It was long and thick, and I don't know if I can take all of him. He is the first man I ever saw fully naked. I remember Vicky and her sisters told me how awkward, uncomfortable, and not enjoyable their first sexual experiences were. I was about to lose my virginity to a gorgeous angel, and I was feeling both excited and nervous-well a bit terrified too. I turn away from him as he crawls into the bed. I was very skittish now.

"I am nervous," I say to him. "Don't be, I will be gentle." He assures me softly. "There will be some discomfort at first, but after that, there will be pleasure, and you will be begging me not to stop. Trust me..." He trails kisses on my legs as his hands caress my thighs and buttocks. He groans deep in his throat as he easily rips the delicate fabric of my underwear off and casts it aside. He pries my thighs apart with his hands and trails his tongue on my inner thighs until I feel his tongue probing hungrily inside me, his mouth feasting and sucking on my clit as his hands tease my nipples. I moan, my fingers entwining in his silky dark hair, feeling like I was about to faint from the pleasurable sensations that infuse my whole body. "Gideon... stop... I think I'm going to..." I gasp in pleasure at a loss for words. Gideon stops probing with his tongue inside of me and chuckles softly. "What's so funny?" I ask him with raised eyebrows. He glances at me from between my thighs with a sly grin. "You're about to have an orgasm, love. Relax and let it happen. There will be plenty more of that to come," He answers, then returns to his task of pleasuring my nether regions with his mouth and tongue. So, this warm, pleasurable feeling of my whole body trembling and wanting to explode in pleasure is an orgasm. He made deep rumbling sounds in his throat as I felt delicious spasms in my body and my orgasm released into his mouth. He hungrily laps every drop of it while making soft sounds of pleasure. "Does this please you?" He asks huskily. "Yes, my Lord," I murmur, biting my lower lip. "Music to my ears. You taste like Nectar and strawberries." His gaze was filled with passion as his hands caress my hips, trailing searing kisses to my stomach and waist, then back to my nipples, sucking and nibbling them. He covers me with his body and gently lifts one of my legs around his waist. His eyes lock with mine for a moment, his gaze intense.

I felt my body tense in nervous anticipation and knew he felt the change, too. "Relax. You will be OK. I will be gentle," He reassures me, caressing my face and kisses me tenderly. I felt the thick, engorged tip of his erect shaft at my entrance. He enters me slowly with a gentle thrust. I let out a cry against his lips at the burning, painful sensation from his thrust as my hands grabbed his biceps. His body went rigid. I felt tears stinging my eyes. "Are you OK? I don't want to hurt you," he murmurs as he gently brushes the tears from my eyes, giving me a look of concern. I could feel the muscles of his body tensing against my body, restraining himself from thrusting further. "I'm OK." I respond nodding at him. "Are you sure?" He asks furrowing his brows. I nod yes. I knew I had to get the uncomfortable part over with. There was a mixture of longing and concern in those ethereal gold-flecked hazel eyes as he kissed me softly. I grasp the bedsheets as he thrusts gently and shallowly, allowing his soft kisses to take my mind off the pain and discomfort.

He closed his eyes, moaning feverishly, and I could tell he was still restraining himself because he didn't want to hurt me. "You can thrust deeper," I say to him. "I don't want to hurt you." He responds between raspy breaths. "It doesn't hurt anymore." I assure him as I lift my hips higher. My movement seems to break the last of his self-control. "OK. Let me know if this hurts." He thrusts deeper slowly, giving my body Tim to adjust to his thick length before fully seating himself inside me all the way to the hilt. I moan in pleasure at the sensation of all of him deep inside me. "Are you ok?" He asks softly. I nod yes. He smiles, as he wraps my legs around his waist then thrusts slow, deep, and sensually locking his gaze with mine. His hands caress my hips and thighs as he kisses me passionately, continuing with his slow, deep, sensual strokes. His deep thrusts were building throbbing sensations as his fullness stretched my insides, bringing pleasure I didn't know was possible. With each pleasurable thrust, I tightened my fingers on his muscled back and biceps and dug my nails into his skin.

He murmurs in an unknown language against my lips as he slides one hand beneath my hips to bring me closer to him increasing his pace. "I've been dreaming of this since I first kissed you. How you feel is beyond what I have imagined." He murmurs, thrusting again and again. I was unable to hold back the moans against his shoulder as I succumbed to the sweet, aching pleasure he was giving me. I writhe beneath him while the guttural cries of his pleasure fills my ears. His mouth devours my lips and breasts with passionate kisses, possessed by raw desire, as his hands anchor my hips to him, thrusting into me hard and fast. I didn't want him to stop. With a cry, I felt the hot release of pure pleasure as I whispered his name. I moaned as I felt him shudder above me, muttering in an unknown language that was fill with need and longing as his irises flares with gold angel-fire. His harsh cries signal his climax, the heat of his release filling me as he kept moving before he collapsed against me, trying to keep his weight from crushing my body. I run a hand down the muscles of his back as my breathing returns to normal. Tonight, he was not the powerful warrior angel and the Lord of the Powers. He was just Gideon—my lover and soulmate.

He moves to my side, pulling me into his arms, kissing me all over as if worshipping my body. His eyes were back to their usual color. "I love you, Seraphina." He murmurs against my lips. "I love you too, Lord Gideon." I snuggle up to him, running my hands on his smooth chest, trailing to the corded muscles on his stomach, enjoying the aftermath of our love-making. My whole body still hummed from his kisses and caresses. My first time with Gideon was not an uncomfortable horror story-it was beautiful. I glance up at his face and smile at him. "Wow… I didn't expect my first time to be so…" My voice falters at a loss for words. "Pleasurable? Mind-blowing?" Gideon finishes for me with a low chuckle. "Well, aren't you self-assured?" I laugh at his cocky attitude. "I perfected that word." His lips quirk in a smile as he traces a line on my collarbone. "You know your irises flare with gold angel-fire when you orgasm, right?" I tease him. "It happens." He give me a half-smile as he entwine my fingers with his. "You think they all noticed we were gone early from dinner?" I ask him sleepily. A rumble of a low chuckle escapes from his lips. "Yes, but I had other plans for you for your graduation celebrations." He murmurs as he brushes strands of my hair from my face. I was too sleepy to respond. He kisses me softly then pulls the bed sheet and comforter over us.

I felt him get up from the bed as I was dozing off. He got

a warm washcloth and used it to clean me off, sensually wiping between my thighs with it, then pulled me to lay on his chest. My body starts to ache for him again. As I lay on his chest, I ran my hands down the ripples of his stomach muscles to his groin. He let out a guttural moan as my hand grasped his hardening erection. "You won't get any rest if you keep touching me like that," He murmurs as he pulls me on top of his body to straddle him, kissing me deeply. Then, his mouth captures a hardened nipple. I moan his name as he grabs my hips and impales me on his hard erection, plunging deeply, making every core of my insides scream with pleasure.

CHAPTER 20

SERAPHINA

"Cael, be quiet. You're waking her up. Knock next time," Gideon scolds Cael in a slightly irritated hush tone. He shushes him not to wake me up. It was too late because I was already waking up. I open my eyes and turn my head to see Cael bustling around the bedroom. Gideon was in a robe, standing by the window with his hands folded, glaring at Cael. His bed and bedding felt so comfortable and luxurious, and I want to stay in them. I groan sleepily, trying to get some clarity. I was lying on my stomach with the bedsheets tangled around my naked body. My whole body felt sore. There was tenderness and soreness between my inner thighs and nether regions. It was a satisfied type of soreness. Cael glanced at our strewn clothes on the floor and then at me lying in Gideon's bed with the sheets tangled around my naked body. He didn't have to guess what had transpired. He was doing a lousy job hiding the huge grin plastered on his face.

"My Lord. Pardon the intrusion. I will knock next time. Lady Anael and her elite squad will be joining us for breakfast." He announces in a formal tone. Gideon glances at me, and I can see the glint of lust in his eyes. "Come back in about an hour, Cael," He says, still staring at me. With a quick bow, Cael smiles, glances at me again, and quickly exits. Gideon drops the robe he was wearing to the floor as he stands naked, his huge erection rock hard, and climbs onto the bed next to me. He props himself on an elbow to look at me as his fingers start stroking my back.

His lust was insatiable because we went three more times again after our first time. I would doze off for a bit, then wake up to him kissing me all over, and my body would be aroused and ready to go again. He did allow me to be on top for a short bit, and then he quickly flipped positions, so he was in control. I didn't think we got much sleep. I barely saw him sleeping for a bit. I found myself staring at his sleeping form, looking so serene, breathing softly with strands of his tousled dark hair falling on his face. He looked like a beautiful angel sleeping. I brushed the hair strands from his face, hoping it wouldn't disturb him. His eyes flew open, and his irises flared with gold angel-fire for a moment before they returned to their hazel gold-flecked color as he grabbed my hands. He saw I was staring, smiled, and pulled me on top of his body. He kissed me hungrily, flipped me on my back, parted my thighs with his own, and we were off again for another round.

He mentioned that he doesn't need to sleep like humans do but enjoys it occasionally to relax. Each love-making session was more pleasurable than the last. Things also got a bit too rough. I blush at the deliciously naughty sensual stuff he did to my body with his hands and mouth. I didn't know such bliss was possible, leaving me without words to describe it. I was warned about supernatural sexual libido and stamina by Vicky. No wonder Laurel is obsessed with him. His reputation for his prowess as a lover precedes him.

I flip on my side to face him. My breasts had hickeys from his mouth, and both nipples felt sore and sensitive. Without my angelic powers, my body was human and did not have the perks of invulnerability and accelerated healing like his. Although my body was sore, and my inner thighs felt bruised and tender, I still longed for him again. The hot, wet liquid of arousal was starting to accumulate between my thighs, and it was aching badly for him. "Are you feeling too sore?" He asks, looking at the bruises on my inner thighs with concern. "I might have gotten a bit too carried away. You make it so hard for me to go slow." He traces his fingers on my inner thighs. "I like making you lose control and love it when you get carried away." I smile flirtatiously at him, running my fingers through his tousled hair. He had morning bed hair and morning wood to go with it. "You do, don't you?" He arches an eyebrow and gives a low chuckle. His eyes gleam with desire as he pulls me toward his body and kisses me with intense passion. Then he flips me on my stomach. He brushes my hair aside, trails kisses on my back, and then lifts my hips toward him. I moan as I feel his fingers and his tongue teasing my nether regions, making circular motions on my clit. I couldn't bear the teasing pleasurable sensations. I grasp his erect cock and beg him to enter me. "Not yet. This is your punishment for making me lose self-control." He takes my hand off his erection as he continues teasing my nether regions with his fingers and tongue. I couldn't hold back the cry of pleasure as I felt the muscle walls of my insides clench one of his fingers that was thrusting inside of me as I climaxed. "You like your punishment?" He whispers close to my ears as he pins my arms to the mattress and spreads my legs with his own. He grabs my hips and buttocks and enters me from behind, making deep guttural groans. With a deep plunge, he fully seats himself and then starts thrusting slowly as my body adjusts to the fullness of his length and girth. He lays down on top of my back, pressing my stomach into the bed, pinning me gently with his weight as his guttural moans fill my ears. "It hurts so good," I moan loudly at the pleasurable sensations of his deep, sensual thrusts. His arm encircles my chest as he positions me in an upright position on my knees. He tilts my face to kiss him as his hands kneads my breasts while still thrusting sensually inside of me. Hot liquid from my orgasm pours all over him as the tempo of his thrusts increases, his hips pounding against my glutes. I cry his name in pleasure as we both climax and collapse on the bed in each other's arms moments later. He strokes my face and hair as I lay on his chest, panting. We just lay in each other's arms in silence for a moment.

"When I first came to Earth, it was Zanael who taught me about the concepts of human emotions. It was all new to me," He says, breaking the silence. I glance up at his face, interested in hearing about this. "So, my dad was your Yoda when you first came to Earth, although you were his Guardian?" I smile at him, amused at that revelation. He nods. "Sort of. I have observed many human relationships and been in many liaisons, but the concepts of intimacy and being in love are new to me. I know that holding you brings me a sense of calm, warmth, and peace. When I thought I had lost you, I experienced something I had never experienced before. Fear. And it was not fear out of duty. But fear of losing you," He confesses as he strokes my hair and cheeks. "So, this is what being in love feels like. Michael warned me about being in love and intimacy as an immortal celestial being on Earth, but experiencing these emotions for you has only strengthened me. He taught me how to be a warrior, but you are teaching me about these emotions." He remarks as he plants a kiss on my forehead. "How am I doing so far?" I murmur, tracing the lines on the Enochian runes and tattoos on his chest. "A great teacher so far." He smiles, kissing me softly. "And you can teach me how to please you in bed," I whisper flirtatiously against his lips. "Hmmmm. I think you are already succeeding in that department." He murmurs against my lips as he deepens the kiss.

There was a knock at the door, which interrupted our kiss. "It's been an hour already?" I whine in disappointment. "That went by too soon." Gideon gives me another kiss before reluctantly pausing and draping his arms around me. I didn't feel like getting up. I just wanted to stay on his warm, broad, muscular chest, inhaling his enticing musky scent, but I was getting hungry, and we had pending visitors. Cael enters, and I quickly pull on the covers to shield my nakedness. He quickly averts his eyes when he sees us cuddling with Gideon stroking my hair. Gideon didn't seem to care if Cael saw him naked because the bed sheet was barely covering his body. "My Lady, I thought you might need these." He set some clothes and toiletries on a chaise lounge for me. I mouth thank you to him. "I will make haste with my duties." He keeps his eyes averted, trying not to smile as he rushes off to prep the shower, then lays out Gideon's clothes and quickly leaves.

"Why are Lady Anael and her elite squad joining us for breakfast?" I asked Gideon as he got up from the bed, took my hand, and led me toward the steaming shower. "I have known Lady Anael for quite some time now, and she doesn't do random things. So, this visit must be important. We better hurry." He pulls me into the shower with him. His shower was the most luxurious shower I had ever seen. It was huge with beautiful tile work and luxurious rain shower heads. "Now, where were we before we got interrupted?" He grins, lifting me, wrapping my legs around his waist as he kisses me passionately and pins me to the shower walls. He positions my body on his hard erection, entering gently as the warm water pours over our entwined bodies. He was gentle and sensually slow with his thrusts, knowing I was still sore from numerous previous love-making sessions. Despite the soreness, I beg him to go faster. That was all the encouragement he needed.

With a growl, he flips my body around as my hands brace against the shower walls for balance. He grabs my hips as he enters me from behind. He made deep groans as he thrusts hard and fast, his hips pounding mercilessly against my buttocks. The combo of pleasure and pain made me cry out in an explosive orgasm that left my knees weak. He groans, climaxing with a final hard stroke as he burrows himself deep inside me. He held me steady against the shower walls, kissing my neck and shoulders with his hands wrapped around my chest. I stayed there for a moment, panting. He continues kissing my neck and shoulders as he soaps my body sensually with a bath sponge. I turned around and took the sponge from him to lather his body with soap. I inhaled the musky with a hint of cedar wood scent from the soap, which usually smells like him. He lets out a sharp intake of breath as I run my hands down his chest and across his back with the sponge. Then I continued down his legs, washing his muscular thighs and calves and letting the water rinse off the soap. His erection was hard again. "We are so going to be late; it's all your fault," He murmurs as he kisses me, nibbling my lips playfully. "Is it now?" I squeal with laughter as he lifts me, wrapping both of my legs around his waist. I playfully splashed his face with water as the overhead shower poured warm water on our writhing, entwined bodies.

Gideon says he has to remember that I am technically still human until my angelic powers return, so he has to refrain from getting too carried away. If the numerous love-making sessions we already had were him restraining himself, I wonder what he would be like with no restraints. My angelic abilities will have to return for me to find out.

Celeste said it was a forbidden dark arts blood hex Cerinda did to me. I could have died if Gideon hadn't stopped her from completing the ritual. To access that particular hex requires a terrible sacrifice, and she wondered what Cerinda sacrificed. Cerinda refuses to say a word to the Council of High Witches.

"What's on your mind?" Gideon takes me out of my thoughts as he wraps me with a soft towel after our shower, kissing my neck. "I don't know how to be a Lady of a faction," I answer as I secure the towel around me, then walk over to sort through the clothes Cael brought for me. He raises his eyebrows at me with a smile of amusement. "That's what I am here for, and so is Lady Anael. We will help guide you. We have been doing this for quite some time." He dries his hair with a towel. "So why didn't you choose Lady Anael as your bond mate?" I ask curiously. "I guess I have only seen Anael as just a good friend, that's all. She is also a good sparring partner. She is like a sister to me." He responds. "You have nothing to worry about with our friendship." He assured me as if reading my mind. I was worried since the Council of Archangels had approved of her as his bond mate." I don't think she likes me. She has always been gruff with me and calls me 'little Nephilim." I scoff, rolling my eyes. Gideon laughs a deep, rich baritone laugh, shaking his head. "You find this funny, don't you?" I throw my hair towel at him, feigning exasperation. "That means she likes you. She has a different way of showing affection." He catches the hair towel, smiling in amusement as he walks over naked to the clothes Cael had laid out for him.

I admire his naked, muscular body, biting my bottom lip. I can see everything clearer now that the room is brighter. I remember clawing his back and arms so many times in the throes of passion, but there was not one scratch on his skin. Having invulnerable skin does have its perks. His muscular glutes are the finest I have ever seen in all the state and the land. His well-sculpted naked body was magnificent to look at.

"Like what you see?" He grins with a playful glint as he notices my gaze. "I have never seen any male naked before." I gave him a shy smile. "I know," he smirks. "Feel free to look all you want." He steps out more in the middle of the room so I can get a better view of his body. "How did you know I never saw any male naked before you?" I raise my eyebrows at him. "I have watched you go on dates, and none have ever made it past a kiss with you." "You watched me on my dates? Hey! That was not fair." "It was not, but it was my duty and still is to watch over you." "What else did you watch me do besides my dates and extra-curricular activities?" "Nothing inappropriate." I had promised Celeste to only watch from afar unless you were in danger. You're my soulmate and the Lady of my faction; you will have duties. And put some clothes on before we end up in bed again." He gives a lascivious smile at my naked body wrapped in the towel as he pulls a T-shirt over his head.

As I was getting dressed, I realized I needed a hair

dryer. Gideon says he didn't have one. "You have been an immortal angel on Earth for how many millennia and still don't own a hair dryer??" I look at him agape in shock. "If you haven't noticed, you have been the first female raised in human society to live with us in this mansion." He started murmuring in an unknown language then there was a knock on the door. He opened it and it was the Cherub twins Elaina and Erella. They giggle at us. "Fetch our lady the best hair dryer you can find." He orders promptly. "Yes, my Lord." They respond in unison and disappear in a fit of giggles. "Gideon, you didn't have to. I could have..." You're my love and the Lady of my faction. I will take care of all your needs." He insists as he kisses me. The Cherub twins returned within minutes with a hair dryer and offered to do my hair.

I blushed with embarrassment when Abdiel asked Gideon if his dwarf wood bed posts were still intact, and then he winked at me. Gideon gives him a look that suggests he shuts up, but there is a hint of a smile on his lips. Gideon's arm was around my waist when we walked into the breakfast area. The seven elite start snickering and giving us amused grins. Kemuel even remarks that we had finally come up for air. Jeb walks into the kitchen and greets us. When he sees Gideon's arm around my waist, he grins widely at him, his dark eyes dancing with amusement. "Not a word," Gideon mutters gruffly to him, but he is smiling.

We were all waiting for Lady Anael and her entourage to arrive. Our absence was definitely noticeable last night, and so was our late arrival for breakfast.

Celeste and Vicky arrive, and Celeste looks at Gideon's arm around me, frowns, and shakes her head at him but smiles at me. I can tell she knows what transpired last night between Gideon and me and will probably have some choice words for me later on. I guess our budding relationship must be a bit weird for her since I am her adopted daughter, and Gideon was the one who entrusted her with my care when I was an infant. Celeste was just getting established with her holistic psychology and tarot card reading business, so finances were tight. Gideon assisted her with my upbringing expenses as a distant benefactor and a protective Guardian angel. Jeb seems more OK with our new relationship since he knows what true soul mate bonds mean for angels and is also very loyal to Gideon.

Vicky mouths, "Did the two of you do it?" I mouth the words "yes" wordlessly to her. Her eyes widened, and she started beaming. Then, she clamped her hands over her mouth to prevent herself from squealing. I know she couldn't wait to corner me privately if she could pry me away from Gideon's side to tell her all the sordid details. She will demand full, explicit details and not a simple watercolor picture explanation. Gideon wanted me to sit by his side at the breakfast table, so she would have to wait to grill me later. Cael served us coffee and juice as Gideon became engrossed in a conversation with Jeb and Kafziel.

"Happiness suits you, my Lady. And so, as Lord Gideon," Cael whispers to me with a smile. "He does make me happy." I glance at Gideon and smile at Cael.

Our moment was cut short by the arrival of Lady Anael and her entourage. Her eight elite Dominion angel warriors consist of five male Dominion angels who all look in their early twenties and three tall and pretty females who also look in their early twenties. They were all good-looking. Are there even ugly-looking angels? So far, I have not met any. Even the fallen Throne Razziel was good-looking despite the scar on his face, compliments of Gideon. They were all dressed casually. Lady Anael was in jeans with a feminine and beautiful long-sleeved top. Even in casual clothing, she looks like a regal supermodel who exudes such enviable confidence. Her mere presence demands attention. She greets Gideon radiantly, hugs and pecks him on the cheek. Then, she acknowledges me with a simple greeting. "What? No hugs? I feel slighted." I tease her sarcastically. "Don't push it, little Nephilim," she says with a slight smile of amusement.

Her elite squad members were giving me furtive glances as they greeted Gideon and the others. The three female Dominions were gazing at Gideon with a look of awe, as if they were seeing their celebrity crush. When he greets them, they act like they are at a loss for words. I thought human women reacted that way with him, but supernatural women, too. I have to get used to the fact that females will respond flirtatiously to him. Not only is he the Lord of the Powers, but he is also Archangel Michael's protege, a bonafide badass warrior, absolutely drop-dead gorgeous; words cannot describe how amazing of a lover he is. He represents prestige, protection, respect, and power, besides the perks of being his lover for any female he chooses. Of course, I know there will be a long line of supernatural women just waiting to have a chance with him. The three female Dominions barely acknowledge me. Gideon holds my hand as he introduces me as the Lady of his faction to Anael's elite squad, which brings a glint of jealousy in the eyes of the three female Dominions.

Lady Anael told us Razziel had escaped custody from Celestial jail as breakfast was served. Gideon was surprised at that revelation because Celestial prison was nearly impossible to escape. Anael informed me that the Cherubim Gamaliel had gone rogue and released him. Lilith seduced him, and they were probably working together. The other faction, Lords and Ladies, all want to convene with the Council of Archangels to decide the best approach to this issue. Gamaliel and Lilith together are a potent combo.

After breakfast, Lady Anael wanted to speak to Gideon privately, so they entered his office space and closed the door behind them. Vicky had to answer a phone call from her uncle, Fae King Aodhan, so I decided to head back to my room after telling her to meet me there when she finished her phone call. I felt exhausted because I hardly slept last night. As I headed to my room, the three Dominion females from Lady Anael's faction cornered me. I asked them if they needed anything. "So, you're the Nephilim that everyone is talking about?" One of them with long, beautiful braids and dark brown skin comments. "In the flesh," I answer with a smile. "Is it true that you are Lord Gideon's true soulmate? How is that even possible? The Powers are warriors. They don't usually have true soulmates." Another with straight black hair and contrasting grey eyes emphasizes shrewdly. "It beats me. That's a question to ask the cosmos." I shrug. All three were at least six feet tall and looked intimidating, but I refused to be intimidated by them. They were eyeing me like apex predators. "I don't know what sort of sorcery you have over Lord Gideon, but he has not been the same since you came into the picture." The third one with brown hair and dark eyes remarks. "You know he is immune to sorcery, spells, and enchantments, right? And what was he like before me? Please enlighten me." I mock them with a laugh. They stare daggers at me. "Lord Gideon and Lady Anael are supposed to be bandmates, but he defied the Council of Archangels and chose you instead. What hold do you have over him?" The strawberry blonde demands in a shrill voice. "I think you should ask him that. Lady Anael and Gideon seem fine with their current arrangements. Please make yourself at home. I have to go." I give them a small smile as I speed walk to my room, leaving them standing in the hallway huffing.

I heard some squeals, and it was Vicky running down the hallway to catch up to me. "Judging by how much you're glowing like a fae lantern right now, I guess Lord Gideon's reputation as a great lover is definitely true." She smiles, hooking her arm with mine as we enter the privacy of my room. I told her I hardly got any sleep and felt exhausted, but it was well worth it. "I need my angelic powers to return already because he is insatiable. My current human body is struggling to keep up." I throw myself on my bed. She laughs at me. "Is it safe to sit on your bed after what happened there?" She jokes. I give her a sidelong glance. "Oh, don't sit there yet. Let me put the handcuffs away," I blurt out in feigning exasperation, trying to stifle a laugh. Vicky's face was horrified, and I laughed at her shocked expression. "I'm joking. We were in his bedroom, silly." I laughed at her, then stopped when I saw some letters on my bed. Vicky squeals. "Wow, it has begun!" "What has begun?" I ask her, glancing at her perplexed. "Think about it this way. You went from a simple college student trying to pay an admission fee to get into a club to automatically upgraded to VIP status." She explains, plopping herself on the bed, delighted with all this. How did the whole supernatural community know about Gideon and me? Was there a mass memo or something that I missed?" I question her, still feeling puzzled. She giggles. I raise my eyebrows at her. "The mass memo was Lord Gideon shoving his tongue down your throat in front of everyone when he saw you were safe. It made my uncle King Aodhan and his hardy fae warriors blush. If any fae saw that make-out session, word would quickly get around in the supernatural community. Then your angelic wings and irises are similar to his, so there are the rumors of a true soul mate bond," Vicky blurts out.

"These are some letters from some members of the

supernatural community who are trying to lobby favors and get into your good graces now that you are Lord Gideon's bond mate and Lady of his faction." She hands the letters to me, smiling. I was stunned as the revelation hit home about the politics I must learn to deal with now. All the letters were addressed to "Lady Seraphina" in fancy lettering. "Let's open them and see what you got!" She says eagerly, grabbing a few from me. A letter from Madam Deirdre's boutique asked if she could be my personal stylist. Another from the Brownie Fae fine dining restaurant Kemuel took me to offer Lord Gideon and myself one of their VIP dining experience booths. Vicky opened one of the letters and was surprised to see it was from her dad, Dwarf Lord Ronan, who offered jewelry design services. She rolls her eyes, saying her dad had always been a suck-up. There was another from a Brownie domestic duties staffing company offering to be part of the staff of my servants. Some Principalities angels were offering spiritual services and some Virtue angels and fae were offering physician services. There was a letter from the Cherub twins, Erella and Elaina, petitioning Gideon to allow them to be my maidservants.

"So how was your first time with Lord Gideon? Rumor has it that he is very well-endowed. Spare me no details. How hot was the sex?" She grins, looking at me with curiosity. I could feel the heat rising to my face. "He was gentle and tender, but after that, we barely slept. Words cannot describe how beautiful it was." I smile at her. "His eyes flare with gold angel-fire when he orgasms ."I continue smiling at her, and she mouths, "Oh my god," and squeals, clamping a hand on her mouth. She still asked for more details and inquired about what Lady Anael's three female Dominions wanted from me. She saw them talking to me. I told her they were upset that Gideon refused to be bond mates with their Lady. She concludes that Lady Anael is still in love with Gideon. She can sense her feelings with her clairsentient abilities. I told her Gideon assured me that I have nothing to worry about with their friendship.

CHAPTER 21

LADY ANAEL

I watch Gideon as he sorts through various requests from other supernatural factions for alliances. He looks pensive, going through each request, frowning here and there, and looking up now and then to ask for my opinion. He even gave me a few requests to sort through. As faction leaders, we can relate to each other through the politics of governing a faction. Seraphina should be the one to help assist him with this, but for some reason, he asked me because he felt there was much she still needed to learn about the supernatural world and its politics. He does want her to get more involved, but not right now.

I have known Gideon since Archangel Michael took him under his wing as his protege. I remembered how he complained to me about Michael's training methods. I was happy to listen to him and allow him to practice his training moves as his sparring partner. Michael was very impressed with what a combat prodigy he was. Gideon helped him, along with the other Archangels, defeat Lucifer and his seven princes. Being the Lord of the Powers, Gideon was the most beautiful, magnificent, and gifted of the Powers, a warrior class of angels.

Michael knew of my affection for him and encouraged it. He thinks we will make a formidable power couple, but Gideon has always only treated me like a sparring partner and a good friend. I was ecstatic to be assigned on Earth also when he told me he would be on Earth as the Guardian for Zanael, the first Earth angel. I was motivated to work diligently, surpass my peers, be promoted to Lady of the Dominions, and be of equal station to him. I remember how happy he was for me and was there to congratulate me at my promotion ceremony.

His compassion made me fall madly in love with him, even as a formidable warrior. I saw how he was willing to beg for the Nephilim boy Cael's life and took the Earth assignment in exchange so that Cael could live. Cael has been a loyal and valuable manservant to Gideon in his gratitude. He also implored the Council to show Caleb leniency when he fell in love with a female vampire. I saw why the other angels would loyally follow Gideon through the fires of hell if he asked them to. His charisma and devastating good looks inspire loyalty.

I remembered taking advice from a Cherub Cupid supernatural matchmaker on acting and making myself attractive so Gideon would see me as someone he desires and wants as his bond mate. He did call me beautiful numerous times before, but never in a way that indicated attraction. One night, Gideon showed up in my chambers and removed his clothing. He wanted to experience the human pleasure of sex with me. Zanael had described how wonderful it was, so he wanted me and him to experience it together. I didn't know what to do since I had never done it before, so I allowed him to remove my clothing. I remembered how glorious his naked body was. I have seen him shirtless countless times but never fully nude. He saw me staring at his body and smiled. I saw desire for the first time in his beautiful hazel gold-flecked eyes as he gazed at my naked body. I felt my whole body was on fire at every pleasurable caress from his hands and every kiss from his mouth. He was a good kisser but swears he didn't know what he was doing.

That night, I was his first, and he was mine. The concepts of earthly human emotions were overwhelming, but we were each other's support system. He was a natural at love-making, always making me crave more of him each time. I was deeply in love with him and desired his body and soul. I can tell he did enjoy our sexual encounters, but there was a void and longing within him that I couldn't fill for him. I asked him if he loved me enough to be my bond mate, but he laughed and said I was more of a best friend to him and nothing more. He said he only loved me as a friend, and the Powers are warriors who don't fall in love and don't do intimacy. He wants to continue our friendship but cannot be my bond mate.

I was crushed and wanted to end our friendship. But Gideon always seemed to know how to charm the soft spot in me for him. He was very hard to say no to. Although we stopped all sexual encounters, I wanted to still be around him because not having a friendship with him hurt a lot more than I realized. I would rather be his friend and not have him than lose him as a friend because I was upset; he didn't want to be my bond mate. I have tried to move on with other males, but none could hold a torch to how Gideon makes me feel in body and soul. Whenever he needed me, I always dropped everything and went to him.

He needed a friend, especially after Zanael's death, which devastated him. He felt that he had failed him. He took his death hard. I comforted him by offering my body and my love to soothe his grief. He took comfort in my body, but he would not accept my love.

I was intrigued when I heard he had a human charge because I saw something I had not seen since Zanael's death —a new sense of purpose. I contacted him through Angelical, inquiring about his charge, but he was very cagey and didn't say much. The other Powers squad leaders didn't know any details about his human charge, and his elite squad was too loyal to him to spill anything.

Then I heard about Caleb's betrayal and how he set some events in motion to have Gideon ambushed and subdued by the fallen Throne Razziel. They should have known better that subduing Gideon would not be that easy. He is the Lord of the Powers for a reason. While they are two steps ahead, he has always been ten steps ahead with unmatched resourcefulness. He escaped thanks to the High Witch Enochian rune's fail-safe protection wards but was severely injured. It was his human charge, the fallen Throne Razziel, and the rogue Gregori Watcher Nathaniel was after. Then I discovered that this human charge gave him refuge in her home and treated his wounds until his celestial powers returned. Then he was forced to reveal his identity and had to escape with her to his compound, and she started living with him.

I was floored when I learned she was a Nephilim and that even the Council of Archangels came days before their deadline because they wanted to meet her. Cael was the only Nephilim, so I was definitely curious about her. I heard rumors from the fae folk that Gideon has not taken any supernatural or angel females to his bed since her. Of course, any supernatural or angel female who had the privilege of being in Gideon's bed will never keep their mouth shut about it. Word will get around. He had Madam Deirdre design a dress for the supernatural Council's banquet, *especially for her*. I knew I had to be there to see this Nephilim girl for myself.

When I saw Gideon walk into the Banquet Hall with her on his arm, looking as majestic as ever in his Lord of the Powers formal attire, my heart stopped momentarily. Why did he have to look so gorgeous? When I saw her, I instantly felt the pangs of jealousy. She was statuesque, beautiful, and regal. She looked like a golden goddess in the dress he had Madam Deidre designed for her. She was the envy of many supernatural females in the room, being on Gideon's arm. I observed all the hostile stares directed at her. She looked a bit like Zanael. If that was his forbidden Nephilim daughter and she was the next Earth angel, why didn't Gideon tell me this? It felt hurtful that he kept this from me, but he always has a reason for doing what he does. I watched how Gideon interacted with her and saw something I never had with him in his eyes. He wanted her and craved her. She looked at him the same way, too.

When he approached me and told me that the Council of Archangels wanted her trained, and he would need my help training her; I was reluctant at first. He still didn't mention her identity to me except that she was the High Witch Celeste's adopted daughter and a Nephilim the Council of Archangels allowed to live. It was hard saying no to him, so out of curiosity to find out who she was, I agreed to assist him with training her. She was a Nephilim, but her powers were not active, so training her was challenging. She was weak as a human but didn't once complain to me, no matter how much she struggled with whatever training I threw at her. Gideon mentioned she was a former gymnast and ballet dancer, so strict training regimes were not new. She had proven herself to be a fast learner, but her body was still that of a weak human. There were times I would overdo it with the training sessions and show my disdain for her by hurling insults because of my jealousy of the way Gideon always looked at her like he wanted to devour her. I always wondered what he saw in her. There were beautiful supernatural women like me who were a better match for him. She lacks decorum, is rude to the fae monarchs, and is a weak Nephilim abomination. There was no way she was the new Earth angel.

As time passed, I saw precisely why Gideon was smitten with her. It has always been the other way around, where many supernatural and human females are smitten with him. But he had never returned much affection to them. I have seen him with many lovers for quite a few millennia. Lovers that were more beautiful and charming than the Nephilim, and I never once felt jealous of him and them. There was no need for jealousy because I was the one he always needed and the only one he confided in besides Jebediah.

Now, something has changed about him, and I saw this change whenever he was around her. She was physically weak, but her resilience, courage, and grit were almost admirable. After all, she took care of Gideon when he was involuntarily teleported to her doorstep, severely injured. Even Gideon's elite squad were all charmed and impressed by her. Kemuel especially was crushing hard on her. I observed how this made Gideon very jealous. He usually doesn't get jealous over anything. He was Lord Gideon. I was intrigued as to why he was so infatuated with a Nephilim he had not even taken as a lover because I could have sensed she was still a virgin.

When I walked in on Gideon on top of her, kissing her with such passion on the floor in the training room, I was beyond jealous. He thought I might not have noticed, but there was no way he could have hidden that huge boner. I tried to take my rage out on her, but she held her ground. At least she paid attention to the combat moves Gideon taught her. They did some training instead of shoving their tongues into each other's mouths after all. I was even a bit impressed at her progress.

I have never seen Gideon so devastated since Zanael's death that he was ready to watch the world burn when he found out Nathaniel and Razziel's forces had abducted her. That's when I knew she was more important to him than what I initially believed. I was ready to be there as support when he contacted me about her abduction. Then he confirmed her true identity, which I had suspected all along.

He has been her Guardian since she was an infant and was the one who gave her to be raised by Celeste. He swore to Zanael that he would protect her and look after her. He watched her grow into the woman she is right now. No wonder he has not taken her to his bed because the Council of Archangels will frown upon their inappropriate relationship. They will never approve of him having a relationship with his charge, and she is not of a similar station as him.

One might think it would have been a fatherly or uncle-type love he would have developed for her since she is Zanael's daughter, and he has always been her protector since infancy, but it was worse. I could have sensed that he was in love with her. He didn't deny it. He ensured to let everyone see she was his after I saw him kissing her when she escaped Nathaniel and Razziel's fortress. It was a full-blown make-out session that caused many members of my elite squad to blush uncomfortably. My elite squad leader, Muriel, turned and looked at me. She could have sensed I was hurting watching them. She made a disgusted, gagging noise and remarked that she was sick to her stomach and wanted to put her eyes out. She knew of my long-standing unrequited love for Gideon and said she would hate the Nephilim girl if I allowed her to. The silly Nephilim girl even threw herself before a hexed spear meant for Gideon, knowing it would have killed her. She was willing to die for him.

Gideon was mad with grief and fought with a fierceness I had never seen since the rebellion. Her angel-fire and irises were gold like his when her angelic powers activated. He looked at her like she was the most precious being in the world. When Cerinda hexed her using her blood, Gideon saved her. I even heard that Archangel Raphael himself came down to heal her. Even Michael and Chamuel visited her. Gideon stayed vigilant by her bedside until she woke up from her coma.

I knew all was lost, especially when there was talk that she was his true soul mate. I hid my jealousy at breakfast at his mansion, watching as he held her hand so lovingly. She was radiant around him, and for the first time, I saw something that I had never seen in Gideon. Bliss and his voids were all filled. I knew he had finally taken her to his bed because she had that same giddy look I had when I first slept with Gideon. I have never envied any other female Gideon had liaisons with, but now I envy her. She was able to give him something I never could. Seraphina had something I never got from him. She had his passionate and consuming love. She has him, body and soul.

"What is troubling you, Anael?" Gideon asks, looking at me quizzically with those ethereal eyes of his as he reclines in his chair, resting his hands casually behind his head. "Anael? Don't play coy with me now." He raises his eyebrows as he scrutinizes me. "We both know you have never been the type to hold anything back, so speak freely."

He has always been able to read me so well. I sigh. "I think they will try to use Seraphina as a weakness against you. They know you care about her. She doesn't know how to use her angelic abilities, which makes her vulnerable and a liability." I finally say to him. Gideon furrows his brows. "Of course, I know they will try to use her to get me. She will need a mentor to help train her to use her angelic powers when they return. Raphael says her abilities will return soon. I couldn't think of anyone more suited than you to help me mentor her." He suggests giving me that winsome, charming smile that is difficult to say no to. Ugh! I rolled my eyes at him. "Yes, she will need a mentor. Someone that will not get a raging boner in training sessions with her." I shake my head at him. He laughs. That deep, rich baritone laugh. "You saw what happened in the training room with her, and I didn't you?" "More than I wanted to see." "Very inappropriate. I know." You know it is hard to hide your raging boner, right?" I give him an amused smile. "Very hard indeed." His eyes dance with a playful glint. His cockiness is quite endearing. That was another trait I love about him. He is quite aware that any female, whether supernatural, angel, or human, that he had as a lover was quite lucky and was very pleased with his skills. "Being in love has not toned down your cockiness for sure." I roll my eyes at him. He laughs again. "I am happy for you and her, Gideon. I will help out with whatever I can," I say softly to him. "That means a lot to me, Anael." He looks at me, his eyes softening. "Now I need to get through all these requests."

CHAPTER 22
GIDEON

I found it hard to focus on the reports from the other squad leaders in the other outposts. My thoughts drifted to Seraphina and how happy I was that we are finally together. I have never been this excited about any female. I cannot wait to have her in my bed again tonight after I return from visiting the Rome outpost. There have been some disturbances at that particular outpost, according to squad leader Agiel's report. Jeb and I will be teleporting into that Rome outpost later on.

Jeb told me that Celeste has difficulty accepting the relationship between Seraphina and me because she feels she is still her little girl. And she doesn't want her to get hurt. I can never dream of hurting Seraphina. Celeste did have a few choice words for me. She still thinks our relationship is inappropriate but has never seen my usual broody demeanor so happy. Celeste also has never seen

Seraphina so happy being with me. She said she would keep a wary eye on me.

The Council of Archangels has convened, and Michael grudgingly agreed with Chamuel to conduct an official bonding ceremony for Seraphina and me when her Earth Angel Powers return. Michael still prefers Lady Anael and me for bond mates, but he blesses Seraphina to be the Lady of my faction and my official bond mate. I cannot wait to share the great news with her tonight.

She has to learn much as the Lady of my faction, along with training to use her angelic powers. I am looking forward to Lady Anael and I being her mentors. There is still a bounty on her now that the supernatural community knows her true identity. We have to step up her training game.

Everyone in the supernatural community was already gossiping about us, and there is even more gossip now that she is the Lady of my faction and my bond mate. When I saw that she was safe after she escaped from Nathaniel, I had to give them all something to gossip about by kissing her in front of everyone, claiming her as mine. Jeb said he wanted to put his eyes out since we were making warriors blush with the kissing. When I thought I had lost her, it was the worst feeling of dread and despair. But her near-death experiences activated her dormant Earth angel abilities. Her angelic irises, angel-fire, and wings are golden like mine. Her angelic form is so beautiful. Celeste and the Council of Archangels examined her, and they said the binding ritual that had bound her Earth angel powers somehow got activated with her near-death experience.

I could have kept making love to her all night, but I knew she needed to rest more than I since her body had been rendered temporary human from Cerinda's forbidden magic blood hex. I couldn't get enough of her body and how amazing it felt being inside her and cuddling with her in my arms after. My lust is insatiable for her. It's been a while since I had taken any female to my bed, so I had to restrain myself from getting too carried away with excitement. Too much tension of attraction had built up between us over the months. The more I tried to reason with myself that what I felt for her was inappropriate, the more I wanted her.

I was getting aroused remembering her cries of pleasure and how responsive her body was each time we made love. I was happy that I was her first. After sensing her nervousness, I knew I had to take my time and be gentle for her first time. She made it so challenging to go slow with her, though. Holding her in my arms after each love-making session was beyond blissful. I don't think I can wait until later on tonight to see her. I have to see her right now before I leave with Jeb. I quickly called Cael to find her and bring her to my office.

Cael did come with her moments later. She was wearing a form-fitting sweater dress, exposing her beautiful, slender, toned legs that I love so much. She smiles at me. My erection was now rock hard and throbbing. I quickly dismiss Cael and close the door behind him. She asks why I want to see her. I immediately cup her face and kiss her passionately, telling her it was because I couldn't stop thinking about her. She returns the passionate kiss, pressing her body against mine, and reaches to pull my T-shirt off my body. Still kissing her, I pick her up, clear the paraphernalia of paperwork from my work desk with a sweep of my other hand, and set her on it. I quickly remove her dress. Her hands trying to unbuckle my jeans feverishly only fueled my lust. I quickly got out of my jeans and pulled her body to mine, spreading her legs. I unhooked her bra, tossed it aside, and eagerly ripped her underwear off. She will have to leave here without those on. I wrap her legs around my waist as my mouth captures one of her breasts, sucking on the hardened nipple, switching from one to the other. I slid my hands up her thighs and entered a finger into her. She was so wet and aroused. She moans as I tease her nether regions with the tip of my hardened erection, then enter her slowly, relishing in the sensations of her tight, warm wetness squeezing my hard erection like a vise. It felt beyond blissful. She cries out in pleasure as I thrust deeper, fully seating myself inside her. I let out groans of pleasure, grabbing her buttocks and kissing her hungrily as I increased the tempo and pace of my thrusts, pounding into her hard. She tightens her legs around my waist, hands clawing my back in a frenzy, moaning her pleasure as I position her body in a sitting position, grabbing her hips and thrusting relentlessly into her. Hearing her cries of pleasure and the warm, slick wetness of her climax squirting on me intensified my pleasure. I am glad my office was spelled soundproof, or the entire mansion would have heard our cries of pleasure.

Moments later, we reluctantly got dressed because I was expecting Jeb to stop by at any moment. She looks at her torn underwear on the floor and shakes her head at me. I smile and shrug. I told her she might be better off not wearing any around me. She gives me an amused smile. I lead her to my office couch and lay back on it, pulling her onto my lap. I cuddle with her, kiss her, and stroke her back. I smile at the content look on her face as she rests her head on my chest, snuggling up to me. I tell her I must teleport to Rome as I stroke her hair and cheeks.

A loud knock on my office door interrupted our cuddling session. I was still shirtless, so I quickly pulled my t-shirt over my head as I opened the door. It was Jeb. He looks at my unbuckled jeans, scattered papers from my desk, the torn underwear on the floor, and at Seraphina straightening her dress, smiling. "I don't even want to guess what I just walked in on." He shakes his head at us as his lips quirks in an amused smile. He gives Seraphina a wave. "I can recall walking in on several inappropriate moments in your work office when you and Celeste started dating," I say to him, giving him a half smile. Jeb smiles at that memory, and then his demeanor changes to a serious one. "We have to leave now for Rome. Agiel's entire squad ran into some trouble. Some are missing. We should take a few others with us just in case." He informs me grimly. Seraphina wanted to know what was happening and even begged to come with us, but I couldn't risk it, especially since she didn't have her angelic abilities back yet. I quickly kissed her, telling her I would return, and went off with Jeb. "Ah, young love. I remember those days..." Jeb remarks with a smile as he glances at me, buckling my jeans. I shake my head at him with a chuckle. "We should take Kafziel, Kemuel, and Abdiel with us. The others can stay back here to maintain order at their posts. Celeste said she would keep an eye on Seraphina," Jeb suggests. I nod my head in agreement with him. "Where are Kafziel, Kemuel and Abdiel?" "They are out training, but I will summon them to the War room right now," Jeb responds as he starts speaking the angelical language to summon Kafziel, Kemuel, and Abdiel.

The Rome outpost was in chaos upon our arrival. Numerous demons outnumbered Agiel's four remaining squad warriors. Jeb, Kafziel, Abdiel, and I donned our celestial armor and ignited our weapons with angel-fire to join the fight. I split my broadsword into two and shot like a twirling missile toward a humanoid demon with several arms, trying to subdue Agiel. My broad swords minced it into a pile of severed body parts. I help Agiel to his feet; he mutters his thanks. He was bleeding from a wound on his stomach. These demons are using High Witch-hexed weapons.

I saw Jeb take a blow to his back, but that only fueled his rage because the demon was minced meat after Jeb had finished chopping it with his Tomahawk. I ask Agiel how the demons got into the outpost since it has many protection wards. He says it was a mystery to him. Only a High Witch can breach the protection wards on the outpost. His angelic healing kicked in for his stomach wound, and he was back in the fight. Abdiel was zooming with his enhanced speed, swinging his copper angel fire Urumi whip sword, and was taking several demons out at a time. Kafziel, in his phased form, was taking several heads and body parts with his angel fire Halberd. Kemuel propelled his body like a torpedo with his enhanced agility and slashed viciously with his double short swords.

We were able to assist Agiel's squad to take out the remaining demons, even the ones that tried to flee. Agiel reports that the High Witch, who was helping them to keep the wards in place, was taken along with three of his squad warriors. This situation was not good at all. Something did not feel right about this situation. To our surprise, we all watch as a bright orb manifests, and then three pairs of grayish-white bloodied angel wings drop to the ground, and then the bright orb disappears. We stared aghast and horrified at the bloodied grayish-white wings because we recognized them from the missing Powers from Agiel's squad. A voice starts speaking to me telepathically in angelical language. A voice that I had not heard in eons.

"I hope you like my welcome to Rome gift Gideon." The voice laughs mockingly. I immediately recognize that voice. *"I see you got tired of Lackeys doing your bidding, so you decided to take a more hands-on approach, Lucifer,"* I say to Lucifer in an

angelical tongue. *"Still very arrogant as ever, Gideon. You have something of mine. I know about your little Nephilim, the new Earth angel. And I will take her from you, and you will watch her die when I take the seal from her,"* Lucifer taunts. *"You could have joined me when I asked but chose my insufferable brother Michael."* *"Sing me a new tune already, Lucifer. I will never join you. Was this attack your handiwork, Lucifer? What did you do with my three warriors?"* I demanded from him. Lucifer laughs mockingly again. *"I have always been steps ahead, Gideon. Were your lowly warriors at an obscure outpost the real target? They were just a distraction."* Lucifer continues laughing, and then it fades away. The others were all looking in anticipation after they heard me speaking in angelical language to Lucifer. A sense of dread overcame me. I knew something was iffy about this situation when a horrific realization dawned on me.

"Jeb, we need to return to the compound to Celeste and Seraphina right now!" I command, feeling a sense of dread. Jeb and the others quickly nodded, and then we tried to teleport, but we couldn't. It looks like a High Witch's spell on the area is stopping us from teleporting. As we look at each other in confusion, a bright flash of white light materializes into a white orb by Agiel's squad building. A portal opens, and several demons with a few fallen angels emerge. The portal quickly disappears. We all look at the demons and a few fallen angels brandishing High Witch-hexed weapons. We were outnumbered.

"What in the hell?" Jeb's voice sounds hollow as his eyes flare with grey-white angel fire. His Tomahawk materialized in his hands, glowing with angel fire. "This was a planned ambush. I can sense a force field ward spelled by a High Witch that will prevent us from even flying out of here," I remark as I feel my eyes flaring with gold angel fire and my broadsword materializes in my hand. "I would rather go down fighting than be taken to a hell dimension by those fallen," Kemuel mutters grimly as his eyes flare copper angel fire and his two short swords materialize in his hands, blazing with copper angel fire. "I second that, Kemuel." Kafziel nods in agreement at Kemuel as his eyes flare copper angel fire and his Halberd materializes, blazing in copper angel-fire. He switches to his translucent phasing form. "Well, at least I know I will be going down with the finest warriors by my side," Abdiel smirked as his eyes flared copper, and his Urumi whip sword materialized, blazing with copper angel fire. "We are not going to get taken or die tonight," I say to them in a steely voice tone to them as I split my broadsword into two and set them ablaze with gold angel fire.

My thoughts went to Seraphina, hoping she was safe with Celeste. We need to survive this so I can get back to her. I look at each member of my elite squad with admiration. I could not have asked for a better set of warriors to have fighting by my side. We were severely outnumbered, but I smiled, feeling the adrenaline rush as my body erupted in gold angel-fire over my golden celestial armor. "What's the plan, boss?" Jeb asks me as the others all look at me expectantly. "I want to start with those fallen angels on the right. They look like they want celestial chain decorations. I say let's give them hell." I let out my war cry as the others erupt in war cries. "Woo hooo! It's showtime!" Kemuels yells with a fierce look on his face. Their wings materialize as they all flew like blazing angel-fire missiles toward the horde of demons. "Let's hope you are watching Lucifer because I plan on giving you hell." My golden wings materialize as I propel toward the fallen angels like a torpedo, brandishing my two broadswords ablaze with gold angel-fire.

WILL LORD GIDEON AND THE POWERS SURVIVE THIS AMBUSH? WAS IT A DIVERSION TO GET TO SERAPHINA, THE EARTH ANGEL? FIND OUT WHAT WILL HAPPEN TO LORD GIDEON, HIS SQUAD, AND SERAPHINA AS THE ADVENTURE CONTINUES IN PART TWO. COMING SOON…

ABOUT THE AUTHOR

Natoya Wayne was born on September 16th and raised in Guyana. She emigrated to the United States when she was eighteen and joined the United States Marines. After the military, she operated and owned a fitness and wellness business while attending college. She has a Bachelor's in Business and a Master's in Psychology from the University of Arizona. She has always excelled in studying History, Literature, Writing, English, Mythology, and Folklore both in Guyana and in college in the US. She is also a SAG-AFTRA stunt performer and remains active in the film industry. Her life is a testament to her insatiable curiosity and passion for learning. Natoya's interests span a broad spectrum, from studying different variations of dance, gymnastics, and martial arts to engaging in gym workouts and arts and crafts. Her love for literature is evident in her choice of reading material, which includes urban fantasy, paranormal, and thriller books. She also embraces holistic health, wellness, spirituality, and fitness as a lifestyle, further enriching her diverse background.